Alley Katz

Second Edition

Alley Katz

Second Edition

Mike Faricy

Library of Congress Control Number: 2023917919
paperback ISBN: 978-1-962080-43-9
e-Book ISBN: 978-1-962080-44-6

MJF Publishing books may be purchased for education, Business, or promotional use. For information on bulk purchases, please contact the author directly at mikefaricyauthor@gmail.com

Published by

MJF Publishing
https://www.mikefaricybooks.com

Acknowledgments

I would like to thank the following people for their help and support:

Special thanks to my editors, Kitty, Donna and Rhonda for their hard work, cheerful patience and positive feedback.

I would like to thank Ann and Julie for their creative talent and not slitting their wrists or jumping off the high bridge when dealing with my Neanderthal computer capabilities.

Special thanks to Ann for her patience.

Last, I would like to thank family and friends for their encouragement and unqualified support. Special thanks to Maggie, Jed, Schatz, Pat, Av, Emily and Pat for not rolling their eyes, at least when I was there, and most of all, to my wife Teresa whose belief, support and inspiration has from day one, never waned.

Prologue

For once, Taylor Cummings woke to the smell of something delicious. At first, he thought it might be the restaurant across the alley. He looked at his watch, just after five in the morning, way too early for them to be cooking. He pulled off the jacket he used as a blanket, rolled off the mattress on the floor, and stood. He hadn't eaten since lunch at school yesterday, and his stomach growled. Whatever he smelled was definitely coming from the other room.

He tucked his shirt into his jeans, tied his shoes, and tiptoed out of the room. The scent grew stronger as he moved down the short hall toward the light. He peeked around the corner and focused on his uncle Eli stirring a pot on the hot plate. His stomach growled again at the scent of whatever was in the pan.

Without turning around, his uncle said, "Sit your butt down, buddy, and I'll dish you up a bowl of your grandma's secret chili recipe. It'll be ready in four minutes. What would you like to drink?"

"What do we have?"

"I'm not sure. Give a look in the refrigerator."

"The refrigerator's empty."

"Well then, we'll just have water. I guess you could add a couple of ice cubes and make it ice water. Your choice."

Taylor took the glass and the coffee mug from the cabinet and turned the water on. There were two empty chili cans in the sink, and he filled them under the faucet. He let the water run for a good long minute until it looked clear enough to drink before filling the glass and mug. He placed them on the table, actually a section of sheetrock resting on a pair of sawhorses, and sat down on the lawn chair.

"Where have you been, Eli?"

"Working. Been coming up with a formula to—"

Taylor shook his head. "You mean you've been gambling again and lost whatever you had. Where'd you steal that stuff you're cooking?"

"Now, why are you starting out so negative? I told you this is your grandmother's recipe. I been cooking this for a couple of hours."

"Eli, I saw the cans in the sink."

"Yeah, well, that company heard about your grandma's recipe, and they stole it from her. They've been making all sorts of money off it. I just figured the least they could do was give me a couple of cans. Now here, this is just about ready to—"

The door suddenly burst open and a very large man with a shaved head and a tattooed neck burst into the room. "Eli Cummings, it's time for you to pay up," he shouted as he stormed past Taylor.

Taylor sat glued to the lawn chair, too frightened to move.

"Now calm down and hold on a second, Lyle. I got your payment right here. Let me just turn this off," Eli said. He suddenly grabbed the pan and tossed the boiling contents into Lyle's face.

"Ahhh-ahh," Lyle screamed and staggered backward a step or two. Eli wound up and hit him on the forehead with the pan, sending him backward. He crashed through the sheetrock table and landed on the floor.

Taylor sat wide-eyed as Lyle groaned and slowly moved his head from side to side. Eli bent down and pulled a wallet out of the man's pocket along with a set of car keys. "Time to go, Taylor, now!" he said, as he pulled a twenty-dollar bill from the wallet and handed it to Taylor. Taylor ran back to the bedroom, grabbed his jacket, and hurried back to the kitchen.

Eli was gone, and Lyle was attempting to sit up. Taylor decided it might be a good idea to leave. He hurried out the door just as Eli backed a shiny red car with two white racing stripes out of the driveway and sped down the street.

One

I was behind the wheel, shouting obscenities at the Mercedes in front of me because they hadn't turned on their left-hand blinker until after the light changed. I couldn't drive around them due to the bus that had just pulled to the corner. I needed the car to pull four feet into the intersection, but apparently, that wasn't about to happen. My curse words and shouting didn't seem to have any effect, but then with my windows rolled up, they couldn't really hear me. A half-dozen cars, an ice cream truck, and some college kid on a motorized scooter drifted past in the oncoming lane, and still, the Mercedes didn't move.

I leaned on my horn, as did two of the cars behind me. The traffic light changed to yellow, the Mercedes finally moved, and I accelerated through the intersection. It was raining, and it took a moment to get any traction. Some jerk waiting on the cross street honked at me.

I was hurrying to the grocery store to buy cut flowers for Gladys. She was cooking dinner tonight, and if I was the least bit late, it would be another night of one-word answers. I figured the flowers would set the mood for an enjoyable dinner and, with any luck, breakfast.

I sped up Grand Avenue just in time to wait for the traffic light on Lexington. At least there was a left turn lane at this intersection, not that it really mattered. The light was exceptionally long, and I was beginning to think it was broken when it finally turned green. I accelerated up the hill past the entrance to the grocery store parking lot and took a right at the corner. Experience had taught me parking in the overflow lot was actually the quickest way to park and run into the store.

I passed the rear entrance into the lot and pulled into the overflow lot, screeching as I turned and sped into the lot. A red SUV, paying no attention, suddenly backed out of a parking place. I slammed on the brakes and leaned on the horn, but with the wet pavement, I slammed my Crown Victoria Police Interceptor into the rear of the SUV.

I sat behind the wheel for a long moment looking at the damage to the SUV, thinking, *'Oh God.'* I got out of my car and hurried over to the driver's door. The window lowered as I approached. A woman with trimmed gray hair and glasses turned toward me. She did not look happy.

"Are you all right, ma'am?"

She seemed to study me for a minute before she answered, "Yes, but what exactly do you think you were doing?"

"What was I doing? I was going to park my car in the parking lot until you backed into me."

"First of all, you were driving at a rather high rate of speed. Was that you I heard screeching around the corner? Secondly, you were traveling in the wrong direction."

"Wrong direction?"

"You entered through the exit."

"Exit?"

She pushed her door open, forcing me to jump back as she climbed out of her car and hurried to the rear. "Oh dear, will you look at this, a broken taillight, my bumper is dented, and that rear quarter panel is going to need replacing. All because you entered through an exit."

"What do you mean an exit? This is the way I always go when—"

She stormed back toward my entrance to the overflow lot, stood in front of the sign, frowned, and signaled me with her index finger. "Would you mind stepping over here, please?"

As I headed in her direction, I said, "Look, lady you backed into me and—"

"I presume you can read," she said, pointing to the sign.

I stepped in front of the sign, ready to protest. Unfortunately, it read,

EXIT ONLY!
DO NOT ENTER

"So, now what's your excuse?"

That last comment prompted a flashback, and for a brief moment, I was back in the hallway outside my high school English class getting yet another lecture from Ms. Wright, my teacher.

She must have recognized the blank look on my face because she suddenly said, "Wait just a minute. Don't I know you from somewhere?"

"I, I'm sure we've never met. I didn't think I did anything wrong, and if you hadn't backed into me, I—"

"Oh. My. God. You're not Haskell, are you? Devlin Haskell? The young man I had senior year? The student who was more interested in the girls in the classroom than what we were discussing in class? I believe I gave you a 'D' just so I wouldn't have to deal with you that final semester. Devlin Haskell?"

"Oh, hello, Ms. Wright."

She glanced at my Crown Vic. "Oh dear Lord, don't tell me you're a police officer now."

"Actually, no, ma'am, I purchased that car at a police auction."

"What on earth are you up to? I've wondered about you for years. You were so… Well, probably best we don't go there. How have you been?"

"Pretty well, thank you. Well, at least up until a moment ago. I still live in the city."

"And you're not a police officer?" she asked and looked over at my car again.

"No, ma'am, I'm a private investigator. Are you still teaching?"

She smiled and shook her head. "No, I retired a few years back. I still hear from a lot of my former students. I volunteer part-time tutoring. I see some things haven't changed with you," she said, glancing at the Exit Only sign.

"Yeah, umm, sorry about that. How about if I give you my details and you contact your insurance company? Your car looks like it should be okay to drive. Here's my card," I said, pulling out my wallet and handing her a card.

"Haskell Investigations. Your office is over on Randolph Avenue?"

"Yes, ma'am."

"Interesting. I remember you very well, Mr. Haskell. I felt I could never quite get through to you."

"I'm guessing all of my teachers would say something like that. I remember there was one guy who would tell his class on the first day that he didn't want any Dev Haskells in the room."

"Oh, yes, Mr. Kennedy. We had a few words about that. Now here, you stand next to this sign and let me get a picture," she said, taking her phone out. Before I knew what was happening, she'd taken two pictures of me. She walked back to our cars and began photographing the damage from a number of different angles.

"Let me check with my insurance company, and I'll be in touch once I hear from them. I'll phone them as soon as I get home. Interesting to meet you again, Devlin. Somehow, I'm not surprised it's under these circumstances."

I held the driver's door for her as she climbed into her SUV. "It was nice to see you again, Ms. Wright. Sorry about the damage."

She smiled and said, "Some things never seem to change, Devlin. Maybe take a moment to read the sign. As I've told you many times before, we all have to follow the rules. I'll be in touch."

As I watched her disappear around the corner, I was thinking back to my high school days. A horn honking brought me back to the here and now. I pulled into the spot she vacated and hurried into the grocery store.

TWO

I was more than twenty minutes late when I parked in front of Gladys' house. I grabbed the flowers, her favorite, cut mums, and hurried up to the front door. I had to ring the doorbell three times before she finally opened the door.

"Oh, finally, it's about time."

"Yeah, sorry I'm late, but I can explain. A woman backed into me on the way to get these flowers for you," I said and held out the bouquet of yellow mums. I figured I still might have half a chance if I splurged and got the large bouquet, twenty bucks worth of cut mums.

"Well, come on in. I've had to keep the dinner warming in the oven for the last half-hour. Steak filets wrapped in bacon, except they're probably all dried out by now," she said as she hurried back to the kitchen.

I opened the screen door and stepped inside, then, in an effort to catch up, I quickly slammed the front door closed, cutting off the bouquet of mums about two inches below the flowers. "Damn it," I whispered and watched the flowers fall to the floor as I opened the door up.

"Dev, what are you doing? I'm putting our overdone dinner on the table."

"Coming," I called and quickly scooped up the flower blossoms and dumped them back into the cellophane wrapper.

"Dev? What are you doing? Get in here."

I hurried into the kitchen. Vintage Gladys, the table was set with her grandmother's china. Sterling silver place settings were arranged on embroidered linen napkins. A Waterford crystal wine carafe was on the table, and Gladys's Waterford wineglass was almost empty. The wineglass at my place hadn't been filled.

"Just put those flowers in the sink, and I'll deal with them later. God, this meal is going to be an absolute disaster."

I couldn't argue, and as it turned out, that was probably the best choice. After the dozen or so one-word responses to my questions, I gave up and focused on my overdone, dried out steak fillet, scorched green beans, and the crusty, overcooked scalloped potatoes.

When Gladys set her knife and fork down signaling she had finished eating, I jumped to my feet and cleared the dishes, arranging them on the counter the way she liked before washing them by hand.

"As long as I'm up, can I get you a dessert?" I asked.

"Sure, Dev, what did you bring?"

It was the most she'd said to me in the past forty minutes and served to remind me that I had offered to bring a dessert. "Actually, I was thinking of pouring you another glass of wine and just listening to whatever you have to say."

"Thanks, but I can pour my own wine, and I don't really have anything else to say."

I glanced at the clock on the wall. If I hurried, I could probably catch my office mate, Louie Laufen, down at The Spot bar. "How about this, Gladys. I know you're upset with me being late, and I don't blame you." Even though I did. "How about you just relax and take it easy after doing all the work on this, this very lovely dinner? And I'll clean up the kitchen. How does that sound?"

"It sounds like you're hoping to spend the night with me, and that's not going to happen, Dev. You were a half-hour late, and because you apparently didn't care enough to call, the dinner I spent the better part of the afternoon preparing was ruined."

"Gladys, I told you. A woman backed into my car, and I had to deal with that."

"Yeah, sure, you probably gave her your phone number. Tried to sweet-talk her."

"Well, for your information, she turned out to be a teacher I had back in high school. I just wanted to make sure she was okay and to get her information, so when I report the accident to my insurance company, they'll know—"

"You know, Dev, I think it would be best if you just leave. I don't want you anywhere near my grand-

mother's china or my crystal. If you hurry, you can probably still catch that Louie character at that dreadful bar
where you two waste so much of your lives."

"You sure I couldn't—"

"Thank you for the flowers. At least you remembered how much I love mums. I'll put them in a vase
once I've finished cleaning up."

That was definitely my traveling music.

"All right, Gladys. Thank you for dinner. Hope to
talk with you later." I bent down to give her a kiss, but
at the last minute, she turned her head, and I ended up
kissing her hair. Anything else I said would just add to
the problem, so I headed for the front door. There were
two mums lying on the floor next to the front door. I
picked them up, closed the door behind me, tossed the
flowers into her front garden, and hurried to my car.

Three

I drove home and pulled Morton off the couch. We went for a quick walk around the block then hopped in the car and headed down to The Spot. As we pulled up, two guys were standing outside smoking cigarettes. We nodded hello to one another, and Morton and I headed into the bar. Louie was seated on his usual stool at the end of the bar.

Mike was bartending, and when he saw us step in, he grabbed a bag of pork rinds from the rack and tossed them in front of Louie. Louie looked up from the newspaper he was reading and watched as Morton began picking up speed, making his way along the bar.

"I thought you were having dinner with that Glad Ass woman tonight. What happened? She get tired of trying to deal with you and sent you on your way?" He tore open the bag of pork rinds, dumped half the bag into his hand, and then leaned down and gave them to Morton. For his part, Morton was careful not to knock any onto the floor. Once finished, he sat and patiently looked up at Louie with mournful eyes.

"Does the word disaster have any meaning? One word answers. Overcooked food, and an unhappy woman pretty much sums up the entire evening." I went on to tell him about the car accident, the ruined bouquet of mums, and the dreadful dinner.

"If memory serves, this isn't the first time you've ended up on 'Glad Ass's' bad side."

"Yeah, I know. I'm not even sure she believed my story about my high school teacher backing into me. I figured there was no point in hanging around, waiting for her to discover how I ruined the bouquet of flowers. That'll probably serve as the icing on the cake and give me about a five-day cold spell before she'll be willing to put up with me again."

"Dev, did you ever think that this might be one of the reasons she's available? Based on the stories you've told, it sounds like she can get pretty negative in a very short amount of time."

"Yeah, there is that, but she's got some good points. She really likes to—"

"Too much information. Buy you a beer?"

"Yeah, at this point, it certainly can't hurt and might just help."

We chatted on about everything and nothing for another round of drinks when Louie said, "Say, maybe just a warning, but I was out of the office this afternoon, and just as I was pulling up, a black SUV pulled away from the curb. I can't be sure, but it looked an awful lot like your close personal friend, Tubby Gustafson, and that Fat Freddy character—"

"Fat Freddy Zimmerman?"

"Yeah, that's the guy. It looked an awful lot like those two. I'd guess they didn't just happen to pull over to make a phone call outside our office."

"The way the day has gone, that's about the last reason they would be there. Bad things seem to happen in threes. I had the car accident, slammed the bouquet in Gladys' front door, and now Tubby Gustafson is looking for me. The perfect end to an already lousy day."

"Sorry to be the bearer of bad news, but I figured it would be better to let you know than to have you blind-sided."

"Yeah, thanks, Louie. I do appreciate the heads-up. Maybe I should just head up to someone's lake place and hide for a couple of days."

"You know someone who has a place you could use for a bit?"

"Actually, no, I don't. I'll just have to hang around tomorrow and see what day brightener Tubby has for me."

Louie took a sip and said, "I'll be in court for most of the morning. Don't think I'm avoiding you, or Tubby, for that matter."

"Not to worry. I think we better head home. I may as well rest up for whatever tomorrow is planning to bring."

Louie nodded, poured the rest of the pork rinds into his hand, and said, "Okay, Morton, a little reward to you for having to put up with Dev. Keep at it. Sooner or later, he's bound to catch on."

I waited a couple of seconds for Morton to devour the pork rinds before we headed out the door. Once home, we settled in front of the TV. I stretched out on the couch, and Morton stretched out on the floor. We fell asleep partway through a movie about pirates. I went up to bed a little after midnight.

Morton woke me about five minutes before my alarm went off. I let him out the kitchen door then went back upstairs to shower and shave. Once I was dressed, I unplugged my cellphone and read the message from Gladys that had come through while I was in the shower. *'Flowers ruined. Thanks for nothing.'* Probably a good idea I left when I did.

I was just dishing up my breakfast when Morton barked at the back door. I let him inside, and forty-five minutes later, we were parking across the street from the office.

It wasn't until I unlocked the door that I remembered Louie had told me he would be in court all morning. I made coffee and settled in at my desk. I began reviewing a pile of job applications I'd received from a friend at an insurance company. I'd be making phone calls checking on previous jobs the applicants had listed. It was slow-moving, boring, no thought required work that paid the bills.

I heard the stairs creaking around 11:30 and glanced out the window to see if Tubby Gustafson's SUV was parked on the street. Instead, I saw Louie's faded orange Ford Fiesta parked at the curb, and a moment later, the door opened and a red-faced Louie stepped into the office.

I knew better than to try to start a conversation just after he'd climbed the stairs to the second floor. So, I said, "Hi Louie, didn't think you'd be back this early. Let me get you a coffee."

I grabbed the mug from his picnic table desk, dumped the remnants down the sink, and refilled it. Louie was seated at this point. Still red-faced and breathing as if he'd just finished a five-mile run. Once I set the mug on his picnic table, he pulled it in front of him, and took a series of sips over the course of the next three or four minutes. Eventually, he sat back in his chair and said. "Any visitors this morning?"

"You mean like Tubby Gustafson?"

"Yeah or Gladys. I was thinking she might come down and return that ruined bouquet you left for her."

"I guess the good news is, so far, neither one has made an appearance."

"Well, the day isn't over yet," Louie said as he pulled a stack of files from his briefcase.

"Things go your way in court this morning?" I asked.

"Yeah, pro-bono work, three cases, just initial hearings, but it takes time. It serves as a reminder to me that

I really don't have anything to complain about. All I have to do is look out the window to find someone who has it worse."

Four

The afternoon passed quickly, and in no time, Louie asked, "Hey, I'm at a stopping point. You thinking about going over to The Spot for one?"

"I could make time in my busy schedule for at least one. Let me take Morton around the block, and we'll join you in a couple of minutes."

Louie headed over to The Spot. Morton and I headed off in the opposite direction. Morton seemed interested in every tree and fence gate along the way. It took the better part of fifteen minutes before we rounded the corner and came in sight of The Spot. We also happened to catch a black SUV pulling away from our office building, heading up the street to the interstate entrance, and disappearing. My first thought was Tubby Gustafson looking for me again.

I debated jumping in the car and heading out of town, but fortunately, a cooler head prevailed, and we made our way over to The Spot. Louie must have seen us through the window because he was in the process of pouring half a bag of pork rinds into his hand. Morton knew there were pork rinds waiting for him at the end of the bar and almost tore my arm out of the socket in an effort to get to Louie. He had Louie's hand emptied and licked clean in a few seconds.

Mike arrived with a beer for me and a fresh drink for Louie as Morton sat and stared at Louie. I pulled a ten from my wallet, the only cash I had, and set it on the bar. Mike smiled and took it.

"Here's to you. Glad you two finally made it," Louie said, raising his glass for a half-second before he took a sip.

"Thanks to Morton taking his time, we missed Fat Freddy and Tubby Gustafson going up to the office. God only knows what they want."

"You think you should give him a call?"

"Tubby? I'm not sure he'd even answer. If he did, he'd probably tell me to get over to his place so he could listen to whatever awful message he has in person. No, thanks."

"Call him and tell him you're out of town. He won't be able to do anything about it, and if he does let you know what he wants, it will give you a day or two to figure out how you're going to deal with it."

"Actually, that kind of makes sense."

"Surprise, surprise. How long ago did you see him?"

"Just a few minutes ago. They headed up the street and onto the interstate."

"Maybe wait an hour and call. Tell him you got word from someone in one of the offices on the first floor, and you wanted to get in touch."

"Great idea, Louie, that's what I'll do, call him in an hour."

We sat and traded stories for the next hour and a half before Louie said, "You going to give Tubby a call?"

"Yeah, like you said, I want to wait for an hour before I call him."

"It's already been an hour and a half."

The jukebox was playing an oldie by the Rolling Stones. "Mmm-mmm, okay, but I better step outside. Order me another beer. This shouldn't take too long."

I stepped outside and speed-dialed Tubby's number. He answered on the third ring. "Just where in the hell have you been, you worthless piece of—"

"I'm out of town, Tub— err, Mr. Gustafson."

"Oh really, out of town. Where? Chicago? Kansas City? New Orleans?"

"No, sir, umm, I'm up in Finland, sir."

"Finland?"

"Yes, sir. Finland, Minnesota. Visiting a friend in the hospital. He's got some rare communicable disease. He's on his death bed, and now that I've seen him, I'm going to head back to town tomorrow, but it might not be safe to see me for a few days. I wouldn't want to risk getting you sick."

"I understand, Haskell, and I appreciate you showing some concern for my health. Wishing you a safe journey home, hope your friend recovers, oh, and one more thing…"

"Yes, sir, what's that?"

"Get your dumb ass over to my car now, you idiot!" With that, the headlights flashed on a black SUV parked across the street and down about two doors. The tires screeched as the vehicle leapt forward into the oncoming traffic lane and pulled up and over the curb, forcing me to jump out of the way.

A thug I didn't recognize slid out from behind the wheel. He was muscular looking, with a shaved head, a tattooed neck, and a face with red blotches and what looked like blisters. He opened the rear door, and I could see Tubby shaking his head, looking like he was ready to explode and still holding his phone.

"Lyle, you have my permission to break every bone in Haskell's body," Tubby shouted.

"Might be a good idea to get in here, dumb shit," blotchy faced Lyle said.

"Oh, nice to see you so soon, Mr. Gustafson. Thank you for making the time to see me," I said as I slid into the backseat.

Lyle slammed the door closed as I was climbing in, pushing me even closer to Tubby. A tray on the back of the passenger seat was pulled down, and it looked like Tubby was in the process of eating a large piece of chocolate cake.

He placed a large forkful in his mouth and said, "Why Haskell? Why? After all I've done for you. Is it any wonder you're nothing but a failure?"

"Good evening, sir. How are things?"

"Not good. Certain people seem to think they can get away with lying to me."

"Oh, umm, I wasn't lying, sir. I knew you were parked across the street. I was just about to walk over, but you saved me the trouble."

"Silencio, you moron," he shouted, spraying bits of chocolate cake in my direction. "God save me. Frederick, give this idiot the Cummings file."

Fat Freddy Zimmerman turned around in the front passenger seat, smiled, and raised his eyebrows, suggesting he was laughing at my predicament. He shoved a manila file folder in my direction.

"Well, take it, for God's sake," Tubby shouted.

"Thank you," I said, hoping I sounded polite.

"Thank you? For God's sake. You idiot, you don't even know what's in there. Open the damn thing and take a look."

"Oh, yes, sir. I was just about to do that, but I thought, you know, being polite and all. I thought it—"

"One more word. One more stupid utterance on your part, and I'll strangle you myself. Now open the damn file," Tubby shouted.

I opened the file and stared at a black and white photo of a nice enough looking guy with dark, curly hair. I studied the photo for a long moment.

"Well," Tubby growled.

"You said you didn't want me to talk, sir."

Tubby closed his eyes, exhaled, and muttered something. I only caught the last word, which was 'Frederick.'

"Haskell, do you know who the hell that is?" Fat Freddy asked.

I studied the image for another moment and shook my head. "He doesn't look familiar. I'm pretty sure I don't know him."

"His name is Eli Cummings, and he owes Mister Gustafson money."

"A lot of damn money," Tubby growled.

"You want me to pay his debt? I just gave my last ten-dollar bill to the bartender. How 'bout I go back in and see what I have for change. It's all I've got, but you're welcome to it, Mr. Gustafson."

Tubby's breathing increased audibly, and his eyes glared. He suddenly shouted, "Get out. Get out. Get out!"

I opened the door and jumped out of the back seat. Tubby threw the file out the door after me as Lyle hit the accelerator. The SUV bounced off the curb and ran the red light at the corner.

"Find him, you idiot, or I'll—" Tubby screamed as they sped down the street.

An oncoming car skidded to a stop, and the driver leaned on the horn. I watched them disappear, wishing this time it would be for good.

Louie looked at me as I stepped back into The Spot. I tossed the file onto the bar and said, "Check this out. That guy ring any bells?"

"You went back to the office?"

"I wish. No, I stepped outside to make Tubby's call. I told him I was up north visiting a dying friend, but unfortunately, he just happened to be parked across the street. They almost ran me over when they pulled up onto the sidewalk. Go ahead, open the file. I'm supposed to find that guy," I said as Louie took the file and opened it.

He studied the black and white photo for a second then lifted it up and read the piece of paper beneath it, mostly addresses. "You know this Eli Cummings guy?"

"Fortunately, no. Not sure I want to if Tubby is looking for him. If they want me to find him, that suggests he's probably hiding somewhere or has left town. With Tubby looking for him, leaving town sounds like the better option."

"What are you going to do?"

"Well, I'm not going to spend a lot of time looking for someone who has probably fled to parts unknown. I'll check around just so Tubby gets the word I'm looking, but I'm not going to waste my time."

"What do you think he did?" Louie asked.

"My guess is Tubby lent him some money at about a two hundred percent interest rate. Now the guy can't be found, and Tubby expects to be paid. Serves Tubby right."

Five

I was on my third cup of coffee before Morton strolled into the kitchen and stretched. I gave him his morning head scratch and let him out the kitchen door. I filled his food and water dish then went back to my computer and continued reading up on Eli Cummings. From what I found online, he was a local, born and raised in town. Employment history was sketchy, to say the least, and nothing of any significance. A couple of oddball construction jobs, taxi driver, Uber actually, until his car was repossessed. No mention of a wife or any family. I came across an address listed for an apartment, and I planned to check it out on the way into the office.

Morton barked twice at the kitchen door, and I let him in. He made a beeline for his food and was licking the bowl clean five minutes later. I placed my coffee mug and breakfast bowl in the dishwasher, and we headed out the door.

The most recent address for Eli Cummings was over on the east side of town. Not the most desirable location. Eli's place was in the middle of the block. All the houses, two-story frame structures, that looked to be at least a hundred years old. Originally built as single family homes, the entire block had been converted into multiple rental units. They all appeared to be in various states of disrepair. I studied the photo in Tubby's file for a moment before I got out of the car.

Nine concrete steps led up a steep hill to the house. The front porch sagged and was missing a railing. Five doorbells were attached to the doorframe. They were labeled with the unit number one through five. I pushed the doorbell for apartment two. Nothing happened.

I figured there were two units each on the first and second floor and the fifth unit was in the converted attic space. I walked around the side of the house to the back. The backyard was small, very small. Based on the lack of grass and the tire tracks, it was apparently used for parking. The back door had the number two painted alongside the door. Not so surprisingly, the door was partially open. Based on the boot print it had been kicked in.

I stepped onto the sagging wooden steps and called, "Hello. Hello."

No one answered, but I could hear pounding, so I pushed the door all the way open, stepped inside, and called again. "Hello, anybody home?"

"No one's here," a voice growled.

I looked around at a broken piece of sheetrock, a lawn chair, a kitchen pan on the floor, and two saw-horses. It looked like someone had thrown up on the floor. There was a small cabinet with a hotplate resting on the counter. A beautiful landscape painting, unframed, hung crookedly on a wall. I headed down a little hall past two more landscape paintings on the walls as I headed toward the pounding.

I entered a grimy room with three portraits of the same older woman leaning against the far wall. Next to the portraits were two brown paper shopping bags that looked to be filled with clothes. A grimy mattress rested on the floor. Two guys were busy nailing an old red curtain over the closet area.

"Excuse me, I—"

"Hey, you hear what the hell I said? No one's here, so beat it," the older of the two said. He had a beer belly, could have been maybe fifty, needed a shave, and given the attitude, deserved a hard kick in the butt.

"I'm looking for Eli Cummings."

"What'd he do now?"

I ignored his question and asked, "Do you know where I can find him?"

"If you find him, you'll have to get in line behind us and probably a dozen other folks. Owes me two months' rent plus damages."

"So he's not here."

"Does it look like he's here? You see him around anywhere?"

"I'm just surprised he left this high-class place. List must be long of folks wanting to get in here and deal with your charming personality."

His partner, standing behind him, smiled at my comment.

"Be a good idea if you got your ass out of here."

"I think you're probably right, for a change. Enjoy the rest of your day," I said and left. As I stepped into the hall, I heard fatty say to his partner, "What the hell are you laughing about?"

I drove down to the office. Louie was seated at his picnic table desk, talking on his cellphone. I gave him a wave and unclipped Morton's leash. Morton headed to his pillow next to the file cabinet and settled in. I poured the remnants from the coffee pot into my mug and took a sip. It tasted like it had been on the burner for the past forty-eight hours. I emptied my mug in the sink, made a fresh pot, and settled in at my desk just as Louie set his phone down.

"How'd it go? You find that guy Tubby's looking for?"

I shook my head and said, "Typical. I went to his last known address over on the Eastside. Not surprisingly, a real dump. The charming landlord was there working. Actually, he was nailing some red curtains over the entrance to a closet."

"What?"

"Like I said, the place was a dump. Tubby's guy owed two months' rent and apparently disappeared. The landlord said, if I was looking for money, I'd have to get in line."

"That figures. What do you plan to do?"

"I'm calling Tubby, right now, and telling him I couldn't find this guy, and he'll just have to deal with it."

"Be careful," Louie said.

I filled my mug with fresh coffee and pushed the speed dial number for Tubby Gustafson. Unfortunately, he answered on the second ring.

"Tell me you've found him," was his opening line.

"Good morning, sir. I've just come from his place, actually his former place. I spoke to his landlord. Cummings owes him two months' rent and took off for places unknown. The landlord seemed to think he left town. He even suggested he may have left the country. He told me Mexico most likely," I lied. "If you want, I would be willing to go down there and try to find him. He seemed to think it was one of those all-inclusive beach resort areas where—"

"Yeah, I'm sure you'd love to go down there and waste your time and my money. No, absolutely not. Now, I want you to find this idiot before I decide to make you responsible for the debt he owes and—"

"Make me responsible?"

"I stand corrected, Haskell. God knows you are anything but responsible. Find him and fast." Click.

"You're off to Mexico?" Louie asked.

"Hardly. Looks like I'm back to square one. I need to find this character. If you skipped out on rent and don't have any dough, where would you go?"

"I'd maybe try to land with a sibling or a pal. You think the guy might have a girlfriend? I'm guessing in today's world, it would be pretty tough to try to rent without any kind of recommendation. Any landlord is going to want at least a month's down payment, references, probably employment information."

"I don't know, maybe he—" My phone ringing cut me off. I glanced at the screen, 'unknown.'

"Tubby calling you back?" Louie asked.

I shook my head and let it ring a couple more times before I answered. "Haskell Investigations."

"I'd like to speak with Devlin Haskell, please."

"Ms. Wright?"

"Oh, Devlin. I wasn't sure that was you."

"Yeah, it's me. Everything okay?"

"Yes, it is. I've contacted my insurance company. Have you contacted yours?"

"Oh, my insurance company? Umm, yeah, I mean yes, I contacted them right after the accident. I'm just waiting for a call back," I said, thinking the last thing I needed was my insurance rates to go up. The damage to my Crown Vic wasn't that bad, and I could live with it.

"Well, I contacted mine. That's the reason I'm calling. I'm wondering if there might be a time we could get together and discuss what we intend to do."

This sounded like it was going to cost me money. "You want to discuss? Isn't your insurance company going to cover you?"

"Oh yes, they'll do that, at least cover a portion. In fact, they'll be more than happy to do that, and then my rates will immediately go up, and in twenty-four months,

I will have paid more to them than if I paid the repair cost myself. Which, I hasten to add, I have no intention of doing."

"Okay, I get that. But what do you want to talk about?"

"I have an idea. I think you may find it interesting. At least, I hope you will."

Oh, God, she probably wants her house painted or something. "Yeah, sure, I suppose we could meet. You pick the place, and I'll be there."

"Are you busy today?"

"Today? Well, I have a number of meetings," I lied. "But you choose a time, and I'll adjust my schedule."

"Wonderful, how does the noon hour sound?"

"Yeah, I'll move things around so I can do that. Where would you like to meet?"

"Let me give you my address."

Six

Ms. Wright lived in the Phalen Park end of town. A nice neighborhood built around Phalen Lake. She lived in a two-story corner house with an attached double garage, a well-kept lawn, a trimmed hedge against the front of the house, and a large, multi-colored garden of flowers.

I spotted the house from a half-block away because her red SUV with the broken taillight and the dented rear quarter panel was parked in the driveway. I parked at the curb, climbed out, and walked up the driveway to the paved path leading to the front door. I glanced at the flower garden. Gladys would have loved it.

I'd stopped at a local florist and gotten a small pot full of some kind of little blue flowers as a gift in the hopes Ms. Wright wouldn't try to get me to pay more than the repair would cost. I still thought at least fifty percent of the accident was her fault. I tried to avoid looking at the damage to her car as I walked past. I rang the doorbell, and she answered the door while the bell was still chiming. "Well, Devlin, come in, come in. You're right on time."

"Here, I know you like flowers, so I got you these," I said, holding out the pot with the little blue flowers.

"Oh, Devlin. Forget-me-nots, so very thoughtful of you. Thank you, that's very kind. Come on into the kitchen. I've got a little lunch prepared for us. I hope you haven't eaten."

"No, I haven't, but don't worry about making lunch. I—"

"It's already made, so you can just relax," she said as we walked through a dining room and into her kitchen.

The kitchen smelled delicious, and I noticed a pan of something sitting on top of the brushed chrome stove. The stove had six burners with two side-by-side ovens below it. The cabinets appeared to be cherrywood with white marble countertops. Two place settings were arranged on the counter. She set the blue flowers on the counter between the place settings.

"Now Devlin, I have coffee on, but if you would prefer a glass of wine, I have a nice chilled Sauvignon Blanc."

"Coffee will be fine for me, but don't let me hold you up if you'd like the wine."

"Mmm-mmm, I really shouldn't, but maybe just one." As she filled a white mug with coffee, she asked, "Do you take cream or sugar?"

"No, black is just fine."

She set the mug at one of the places at the counter and said, "Grab a seat." I walked around the counter and pulled out a stool as she took a wine glass from a cupboard. She opened the double door refrigerator and pulled a half-filled bottle of white wine from the shelf on the door. She filled her glass, returned the bottle to the refrigerator, and settled onto the stool at the end of the counter. "Well, thank you for coming, and thank you for the flowers," she said and raised her wine glass.

I raised my coffee mug in response.

"So tell me what you've been up to since graduation."

"Oh, a little of this and that. I tried college for a bit, but I just wasn't cut out for it."

"Oh, but you were so smart in high school. I think that was one of the things that caused you to be bored with classwork. You could see well beyond it and became easily bored. You were known as the class clown. Anyway, enough of that. So, where did you go to college?"

"I was at the U, but it just wasn't for me. I didn't enjoy it at all. I dropped out after three semesters, went in the service, got out, and was looking around at things, the trades and whatnot. Eventually, I wound up where I am."

"And your business is called Haskell Investigations?"

"Yeah, it puts food on the table. I occasionally meet some interesting individuals."

"I can only imagine. But you enjoy it?"

"Most of the time. Sometimes I end up dealing with either an individual or a situation that isn't all that great, but yeah, all in all, I enjoy it. I office with an attorney pal. I have friends on the police force, and like I said, I meet a lot of characters."

She smiled at that last bit and said, "You must meet some dreadful people, too."

"Once in a while. If someone is hiring me, it's usually because of a problem, someone missing, a spouse maybe misbehaving, a court case with a decision they didn't want, all sorts of things. It's never dull for very long."

She nodded as I spoke and eventually said, "It's interesting you do what you do, and in a way, I'm not at all surprised. I could tell when you were in my class that you would be taking the… How can I say it? You would be taking the path less traveled."

I chuckled and said, "You make it sound like I would be looking for buried treasure or something."

"No, not exactly, but it sounds as though you're always searching for answers. Where did someone go? Is someone true in their relationship? Was thus and such done fairly, legally?"

"I never thought of it like that, but I suppose you may be right. What about you? You told me you had retired."

"Yes and no. I did retire from actively teaching and earning a paycheck. Now I volunteer, essentially doing the same thing, helping children, only now I'm not paid."

"You didn't get your fill of that, dealing with kids like me?"

"Every student I've had is a unique case, a special entity, and if I can just unlock the door for them, the world would be their oyster. In fact, that's why I wanted to chat with you. I've wondered about you often over the years, and to be honest, I had always thought you were one of the ones who got away. Someone I didn't quite connect with."

"The teachers used to say they didn't want any Dev Haskells in their classroom."

"Yes, Milton Kennedy, our chemistry teacher if you'll recall. I told you, he and I had a little talk about that."

"Yeah, I think he was always mad about the bag of dog poop I put in his desk."

"You're the one who did that?"

"Oh yeah. I did it on a dare. He knew it was me, but he could never prove it. I think he even had someone come in and try to pull fingerprints off his desk. Not that it did any good. Well, except it kind of got me interested in the crime and evidence aspect."

She laughed at that as she got off her stool and went over to the stove. "I remember the fingerprint episode. He was obsessed with finding out who did it. Now, I made a lasagna, and before you say anything, let me warn you. It was my mother's recipe, so eat it and don't complain." She placed a large piece on a plate and pushed it across the counter to me. She dished up a

smaller piece for herself, topped up her wine glass, and
sat down.

Seven

We ate and talked some more, just catching up. I told her about a couple of people who had been in my class and what they were doing. It turned out she knew about a lot more people than I did and filled me in. Nine people had died, three in the service. Two guys had died of cancer, another guy of a heart attack. A couple who were high school sweethearts died in a car accident. One girl went off a mountain while skiing out in Colorado. We talked about a number of people who disappeared, which probably meant their families had moved out of town.

Eventually, we came back around to the reason I was there, the damage to her car. "So, the estimate I got was thirty-eight hundred dollars to repair the damage to my car," she said.

"Thirty-eight hundred to fix a broken taillight?"

"Yes, along with replacing the back bumper and a new rear quarter panel. Thirty-eight hundred dollars. You are more than welcome to get your own estimate on what it will cost. But I think you know as well as I do that the cost will undoubtedly be in that neighborhood."

"That's an awful lot of money," I said, thinking about all the trips I could take for thirty-eight hundred dollars. The dates I could go on, the drinks I could buy. I could pay in advance at The Spot and run a tab there for the better part of six months. I thought of a couple of women I could take to a topless beach, maybe two at the same time, and we…

"I have a couple of thoughts," she said, bringing me back to the here and now. "You could always write me a check for that amount and go your own way. You could pay me in monthly installments, say a hundred dollars a month for thirty-eight months. Or, I may have one other idea."

Against my better judgement, I asked, "What's the other idea?"

"A few of us volunteer twice a week at the high school, helping students with homework. But the group is much more than simply helping with homework. It's more or less a last-ditch effort to keep the students from dropping out. We've got a few bad actors. There's the occasional student that's having a problem with a particular class. We've got students who speak English as a second language, and the help they would normally get from, say, parents or other family members just doesn't exist. And, we've got students like you, who, for whatever reason, don't seem to be the least bit interested. It doesn't mean that they're stupid. On the contrary, they're oftentimes very bright, but nothing seems to catch. I'm wondering if you would be interested in help-ing us?"

"Me?"

She looked around the room for a moment then said, "I don't see anyone else in here, Mr. Haskell."

"What's this group called?"

"It's called a lot of things, and officially it's referred to as the Independent Learning Initiative."

"And unofficially?"

She smiled and said, "Something near and dear to your heart, those of us in the group call it After School Detention or simply, Detention."

"I think I spent a good part of my high school years in detention. I'm not sure I could be of much help to any of these kids."

"Why don't you let me worry about that? I happen to think you could be exactly the sort of person we need and so seldom get. If I may be so bold, you usually were in detention for things you were caught doing, the dog poop episode with Mr. Kennedy aside. It's a different world today, Dev. It's actually a lot harder on these kids than it was in your day and certainly a lot harder than my day. Even the word detention has been softened to Inde-pendent Learning Initiative."

"How often would I be doing this?"

"We meet twice a week, Tuesday and Thursday eve-nings for two hours, six until eight o'clock. A number of us interact with the kids on the weekends or other times, but usually, that's just for a project or maybe a paper they have to write. As for how long you would have to do this? Let's just take it one day at a time, but certainly, no longer than fifteen weeks. That's a semester. If you wanted to continue after that, we'd love it, and if not, that would be okay, too."

"Tuesdays and Thursdays?"

She nodded. "Yes, from six until eight, your first day would be tomorrow."

"And it's at the high school?"

"We meet in the cafeteria at five forty-five. Fifteen minutes before the students arrive. It's not mandatory anymore, so we never know how many students we'll have on any given evening."

"Okay, Ms. Wright, I'll give it a try. I might be coming to you for help when they ask me about punctuation, history, or God forbid algebra."

"I think you'll find you might just enjoy it. Oh, and Devlin, please call me Barbara."

"Oh, thanks, and you can call me Dev."

"Deal?" she asked and held out her hand to shake.

I extended my hand and said, "Deal," as we shook.

Eight

I spent the better part of the next day trying to find anything on Eli Cummings. I pretty much came up empty-handed. I placed a call to my pal on the police force, Lieutenant Aaron LaZelle, but ended up leaving a message. I drove back to the house on the east side where Cummings had skipped out on the rent, but the crabby fat landlord wasn't around, the door to unit two was padlocked, and no one answered when I rang the other four doorbells.

I drove back to the office and looked up the property tax records and got the name of the LLC listed as the owner of the property. I called the phone number listed.

"Yeah," a raspy voice answered, and an image of the crabby fat guy flashed in my mind. I heard a horn honk on the other end of the line, suggesting he was driving while talking on the phone, which was against the law in Minnesota.

"Good afternoon, thank you for taking my call. We're calling regarding a tenant of yours at nine forty-seven Burr Street, and—"

"Is this the cops?"

"We have some questions regarding an individual by the name of Mr. Eli Cummings."

"Cummings? Let me tell you. You should arrest that son-of-a-bitch. He skipped out on two months' rent. Left my apartment in a terrible mess, and it's going to cost me a hell of a lot of money to repair the damage."

"If we can get ahold of him, we could certainly add that to our list of offenses. Now our records indicate he resided in unit number 2, is that correct?"

"Yeah, he was only there for four months, owed me two months rent, and ran out."

"Any idea where he may have gone?"

"Where? Hell, if I knew the answer to that, I'd be there looking for him right now."

"Do you have any information on next of kin or a place of employment?"

"Place of employment? Who the hell would hire that loser? When he disappeared, I called the job site he'd listed, and they told me they'd never heard of him— my fault for not following through to begin with. I knew the bastard was shady from the moment I first laid eyes on him. Being a nice guy, I rented a gorgeous unit to him anyway, and now I'm paying the price, damn it."

Images of the 'gorgeous unit' flashed in my mind. The single cabinet with the hot plate, the sawhorses, whatever it was splattered across the wall and floor, the grungy hall and the room with the grimy mattress on the floor and the red curtain nailed to the wall covering the closet. "It's absolutely unfair, sir. If I may, I'll make a note of your phone number, and should we get hold of Mr. Cummings, we'll contact you."

"That would be great. Can I charge him interest on the outstanding rent?"

"Absolutely. In fact, that's one of the ways we can help. Now, all we have to do is send a city inspector over to inspect the premises for any code violations. I'll file a request and get that procedure underway immediately—"

"Wait a minute, did you say a city inspector?"

"Thank you for your time, sir."

"Wait a damn minute. I don't want—"

I disconnected and quickly blocked his number. I heard the staircase creaking, a moment later the office door opened, and a red-faced Louie entered. He gave me a slight wave, set his briefcase on the picnic table, and settled into his desk chair. I grabbed his coffee mug, dumped the remnants in the sink, and poured what was left into his mug. Once I set the mug down, he slid it over and then sipped and grimaced for the next three or four minutes.

"How's your day going?" he eventually asked and pushed the mug off to the side.

"Still trying to locate this Cummings character Tubby wants me to find."

"You're going to turn him over to Tubby Gustafson?"

"You kidding? If that news got out, I could be listed as an accessory to murder. No, I'd just give the guy a heads-up and tell him to leave town. Maybe wait a couple of days and tell Tubby I couldn't find him."

"But no luck so far?"

"None. Just got off the line with his former landlord. Apparently, Cummings lied about his place of employment. Wherever it was, they'd never heard of the guy. Not that the landlord is any great shakes. The apartment was a real dive, and the landlord is a major jerk."

Louie nodded, suggesting the two maybe went hand in hand. "You interested in going over to The Spot for one?"

"I'd love to, but I'm helping some folks at the high school, so I'd better take a pass," I said, not wanting to tell Louie I was back in high school detention. "If I can finish up at a decent time, I may stop down, but it wouldn't be until sometime after eight."

"I don't even want to know what you got yourself into. If you feel like it, I'll probably still be there."

Nine

As I pulled into the parking lot at my old high school, it didn't look like much had changed other than the fact I was driving my own car. Eight cars were parked in the area marked for staff, including Barbara's red SUV. I parked at the far end of the lot and felt like I was sneaking in.

There were four cars in the main parking lot with a half-dozen kids hanging around, but I couldn't tell if they were waiting until six to come into the detention meeting or if they were just hanging around after one of the team practices.

Rather than entering the building through the main door, I headed for the door that led to the cafeteria. Fortunately, it was unlocked, and as I stepped into the building, I was immediately transported back twenty years. The place looked pretty much the same other than the metal detectors positioned on either side of the entrance, a sign of the times, I guess.

I walked down the hallway. Buff-colored student lockers with black combination locks lined both sides of the hall. It was a short thirty-foot walk to the double doors that led to the cafeteria. I pulled the door open and stepped in. Dozens of Formica topped tables were neatly arranged with five chairs on either side. Over in the far corner, seven people, five women and two guys, all turned as one to see who had just entered.

Fortunately, one of the women was Barbara, and she waved a hand and called, "Over here, Dev, join us."

I headed over to the table, not recognizing any of the people sitting with Barbara. "Any trouble finding the place?" she asked, then laughed. "This is the man I was telling you about, Dev Haskell. He's offered to join us for a semester to help out. Dev went to school here."

"Yeah, but wisely, the school never mentions me," I said, which brought smiles to almost everyone seated.

"Dev," Barbara said, "this is Marjorie Murphy and…" She went around the table, introducing everyone. I got a smile and a nod in every case, but one, a guy named Harold Kennedy gave a half-frown as he nodded. I wondered if maybe his father was the chemistry teacher whose desk I'd placed the dog poop in my senior year.

"Nice to meet you," I said once Barbara was finished. I looked at everyone around the table and studied Kennedy for a long moment. I pulled up a chair and listened for all of five minutes before two girls walked in, and everyone stood and hurried to different tables.

"All right, Dev, why don't you grab the table next to me? The students go to someone for specific help, like Harold for chemistry, or Rosa for Spanish, or they head for a table that doesn't already have someone. You're going to be the last person they'll go to only because they don't know you yet. Don't be discouraged. In their own way, they're still somewhat shy. Once the word is out on you, you'll be very busy. Here you can use this," she said, handing me a yellow legal tablet and a pen.

She wasn't kidding about me being the last person. There were two or three students waiting at every table except mine and, at no surprise, Harold Kennedy's. The door opened, and a pretty girl walked in. She looked at the various tables with students waiting and then chose me instead of Harold Kennedy, making a beeline in my direction.

"How's it going," she said, pulling a chair out and sitting across from me. "Who are you? I haven't seen you around here before."

"Yeah, well, I graduated from here about twenty years ago, but I got a notice that said I skipped a detention, and I still had to serve it, or they were going to revoke my graduation."

Her eyes widened as she leaned forward, gave a quick look around, and half-whispered, "Really?"

"No, just kidding."

"Oh man, that was good. You got me, dude."

"So what brings you in here on a nice night like tonight?" I asked.

"I'm having some real problems with a paper I'm supposed to write, and it has to be three thousand words long."

"Okay, so how far along are you?"

"I got two words down so far. My name, Ramona Williams."

"Mmm-mmm, I hate to tell you this, Ramona, but I'm not sure your name is going to count."

"Are you kidding me?"

"I wish. Hey, I've been there. So what topic did they give you to write about?"

"Well, that's part of the problem. She didn't give us a topic. We're supposed to come up with one, and I just can't."

"What do you like to do?"

"Huh?"

"If you can write about anything you want, why don't you pick something you like to do? You into certain kinds of books? You know, romance or horror or—"

"That sounds like the same thing," she said and laughed.

"Yeah, there are times," I said, recalling my last text from Gladys. "But what do you like? Maybe a particular kind of music or a band. You like looking at clothes or hairstyles. Do you know how tattoos are done?"

"Tattoos?"

"Just throwing out ideas, here. I didn't say you have to get one."

"No, no, I really like tattoos, my boyfriend, well, ex-boyfriend had one. A great big pair of wings across his shoulders. It turned out to be about the only good thing about the guy."

"Well, maybe you could write about tattoos. There's all sorts of information and images online you could check out."

"Mmm-mmm, yeah, my mom can't afford internet access in our apartment, and we don't have a computer anyway, so that's kind of out."

"You got a driver's license?"

"No, not till next year, then I'm blowing out of this town."

"You take the city bus?"

"You kidding? Every day, but I don't want to write about being on the bus. Talk about boring."

"Yeah, I get that. You live near here."

"Kind of," she said, suddenly sounding cautious.

"I'm just thinking. I got a pal with a tattoo shop. He's pretty good. He's won all sorts of awards and contests. He's got at least a half-dozen albums full of original tattoo designs. If you want, I could call him and see if he'd talk to you, and you could write about that, or I know a lady who runs a bakery and—"

"I'd love the tattoo dude. That would be so awesome."

"You want me to call him?"

"Yeah, please, that would be really cool."

"Okay, hang on. I'll do it right now." I pulled out my phone and speed-dialed my pal Dennis Richards. He answered almost immediately.

"Dev Haskell? To what do I owe the pleasure?"

"Hey, Dennis, too long since we spoke. I'm calling to ask a favor."

"Fire away."

"I've got a friend named Ramona and—"

"She looking to get inked in a private area?"

"No, actually she's looking to write a high school paper on tattoos. Would there be any chance she could talk to you?"

"You kidding? I'd love it. Have her stop down any time."

"I'll pass this on to her, Dennis. Much appreciated."

"You still showing up at The Spot, Dev?"

"Yeah, I office right across the street from there."

"Good, I'll stop in one of these nights and you can buy me a beer," he said.

"Consider it done. Hey, give me your address," I said then wrote it down on the back of one of my business cards, and we disconnected.

"What'd he say?" Ramona asked.

"He said he'd love to have you stop by." I slid my business card across the table to her. "Here's my card. His name and address are on the back along with his cell-phone number."

She turned my card over and read Dennis's information. "Inkredible, that's the studio's name?"

"Yeah, it's kind of famous."

She nodded. "I've heard of it. Oh, this is going to be so cool. Thanks so much." She turned my card over as she stood. "You're a private investigator, Mr. Haskell?"

"You can call me Dev, and yeah, that's what I do."

"Like in the movies?"

"Nothing that crazy, actually, I'm a pretty boring guy. Good luck talking to Dennis. He's a good guy. Nice to meet you, Ramona. You let me know how the paper turns out."

"I will. I promise. Thanks again, dude," she said and hurried out the door.

Ten

Two more students ended up at my table, only because no one else was available. One wanted help with an algebra equation, which immediately informed me she knew more than I did. Fortunately, some kid was just leaving another table, and I strongly suggested she would be better served by the individual over there. She must have been, because as she left, she smiled and gave me a thumbs-up. A ninth-grader got stuck talking to me about social studies and the American Revolution, and I think I more or less held my own in that conversation.

Things clearly began to slow down after 7:30, and by 8:00, there were just two students finishing up. Everyone stayed seated at their tables for another ten minutes until the students left. Apparently, they always met at Tiffany's for a post-session conference. I decided I would hurry home to let Morton out and then join them. While they were still talking, I headed out the door and ran into a student just coming in. He was a lean kid with dark curly hair and blue eyes. Based on his clothes, I figured grunge was apparently his thing.

"Oh, hey, I think they're pretty much finished for tonight. Anything I can help you with?"

"Oh, umm, no, not really. I just have to turn something into Ms. Jackson. I had to leave school early this afternoon and missed her class."

"She's right inside, can't miss her," I said and headed out the door.

I went out to my car and drove home. Morton was watching out the window as I pulled up. He met me at the front door. We went for a two-block walk. I let him back into the house and headed over to Tiffany's on Ford Parkway.

The official name of the place is Tiffany's Sports Lounge. Fortunately, it was a pleasant enough evening and the group was assembled at two outdoor tables. Barbara waved me over as soon as I stepped out of the parking lot. A number of glasses of white wine rested on the tables. I ordered a beer. Interestingly, Harold Kennedy wasn't in the group, and over the next hour, I never heard anything suggesting he was missed.

People chatted about various students. Collectively, the group was old enough that there was a good chance they knew and possibly had even taught one or both parents of the kids that had stopped in tonight.

I asked the woman next to me if Harold Kennedy's father had taught at the school. She replied with a yes that suggested no further questions on the subject were needed.

I looked at the woman across the table from me and asked, "Excuse me, are you, Ms. Jackson?"

She smiled and said, "Please, call me Janet. Your name is Don?"

"No Dev, short for Devlin. Nice to meet you. I wanted to ask if the boy at the end of the evening was able to turn in his paper to you."

She got a confused look on her face and said, "A boy tonight?"

I explained the situation, running into the kid as I headed out the door.

"That doesn't make any sense. I retired two years ago. I occasionally sub for a day or two, but no one has to turn in a paper to me. Almost all of us are retired, well except for Harold, I think you met him and then Ann sitting down at the end of the table. Are you sure you got the name correct?"

"Yeah, he said Ms. Jackson. Is there someone else with the same name?"

She shook her head and said, "No, no one else by that name. I'm the only one."

"Hmm, I must have misunderstood. I was in a hurry to get home and let my dog out."

"Sometimes it can be a long night, a very long night. How did things go for you?"

"Fine. Barbara warned me it would take some time, but I talked to a couple of nice students. One girl had an algebra question. She was a ninth-grader, and it was instantly apparent she knew way more than I did. Fortunately, she hurried over to another table and I think got the answer she wanted."

I actually stayed for two beers and walked Barbara to her car. "Well, how did the first night go?" she asked.

"You know, a lot better than I expected. Nice kids, great group of people."

"So, you'll be back?"

"Oh, yeah, wouldn't miss it for the world."

"Liar," she said but then smiled. "Thanks for coming tonight, and as I said, word will spread among the students, and you'll suddenly have a line of them waiting to talk to you about everything. Just be prepared. All of a sudden, you'll be handing out non-school advice, and that can sometimes get a little dicey. When that happens, we usually recommend they speak to one of the school counselors."

"That seems to make perfect sense." I held the car door for her as she climbed in.

"Oh, Dev," she said, pulling a manila envelope off the passenger seat. "Don't open this until you get home. Something I found rummaging around in my files this afternoon."

The envelope had some weight to it, and I said, "What's this, a list of things I did wrong in school?"

"You're not to open that until you get home. That's all I'm going to say. Thanks again for coming this evening."

"Thanks for suggesting it," I said and waved as she drove off. I thought about going home but decided maybe just one at The Spot wouldn't be such a bad idea. I tossed the envelope on the passenger seat and pulled out of the parking lot.

At no surprise, Louie was seated on his favorite stool at the end of the bar. Mike nodded at me and poured a beer as I headed toward Louie. He lowered the newspaper he was reading as I approached.

"So, did you tell some kid the secret way into the girl's locker room?"

"No, Louie, if you must know, I was helping students. I arranged an interview for a girl writing a paper and directed another girl over to someone who knew about algebra."

"Good idea on the algebra. Who is the kid going to interview?"

"She can write a paper on anything she wants and was stuck on a subject, so I called Dennis Richards, and he said have her come down anytime."

"Richards, is he the tattoo guy?"

"Yeah, Inkredible is his studio. Nice guy, one of the top ink guys in town. He's looking forward to it, and the girl was all excited. So it worked out."

"Yeah, until she shows up at home with her boy-friend's name tattooed on her chin," Louie said and laughed.

"That's why I called Dennis. He's a straight arrow. Plus, he'd actually be interesting to talk to."

"So it went well?"

"Yeah, pretty much. Nice group of people, just trying to help kids. I'm glad I did it."

"So, you're finished after the one night?"

"Hardly. I'm doing it all semester, working off the damage to Barbara's car. I gotta tell you, I liked it. I only talked with three kids, but it felt good."

"Who knew?" Louie said as Mike set down my beer and another drink for Louie.

Morton was asleep on my bed when I got home. I tossed Barbara's envelope on the kitchen counter and turned on my computer to check emails. There were six emails, one more worthless than the next, a cruise promotion, a request to phone my state representative to protest an upcoming bill, a twenty percent coupon for a local hairstylist. Unfortunately, nothing from Gladys. Apparently, she was still upset with me about showing up twenty minutes late with the ruined bouquet of flowers, which I was starting to think was pretty funny.

I turned off the computer, got the coffee ready for the morning, and went up to bed. I had to move Morton, not that he woke up to notice. I set my alarm and fell asleep in less than five minutes.

Eleven

The following morning, I was up before my alarm went off. Surprise of all surprises, Morton came into the kitchen as I was pouring my first cup of coffee. He was up an hour before his usual time. After I gave him his morning head scratch, I let him out the kitchen door. I turned on my computer and checked the local news.

There was another bank robbery on my end of town— the second in as many weeks. The article I read suggested a number of similarities. Two armed, masked men entered the bank and told everyone to get down on the floor. In this instance, 'everyone' consisted of six people, two bank officers, two customers, and two bank tellers. Once again, this was a branch bank, and there were no guards. The robbers took the cash from the teller drawers, headed out the door, and ran off in opposite directions.

Fortunately, no one was hurt. The robbery got me thinking, taking cash from two teller drawers, what could that amount to? A thousand dollars, maybe fifteen hundred dollars on a good day? Split that two ways, and it's an awfully big risk for a few bucks. It sounded like the robbers were some pretty desperate, clueless guys.

Robbing a small branch bank, you wouldn't be getting much to begin with, and compared to the jail time you'd face, it seemed like one of the dumber recent crimes. Our state legislature was in session, but I skipped those two articles just to keep my blood pressure in check.

I poured myself another cup of coffee and noticed the envelope from Barbara I'd set on the counter when I got home last night. I opened it and pulled out a sheet of paper dated October tenth, 1999. The paper was a set of directions about writing a book report on <u>To Kill A Mockingbird</u>. I tipped the envelope upside down and out slid the paperback book, complete with aged, yellowed pages and a yellow Post-it Note.

The Post-it note read, *'You never completed this book report and therefore received a 'D' in my class. If you read the book and write a report, I will adjust your grade accordingly.'*

She must think I have a lot of time on my hands. Besides, why read the book? I recalled watching the movie starring Gregory Peck at a pal's house back in high school so we wouldn't have to read the book. I set the book aside and let Morton in. Forty minutes later, we were parking across the street from my office. The coffee was on, and Louie was already at his desk.

"Good morning, Louie," I said as Morton headed for his bed. I filled my mug and settled into my desk chair.

Morton's eyes were already closed, so much for being an early riser. "Aren't you in court this morning?"

"Yeah, later. Literally, all I have to do is stand there, look halfway interested, and say 'Yes, Sir' the three times I'm supposed to. Then, if my client remembers not to utter a word, we'll be out of there with a small fine, and I'll be back before the noon hour."

"You're making it sound like that last part could be a big 'if'."

"She always seems to have some wisdom to impart, and the guy we're appearing in front of is not the person to push. I'll meet with her fifteen minutes before our appearance and offer some advice."

"Hopefully, she'll listen."

"That's always the question," Louie said. He headed out the door forty-five minutes later. I drummed my fingers on my desk, made two phone calls, and left a message each time. Morton woke from his morning nap, stretched, and then stood by the door, suggesting it would be a good idea to take him for a walk.

We took our usual two-block route. Morton investigated the base of every tree, both fire hydrants, and most of the gates leading into front yards. We rounded the final corner about to head back to the office when I noticed a black SUV in the process of parking across the street from the office.

The SUV left no doubt in my mind. Tubby Gustafson was about to pay a visit, and I had absolutely no information to tell him about Eli Cummings. I made a quick about-face and headed back the way we'd come. Ninety seconds later, I heard tires screeching around the corner and glanced over my shoulder.

Fat Freddy Zimmerman, wearing an evil grin, sped down the street and screeched to a stop alongside us. He lowered the passenger window and said, "Hey, dumb shit, nice try. Too bad it didn't work. Might be a good idea if you got your worthless ass in here."

I smiled, nodded, stepped over to the curb, and opened the front passenger door. "Okay, Morton, up you go. Inside boy, hop up."

Morton hopped up onto the passenger seat. Fat Freddy stared wide-eyed, as Morton licked his face.

"Frederick!" Tubby screamed from the back seat. "Watch him. Haskell, you lunatic, as much as I'd enjoy chatting with your four-legged friend, unfortunately, I have words for you. If you'd be so kind as to exchange places, Frederick will watch your friend."

The car rocked from side to side as Fat Freddy oozed out of the driver's seat. He hurried around the front of the car and held out his hand for the leash.

"Careful, he likes to bite," I said, handing the leash to Fat Freddy.

"Good luck," Freddy said and gave a hip check to the passenger door before I was all the way in.

"Good morning, sir," I said as I turned and looked at Tubby seated in back. His baked potato nose appeared redder than usual, and what looked like grains of sugar surrounded his mouth. I noticed the white bakery box resting on the seat next to him. It was large enough for maybe a half-dozen doughnuts although there was only one left in the box.

Tubby held what was left of a sugar-coated doughnut in his right hand. He promptly shoved it into his mouth and said, "So, Eli Cummings, what have you found out? Where do I find him?"

"Actually, sir, I'm still working on that. All indications suggest he seems to have slipped beneath the radar and has quite possibly left town, maybe even the country. I'm in the process of investigating Playa Del Carmen in Mexico, but thus far I—"

"In other words, you're looking at topless beaches because that's where a ne'er'-do-well such as yourself would go." Tubby shook his head and said, "You never fail to disappoint, Haskell. Perhaps, I didn't make myself clear the other day. I want you to listen carefully. Are you listening, Haskell?"

I thought it best not to reply.

"Well, are you?" Tubby suddenly shouted, spraying bits of sugar covered doughnut into the front seat.

"Yes, sir, I'm listening. I'm all ears."

"You're an idiot is what you are. Cummings is not in Mexico. He's somewhere in this city. For God's sake, he just robbed a bank the other day."

"Robbed a bank?"

"Yes, robbed a bank. Other than yourself, who else would be stupid enough to rob a bank and only take the funds from the teller's drawers? Find him, you moron.

Now get out of my sight. I can feel my blood pressure rising just having to look at you sitting there, clueless to the workings of the world. Go on. Get out of my sight. Get out. Get out. Get out. Frederick, lend a hand for God's sake," Tubby shouted.

Fat Freddy opened the passenger door, took hold of my shoulder, and yanked me out of the front seat. I landed next to Morton, who growled and snapped at Fat Freddy.

"I should call the cops on you. That dog is a danger to society," Freddy said, tossing the leash in my general direction and quickly waddling around the back of the car.

"He just likes to bite jerks, Freddy. It's a gift he was born with, nothing I can do about it," I said as I closed the passenger door, and Freddy sped away.

"Good job, Morton. Come on. Let's find you a treat and get the taste of Freddy out of your mouth."

Twelve

I'd been on my computer for the better part of an hour when Louie came back to the office. I let him catch his breath for a few minutes while he sat at his desk. Eventually, I asked, "Everything go okay in court?"

"Yeah, couldn't have been better. She followed my advice to the letter, didn't say a word, smiled, nodded, and paid her fine on the way out. We grabbed a nice lunch afterward, her treat."

I went over to the coffee pot and filled my mug. "You want some? I put on a fresh pot a little while ago."

Louie looked at me for a long moment then held out his mug. I filled it, almost draining the pot, then dripped a trail of coffee across his picnic table desk that he didn't seem to notice. "So what's with the knees on your jeans? Were you out pulling weeds?"

I glanced down and, for the first time, noticed the dirt stains on the knees of my jeans. "Oh, yeah, a little run-in with Tubby Gustafson."

"What? Now he's making you crawl to him?"

"No, actually, I was sitting in his SUV, the front seat, and when he yelled at me to get out, Fat Freddy was out of the car hanging onto Morton's leash. He opened the door and pulled me out of the front seat."

"What did those two idiots want?"

"Info on Eli Cummings. I didn't have anything to tell them, and Tubby blew up."

"No surprise there, that guy is certifiable."

"Can't say that I disagree. He did say something interesting, though. I told him Cummings probably fled out of town and might even be down in Mexico. That sent him over the edge, and he started yelling at me. Told me he knew Cummings was still in town because he pulled that bank robbery the other day."

"Is that the one I read about in the paper?" Louie asked and slurped coffee.

"Yeah, two guys taking cash from the teller drawers. By the time they split the money, they'll be lucky if they each make a grand."

"You think it was Cummings, or was Tubby just making it up?"

"I'm not sure. I suppose it's possible. I left a message with Aaron LaZelle to call me, and I've been online trying to find information on the robberies. So far, there's nothing that mentions Cummings. For whatever reason, he owes Tubby a chunk of change. I'm thinking maybe a gambling debt or something. Now I'm wondering if he was going to rob a bank to pay back Tubby."

"Just be careful where Tubby is concerned. He's never heard of the crime he wouldn't commit."

"It would still be interesting to see if this Cummings guy is—" My phone suddenly rang. I put the almost empty coffee pot back on the burner, turned the burner off, and hurried over to my desk. My pal in homicide, Aaron LaZelle, returning my call. "Haskell Investigations," was how I answered, hoping I sounded professional.

"Hi, Dev, I'm returning your call, and before you say anything, let me remind you it's your turn to buy dinner."

Damn it, once again, I'd completely forgotten. "Umm, yeah, Aaron. That's why I was calling. Wondered if you might have time to grab dinner one of these next nights."

"Seriously?"

"Yeah, why, is that a problem?"

"No, not a problem. It's just that you usually forget and—"

"Not this time, that's why I called," I lied.

"Actually, I don't have anything scheduled for tonight. You open?"

"Yeah, I am. Tell you what, you pick the place, and I'll meet you there."

"Mickey's?"

"Mickey's? You mean as in Mickey's Diner?" I asked.

"Yeah, I'm in the mood for a delicious, greasy cheeseburger, some oil-soaked fries, and maybe a piece of caramel chocolate cheesecake for dessert."

"You got it, man. How does 7:00 sound?" I asked.

"Sounds like a plan. Oops, gotta run, Dev. I'll see you there."

I was going to ask him about Cummings and the bank robberies, but he'd already hung up, so it would have to wait.

"Did I hear you mention Mickey's Diner?" Louie asked.

"Yeah, lucky me. Actually, it's my turn to buy. Other than the drive-thru at McDonald's, I can't think of a less expensive place. We can get out of there for less than a bottle of wine would run me at any other restaurant, so I'm a happy camper."

Louie headed off to The Spot toward the end of the day. I told him I might stop in after my dinner with Aaron. I did more online searching for Eli Cummings but couldn't find anything.

I took Morton home around 6:00. We did a two-block walk, where I kept looking over my shoulder, expecting to see Tubby's SUV speed around the corner. Thankfully, he never showed. I tossed Morton a biscuit when we got back home then hurried upstairs, changed jeans, and headed down to Mickey's Diner.

Thirteen

Mickey's is a downtown city landmark. It's a somewhat famous yellow and red, art deco styled dining car that's appeared in movies and TV shows. The place is open twenty-four hours a day, has free parking for maybe a half-dozen cars, and is filled with characters. The food isn't half bad either.

I was ten minutes early and able to grab a booth. Since they don't serve alcohol, I ordered a chocolate shake and waited for Aaron to show up. He arrived twenty minutes later. As he walked in, one of the guy's behind the grill shouted, "Hey L.T., how's it going?"

"It's going well, Rashad, but then it's still early in the night," he yelled. He saw me wave and headed for the booth.

"God, you're mister popular everywhere you go," I said as he slid in across from me.

"He's a nice guy, got into some trouble as a kid, and I was able to point him in the right direction. You been here long?" he asked and glanced at my half-finished chocolate shake.

"Not that long, and it's always great people watching," I said and indicated the two women behind us, a blonde and a redhead. They looked like working girls, as in working evenings on the street.

A waitress suddenly appeared. She tossed plastic-coated menus in front of us, placed a hand on her hip, and said, "Haven't seen you for a while, Lieutenant. Where you been hiding?"

"Just been putting in my time, Doris."

"Hardly," she said and laughed. "You want the usual?"

"Yeah, cheeseburger, fries, and better add a strawberry shake. I need the sweetening."

"Got it. What about you? You begging for mercy from the chief of police here?"

"I know better than to do that," I said. "He's just looking for a reason to lock me up. I'll have the same, minus the shake. I'm already sweet."

"Mmm-mmm, I bet you are," she said as she picked up the menus and stepped over to the booth behind us.

"Is there anyone working here who doesn't know you?" I asked.

"What can I say? I'm a nice guy."

"Yeah, well, I could tell them some stories. Hey, you ever hear of a guy named Eli Cummings?"

"Eli Cummings? Local guy, dark curly hair, maybe five-ten, late thirties?"

"If you say so."

"No, never heard of him," he said, shaking his head.

"You know more than I do, and I was searching online for the better part of the afternoon."

"What's your interest in him?"

"More or less forced on me. Tubby Gustafson has been looking for him and asked me to try to find him."

"I'm sure he asked nicely," Aaron said.

"Tubby doesn't know what nice is. He didn't tell me why he wanted the guy, but if I had to guess, I would think maybe a gambling debt. I checked out the most recent address, a dive over on the east side. He'd split owing two months' rent."

"No idea where he went?"

I shook my head and said, "If Tubby Gustafson was looking for me because I owed him money, I don't think I'd still be in town."

"Of course, by saying that, you're suggesting this guy has some smarts."

"I'm getting the feeling you maybe know more than you're letting on, Aaron. Let me level with you. This bank robbery the other day, two guys hitting that branch bank, Tubby suggested to me Eli Cummings was involved."

Instead of looking surprised, Aaron simply nodded.

The waitress suddenly arrived with his strawberry shake. "Here you go, darling," she said, setting it down in front of him. "Little something extra to tide you over 'til your dinner arrives. Shouldn't be more than a couple of minutes," she said and set down a small plate with what looked like three chocolate chip cookies.

"Thanks for looking after me, Doris," Aaron said. She smiled and hurried over to another table.

"You gonna share those?" I asked, nodding at the cookies.

Aaron pulled the plate closer to him and didn't answer. "You said Gustafson told you Cummings was in on the bank robbery?"

"Yeah, and the way he said it suggested he wasn't too impressed. Do you think Cummings was involved?"

Aaron shook his head and picked up one of the cookies. "No, we don't think, we know. We were able to pull his prints from one of the teller windows. They were wearing masks, but the images on the security cameras correspond to his physical description, and then with the fingerprints, it's him, Eli Cummings, in both bank robberies. A lot of risk for not a lot of money."

"Yeah, and figure he's got to split it with the partner. Are they even clearing a grand apiece?" I asked then quickly reached across and stole a cookie.

"No, more like maybe eight hundred bucks. Fortunately, no one has been hurt yet. But it's only a matter of time before something will happen. Trying to find him is like looking for the proverbial needle in a haystack."

Doris suddenly returned with two platters weighed down by gigantic cheeseburgers and a mountain of French fries. As she set them down, the delicious smell wafted up, and I could almost feel the heat.

Aaron grabbed the Ketchup bottle, turned his cheeseburger upside down, and lifted the bottom of the bun. He squirted Ketchup, slapped the bun back on the cheeseburger, and pushed the Ketchup bottle over to me. I followed suit. We didn't say anything for the next few minutes.

"Any idea where he might be?" I finally asked.

Aaron made an audible swallow and said, "Who?"

"Cummings. Who do think we were talking about?"

"Sorry, I missed lunch today and was focused on re-gaining my strength." He grabbed a couple of French fries, dragged them through a puddle of Ketchup, and shoved them in his mouth.

"I know we've checked the usual known acquaint-ances, but we've come up empty-handed. Not a lot of family around. His brother and sister-in-law were killed in a car accident some years back. Parents are deceased. There's a sister living down in Winona, but all indica-tions are there's been no contact between them for a number of years."

"It seems like a stretch that he would drive up from Winona to rob a bank where he wouldn't get much money."

"Yeah, we're pretty sure he's laying low somewhere in town, maybe working on paintings."

"Painting? You mean he's painting houses?"

"No, Dev, paintings as in art. The type of things that hang on walls in museums and people come and look at them."

"The guy is an artist?"

"Yeah, maybe, but he never seems to stick with it. Last year, there was a question of a forgery, but it was never pinned on him. He was maybe one of four or five people that were being checked out."

"And it turned out not to be him?"

"If I recall, no one was ever held responsible. A portrait of a Governor's wife from a hundred years ago. They couldn't pin it on anyone. It's still an unsolved case."

"And now the guy is robbing banks?" I asked.

"Another very poor choice. If we had all the facts, it wouldn't surprise me if he's one of those guys who is actually pretty smart, but he has this habit of making one bad decision after another."

I was thinking back to the dumpy apartment on the east side with the landscape painting on the walls and the portraits sitting on the floor. Was Cummings involved in a forgery? More importantly, had he forged something for Tubby and gotten caught?

"Hey, Dev, come back to the here and now, buddy. Where are you?"

"Oh, sorry. I was just thinking about the other day when I went to that dive apartment where Cummings had been living. There were maybe a half-dozen paintings, three landscapes, all pretty similar, and three portraits of an older woman that were leaning against the wall in a grubby bedroom."

"Hmmm-mmm, it would be interesting to run those past someone in the biz who could tell if he was working on a forgery."

"You aware of any forgeries or thefts from a museum lately?"

Aaron shook his head as he took the last chocolate chip cookie. "No, I'm not aware of anything, but then we're spending all our time on nutcases shooting someone for ten dollars. That or someone looked at them wrong, so that becomes grounds to shoot. It's crazy, man."

Doris suddenly arrived. "What about some dessert tonight, gentlemen?"

"None for me," Aaron said.

"Yeah, I'm out too. I think just the check when you've got a moment," I said.

She reached into her apron pocket and set the check in front of me. "Pay me when you're ready, fellas."

I looked at the bill. Twenty-four bucks, and Aaron's strawberry shake and chocolate chip cookies weren't on the bill.

"You want to split that?" Aaron asked.

"No, I got it, and next time we'll go somewhere fancy, and you can pay," I said and pulled out a twenty and a ten.

We chatted for a couple more minutes then headed out the door. Aaron was parked right next to me, and we talked for another minute or two then took off in opposite directions. Aaron, being sensible, was probably headed home. I decided that one beer couldn't hurt and headed toward The Spot and Louie.

Fourteen

There were only a couple of people in The Spot—two guys on stools and a husband and wife seated in a back booth. Louie was sitting on his favorite stool reading a two-day old copy of the local paper, the Pioneer Press. He didn't notice me until I pulled the paper down.

"Oh, hey, Dev, how'd your dinner go?"

"Good, had a nice chat with Aaron, learned a little bit about Eli Cummings."

"I don't suppose that little bit includes an address or what hotel he's staying at."

"I only wish. But, he did confirm that Cummings is one of the bank robbers. They got a set of fingerprints at the last robbery, and they belong to Cummings. Turns out, he's also a person of interest in an art forgery case. I told Aaron there were some nice looking paintings in that dive place Cummings skipped out of over on the east side."

"So when you say a person of interest, does that mean he actually forged something or that he *might* have forged something?"

"More like he might have, he's never been convicted of art forgery, but it's another bit of information on the guy. Now I'm wondering if some aspect of that, might be what has Tubby Gustafson's attention. I just may have been way off-base with the idea of a gambling debt."

Mike suddenly set a beer in front of me and a fresh drink for Louie.

"I got this. Put it on my tab, Mike," Louie said and handed Mike a five-dollar tip.

"Thanks, Louie," I said and took a healthy sip.

"So what's your next move on Cummings?"

"I don't know exactly. I'm thinking I'll call the Art Institute and see if there's someone there I could talk to regarding forgeries, maybe start in that direction."

"I know someone who was involved in investigating forgeries," Louie said. She works for an insurance company. She was on a case maybe a year or two ago, some guy over in Northern Michigan who ran an art forgery ring. I think he had forged the work of two or three artists. I don't know who they were, but she might be a good place to start."

"Yeah, that sounds like just what I'm looking for. You got a phone number or an email address?"

"I do," Louie said and pulled out his phone. He began typing in a name. "Oh, yeah, here we go. Her name is Annette Dinicci. She lives over off of Highway 10." He proceeded to give me her phone number and then the correct spelling of her last name. "She's a nice lady, a lot of fun, and after her second glass of wine, she'll talk for hours about the cases she's been involved in. Art forgery is a lot bigger business than we realize, at least based on what she's told me over the last couple of years."

"Thanks, Louie. I'll give her a call tomorrow. Great, this guy Tubby wants me to find is a bank robber and an art forger."

"You ever think maybe Tubby wants to hire him? Sounds like he might be a great fit for Tubby's organization," Louie said.

We chatted on for two more beers. I stayed at The Spot longer than I should have. When I finally made it home Morton was asleep and I joined him in bed.

Fifteen

I was up the following morning just in time to turn off the alarm before it sounded. I shaved, showered, got dressed, and was down in the kitchen on my second cup of coffee when Morton finally made his appearance. After his morning scratch behind the ears, I let him outside and poured myself another coffee. We were down in the office by 8:30. Louie hadn't made an appearance yet, so I made a fresh pot of coffee and settled in at my desk. I phoned Annette Dinicci at exactly 9:00. She answered on the third ring.

"Dinicci."

"Hi, Annette. My name is Dev Haskell. I share an office with—"

"With Louie Laufen. Oh my God. Dev Haskell, Louie has told me all sorts of stories about you."

"Well, don't believe any of them. I'm actually a very nice guy."

She laughed at that and said, "Listen, we all need a friend like Louie. He's a big fan of yours. What can I do for you?"

I went on to explain the little I knew about Eli Cummings and how Tubby Gustafson was after me to find him.

"Eli Cummings, the name rings a distant bell, but that's about it. As for your Mister Gustafson, I'm a little more familiar with him but mostly based on what I've read in the papers. Interesting all the same. I'm wondering if you might have time for lunch. I'd love to finally be able to associate a face with all the tales Louie's told me."

"Lunch? Yeah, sure. You name the day."

"Would you be available today?" she asked.

"As a matter of fact, I think I can. Let me make a couple of calls and clear some time," I lied.

"If it's not too much trouble, that would be great. I've got an afternoon appointment in downtown St. Paul today. If we could meet a little early, say 11:30 or so?"

"That will work just fine. You have some place in mind?"

"Not really."

"Okay, how about this? We'll meet at the Gnome…" I proceeded to give her directions and finished up with, "Any problems, just give me a call. I'm wearing a black t-shirt with Bob Seger written across the front in red letters. There'll probably only be two or three guys at the Gnome wearing t-shirts like this."

She didn't respond.

"Hello, Annette?"

"Yeah, I heard that last bit. God, Louie wasn't kidding. See you at 11:30."

The Gnome is within sight of my front porch. I took Morton home and let him out into the backyard then walked over to the Gnome. It was a warm, sunny afternoon, and I grabbed a table on the back deck. I sent Annette a text message telling her where I was sitting.

Five minutes later, an attractive, dark-haired woman stepped out of the restaurant and onto the deck. She glanced around for a second or two then smiled and headed toward my table. Her straight, dark hair was neatly trimmed at about her jawline. She was dressed in blue jeans with a striped black and white top and a black blazer.

"Dev Haskell?" she asked from about ten feet away.

"Yeah, that's me, nice to meet you, Annette," I said as I stood.

"I wasn't sure. There are two guys in the bar with Bob Seger t-shirts," she joked.

"Yeah, they follow me around all the time."

She shook her head as she sat down, glanced around, and said, "You really are pretty funny. Hey, nice choice. This place looks gorgeous."

"The food is pretty good, too. Thanks for making the time to meet with me." We took a moment to look at the menu, ordered, and chatted back and forth. We talked about Louie and some general things for maybe ten minutes until our lunch arrived. A salad for Annette and a shrimp taco for me.

Annette took a bite of her salad and said, "So, you think Eli Cummings is involved in a forgery?"

"No, not exactly. As a matter of fact, I'm not sure what he's involved in. Like I told you, I'm supposed to find him for Tubby Gustafson, and I have no idea where to start looking."

"Yeah, you mentioned him on the phone. I read about him in the paper from time to time. Do you deal with him often?"

I nodded, wiped the taco sauce from my chin with my napkin, and said, "Certainly more than I would like. He seems to have taken an odd liking to me, unfortunately."

"And what will you do if you find Eli Cummings?"

"If you're asking will I hand him over to Tubby, the answer is no. I'll probably give him a warning. Tell him something like, if I can find him, Tubby can't be far behind, and he'd better leave town. That said, he's also a suspect in a couple of bank robberies that took place over the past couple of weeks. Fortunately, no one has been hurt, and they didn't take much money, but sooner or later, somethings bound to go wrong."

She nodded, taking it in, and said, "Well, after your call this morning, I did a little research on Mr. Cummings." She reached into her purse, pulled out an envelope, and handed it to me.

"I've detailed what I learned in there. It's not much. He's recently been named as a suspect in three cases over the last two years. I should mention other people are suspected as well. Eli Cummings is the new kid on the block in forgery. The paintings involved were definitely forgeries, excellent forgeries. Cummings was one of a number of suspects. No one has ever been charged in any of those cases. That said, there does seem to be a pattern."

"A pattern, you mean his particular style of painting? Is it something that's identifiable?"

"Not exactly, I was referring more to the market aspect of the forgery. Let me start by saying he seems talented and can copy a number of different styles. Here's one of the keys to his suspected forgery career, and it's actually pretty smart. The forgeries he's been suspected of are works done by second-tier American artists. Not that they aren't talented. In fact, they're extremely talented. But, for whatever reason, they're known more regionally than nationally."

"Can you give me an example?"

"Oh yeah, the three recent forgery cases he's been suspected in were sold as works by a Surrealist artist named Gertrude Abercrombie and two Precisionism painters, a man named Ralston Crawford, and another man named George Copeland Ault. They were all part of the representational movement that embraced geometric compositions with clear outlines and simple shapes."

I must have had a blank look on my face.

"So, picture block buildings, simple square structures, that's what these folks do. They painted in the first half of the last century, say from maybe 1910 to 1950.

Gertude Abercrombie had a 1947 painting entitled *'Coming Home'* that sold for, I think, two hundred and fifty thousand dollars just a few years ago. It has since been identified as a forgery. Crawford's *Smith Silo* sold for almost four hundred thousand, and Ault's *Morning in Brooklyn* sold for two hundred thousand, and both of those paintings have been labeled forgeries as well.

"How is it determined that they're forgeries? Do the original artists get involved?"

"No, the original artists have all passed away. Usually, careful examination by experts makes the determination. Ault's *'Morning in Brooklyn'* was actually done in 1929. Examination of the canvas in question contained materials that weren't available back in '29. In that case, it was a Hansa Yellow pigment and acrylic paint. Don't get me wrong, the work on the forgeries was excellent, but, at the end of the day, they're still forgeries."

"And these things sold for two to three hundred grand?"

"Almost four hundred for Crawford's *'Smith Silo.'* They were all sold at auction. Usually, but not always, to private collectors. The auction house was not involved in any way, shape, or form, and indeed had competent, responsible individuals initially certify the paintings. In the art world, it's not uncommon for the auction house to purchase the paintings and then auction them off at a later date, which means that the auction house was out a big chunk of change as well, not to mention the damage to their reputation.”

“Just for the sake of argument,” I said, “let’s say Eli Cummings was the forger. We’re still talking a lot of money on these paintings. Why would the guy be living in a two-room dive? Why is he suspected of being involved in bank robberies that can’t be worth more than six to eight hundred bucks?”

Annette shook her head and said, “Who knows? Drugs, gambling, maybe a bad investment. He may have sold the forgeries five or six years ago to a middleman who held them for a few years. Cummings may have been paid pennies on the dollar if he didn’t have the connections.”

“You think Tubby Gustafson might be a middleman in all this?”

“It’s quite possible. The little I know of him, he strikes me as someone who would be quite capable in that vein.”

We chatted some more over lunch, and just as I was about to suggest a dessert, Annette said she had to leave for a meeting. I gave her directions to her meeting.

“Thank you for lunch, Dev. A real pleasure to meet you, especially after all the stories I’ve heard from Louie. I hope we can get together again sometime when I don’t have to run off.”

“Yeah, I would enjoy that.”

“Don’t forget to read through my notes and let me know if you ever find Mr. Cummings.”

"I'll be sure to do that. Thanks again, Annette."

She leaned in and gave me a peck on the cheek then hurried back into the restaurant. I sat at the table for a few minutes waiting to pay the bill then headed out the side entrance on the deck. I was just about to go down the three steps to the parking lot when a voice called, "Haskell?"

There at a corner table sat a woman I didn't recognize. Unfortunately, she was seated across from a woman I did recognize, Evelyn Marco, AKA Evil Evelyn. One of Gladys' close friends. Her mission in life seemed to be to rain on everyone's parade. If someone was enjoying themselves, it was Evelyn's job to put a stop to it.

"Oh, Evelyn, I didn't see you back there."

"Apparently you were involved in an out of the way lunch?"

"Out of the way? No, I live just down the street. Business meeting on a case I'm working on."

"Mmm-mmm, interesting," she said and appeared to be waiting for an explanation.

"Nice to see you. Enjoy the afternoon, ladies," I said and hurried down the steps. I debated calling Gladys to explain my luncheon with Annette but figured that would only add fuel to the fire. I walked back to my place, grabbed Morton, and we headed down to the office.

Sixteen

Louie was seated at his picnic table desk when we walked into the office. I picked up on the scent of burning coffee the moment we entered. I stepped over to the empty coffee pot, turned off the burner, and set the pot on top of the file cabinet.

"Were you in earlier this morning?" Louie asked, not looking up from his computer screen.

"Yeah, I'm just back from lunch with your friend Annette Dinicci."

"Oh, really, that's great. Was she able to help?"

"Yeah, she gave me some pretty good information," I said, pulling her envelope out of my back pocket and tossing it on my desk. "Unfortunately, it brings up more questions than answers." I went on to give Louie a quick recount of our luncheon discussion.

"Well, it maybe gives you some other areas to look into. She have any idea where this Cummings character might be?"

"No, but now that I think about it, I might head back to that unit on the east side where he skipped out on the rent. I'd like to take a look at some paintings that were in there. Maybe take them off that crabby landlord's hands."

"Just from your description of that guy, I wouldn't count on him doing you any favors."

"Yeah, probably right, but no harm in trying. You going to be here for an hour?"

"I'm here for the rest of the afternoon. Go on, take off. Morton will be under my watchful eye."

"I'm thinking it might be the other way around. I'll be back as soon as I can," I said and opened the door. Morton was already sacked out on his pillow. He opened one eye as I opened the door and made no effort to follow. I drove over to the east side and parked in front of the house with the sagging front porch.

The nine steps leading up to the front of the house were still in disrepair, and I didn't expect that to change anytime soon. I walked around the side of the house, stepped over two black trash bags, and stood on the sagging wooden steps at the backdoor.

The door was closed, but it was obvious the damage to the doorframe hadn't been repaired yet. As I knocked on the door, it squeaked open. The saucepan and whatever had been on the floor was partially cleaned up, and the broken pieces of sheetrock were now leaning against the wall. The landscape painting still hung at an angle on the back wall.

I heard a noise coming from the other room and walked down the hall. At first, I thought someone might be moving a piece of furniture, but when I looked in the room, all questions were answered.

The soiled mattress was still on the floor of the room. The crabby fat landlord was on the mattress, snoring away. An empty cheap bourbon bottle, was on the floor next to him. The three portraits of an older woman were leaning against the wall exactly where they were the last time I saw them.

I thought for a half-second before I quietly tiptoed in, gathered the three paintings and hurried out of the room. Crabby never stopped snoring. I took the two landscapes hanging in the hall and stepped into the kitchen. I lifted the landscape off the nail in the wall and hurried out the door.

I had just settled into the driver's seat when my phone rang, Barbara Wright. "Hi, Barbara, what's up?"

"Just calling to remind you it's detention night. I hope you didn't forget."

"No, I didn't forget," I lied. "As a matter of fact, I was thinking of bringing <u>To Kill A Mockingbird</u> so I could continue reading if no one shows up," I lied again.

"Oh, so you actually are reading it?"

"Yeah, of course."

"Wonderful, well, I'll look forward to seeing you this evening."

"I wouldn't miss it for the world. Thank you for the call. See you tonight," I said and thanked God for her call reminding me. I headed back to the office, carried the paintings up the stairs, and leaned them against the wall behind my desk. Louie had left a note on my desk, saying he'd been at a stopping point and decided to refresh himself over at The Spot.

I put Morton on his leash, and we took the long way around the block to The Spot. Louie was on his favorite stool, and he signaled Mike for a bag of pork rinds when we entered.

"Get you a beer?" Mike asked as Morton pulled me along the bar toward Louie.

"Thanks, Mike, but I've got a meeting tonight, so I better take a pass."

"Morton," Louie said as he leaned down with a handful of pork rinds. Morton licked his hand clean in about two seconds. Louie sat up and said, "Were you able to talk to that landlord?"

"He was otherwise disposed," I said. "Fortunately, he told me to help myself to any paintings. Just one more thing he won't have to deal with when he gets around to cleaning out the place, if he ever does."

"He have any idea where the guy may have landed?"

"No, unfortunately."

"You sure you don't want a beer? I'm buying."

"Thanks, but I better not. In fact, I should probably take Morton home. It's a detention night, so I'll be over at the high school."

"Well, I'll be here for a while, so feel free to stop back down once you get out of there."

"Thanks, I'll play it by ear. If nothing else, I'll see you in the morning."

Morton scammed the remainder of the pork rinds from Louie, and we went home. I took him on a two-block walk, rewarded him with a biscuit in the kitchen, and then drove over to the high school.

Seventeen

A text message came through as I drove to the high school. I parked in the staff only parking lot and checked my phone. The text was from Gladys. I called and ended up leaving a message. "Hi Gladys, got your text. I'm doing what I'm told, calling you back."

I didn't see any cars in the larger lot and wondered if it would be a quiet night. I was the third person in the cafeteria. Barbara and Janet Jackson were seated at a table. Barbara gave me a wave when I walked in.

"Good evening, ladies, how are you doing tonight?"

"Nice to see you," Janet said.

"Dev, you're an early bird tonight. Who knew?"

"Wouldn't want to miss it, Barbara." We chatted for a bit as more people drifted in then took up positions at separate tables a few minutes before 6:00. I pulled out the aged copy of <u>To Kill A Mockingbird</u> and opened the book to page one. At 6:01, four girls wandered into the cafeteria, looked around, and headed straight for my table. I recognized the girl leading the pack as Ramona

Williams, the girl I lined up with Dennis Richards, my tattoo artist friend.

"Hi Ramona, were you able to meet with Dennis yet?"

She grinned and said, "I went down there today. We all did."

"I drove," a redheaded girl said.

"Well, sit down and tell me about it. Did you get enough information to write a paper?"

"We all did," Ramona said. "I'm doing a paper on Dennis, how he got started in the business, and what it's like to build and run a tattoo parlor."

"We're doing a paper together on his customers. You know the people that get tattoos. What kind of tattoo's, why they get them," another girl said and indicated the blonde girl next to her as the partner on the paper.

"I'm writing about the artwork," the redhead said.

"So everyone has a subject. That's great. Did you two check with the teacher to see if it's okay to do a paper together?"

They nodded, and one of them said, "She said if we were going to do it together, it would have to be forty-five hundred words, but I think we can do that." She looked over at her friend, who nodded.

"Oh, that's great, so are you going to go back there or do you have enough information already?"

"We're all going back there tomorrow night. He's got two other people working there, and we get to interview them, too."

"If they're not busy," another girl added.

"They close Inkredible at eight on Friday night, and Dennis said he would hang around and answer any questions we might have."

"Hey, that's good news. What did the teacher say when you told her you were writing about a tattoo parlor?"

"She thought it was pretty cool."

"Oh great, let me know how it works out. Anything else I can help you with?"

Ramona shook her head and said, "Just wanted to stop in and thank you. We're gonna get a pizza, and a bunch of us are meeting at Kendra's later tonight."

"To work on our papers," one of the girls added, not that I believed her.

"Yeah, you can work on the outlines before you talk to Dennis tomorrow night. When are the papers due?"

"Not till a week from Monday," one of them said, which suggested they could put off writing for an entire week, until late Sunday night or early Monday morning. One of the girls gave a signal, and they all stood at once and smiled.

"Say Ramona, could I have a private word with you for a moment?"

She gave me a look, but waved the other girls off. "So what is it?" she asked as the girls headed for the door.

"I'm wondering if you could help me. The paper you're doing, would you consider writing one for me on this?" I said and slid <u>To Kill A Mockingbird</u> across the table.

"Why would I write a book report for you? I'm not in your class."

"No, I have to do it for a teacher, well former teacher, kind of a long story. But if you could write it, I'd pay you."

"How much?" she asked.

"How does twenty bucks sound?"

"Thirty sounds better, in advance."

I thought for a moment and then nodded. I pulled out my wallet, and took out two twenties, all I had. "You owe me ten," I said and slipped the bills into the book.

"I'll get on it right way. I've got your card. I'll email you a copy," she said and hurried out the door.

I had a pretty steady stream of students for the next two hours. A couple of chemistry and algebra questions that I sent to other tables, but all in all, it was about five times the kids I'd had on my first night. We shut things down at eight, stood around chatting for ten minutes before heading over to Tiffany's Sports Lounge.

I ran home, let Morton out into the backyard for a few minutes, and then drove over to Tiffany's. Once again, everyone was sitting outdoors around two tables. White wine appeared to be the beverage of choice. I ordered a beer from the waitress and sat down.

I had barely settled into my chair when a woman asked, "So what were you giving away that gave you a steady stream of students tonight?"

"Me? Nothing really. One of the girls had to write a paper, and I lined her up with a guy to interview." I went on to tell the tattoo tale.

"Inkredible? I know that place, or well, I know where it is. Of course, I've never been there," one of the women said.

"They're supposed to write about a tattoo parlor?" someone asked.

"They could write about anything. My pal owns a tattoo parlor, and now four of them are writing on different aspects of the business."

"What happened to the days when we assigned the constitution or state capitol as the subject?" a woman asked.

"I think it's wonderful. They have to interview the owner of a business. One can only imagine what preexisting thoughts they have on the subject," someone said.

The discussion continued for two more drinks, and then it was time to go. Barbara seemed to be searching in her purse for something.

"Lose your car keys?" I asked.

"Thankfully, no, but I think I left my cellphone back at the school. I'd better head over there and get it."

"You can't wait until tomorrow?"

"I don't want to do that. It will just take a minute to run in. I've got the key."

"I'll follow you over, just to make sure you make it out of the building."

"Oh, that's very kind, but this will just take a moment. You don't need to—"

"Humor me, Barbara."

She shook her head then smiled and said, "Thank you."

I walked Barbara to her car, held the door for her, and told her I'd follow her over. She pulled to the exit in the parking lot and then waited until I pulled in behind her. It was less than a ten-minute drive back to the school. The main parking lot and the staff parking lot were empty. We pulled into the staff parking lot, and I climbed out of my car.

"Oh, Dev, that's sweet of you, but you don't have to stay. I can—"

"Not a problem, Barbara, let's find that cell phone."

We walked over to the cafeteria door. Barbara unlocked the door and flipped on the light switch. The fluorescent lights in the hall flickered for a moment and then came on. We walked down the hall, and I opened the cafeteria door. Barbara stepped in and turned on the light.

"Now, let's see," she said, looking over to the far corner of the room where we had been sitting.

"I got a better idea," I said and pulled out my phone. I called her number, and a moment later, the phone lit up on a distant table. The opening chords to 'Bad to the Bone' identified me as the caller and continued to play until she got to the phone and quickly turned it off.

"Oh, goodness, thank you. I don't know how I could have forgotten this," she said, walking back toward me.

"'Bad to the Bone'? You've got George Thorogood's 'Bad to the Bone' identifying my phone call?"

"Consider yourself lucky. Some people just get the standard ring," she said and turned off the cafeteria lights.

We headed for the door leading outside when I heard a noise coming from the small cloakroom behind the lockers. "You hear that?" I said.

"What?" she said and shook her head.

"Wait a second." I walked back to the cloakroom entrance and flipped on the light. A jacket with a torn sleeve hung from a hanger in the far corner, and beneath it was a wide-eyed kid with dark curly hair sitting next to a McDonald's bag. The same kid who told me he had a paper to turn into Ms. Jackson the other night.

"What are you doing here?"

"Oh, I kind of got locked inside, and I was just calling my mom to come and get me."

"Dev? What are you—" Barbara said as she stepped in behind me and then just stopped and stared. "How did you get in here?"

"I was down in the locker room, and I maybe fell asleep for a couple of minutes. When I woke up, the school was closed, and all the doors were locked."

"Well, you can get out now," she said. "How long have you been in here?"

"A couple of hours, I guess."

"What's your name, dear?"

"Taylor, I'm in eleventh grade."

Barbara nodded and said, "Taylor, we can't let you stay here. Did you reach your mother?"

"Her line was busy. She's probably calling around looking for me. I left her a message."

"Okay, why don't you come with us, and you can wait for her outside."

He stood, pulled the worn jacket from the hanger, and reluctantly followed us out of the building. Once we were outside, Barbara locked the door to the school and said, "Taylor, can I give you a ride home?"

"Oh, thanks, but no. I left a message so she's probably on her way now."

"Do you want to call her again, just to be sure?"

"No, that's okay. I'll just wait for her here. Thanks."

"You're sure you're okay?"

"Yeah, fine."

"Okay, have a good night," she said, and we walked to the staff parking lot. "Oh, I don't know, Dev. Something doesn't sound right."

"You picked up on it, too? Listen, go on home. I'm going to go back and talk to him. No way he fell asleep in the locker room. Something's up. Maybe there was a problem at home, and he ran away, and now at close to ten that doesn't seem like the best idea. I'll check it out and keep you posted."

"You sure? Maybe we should get the police involved or child welfare or someone?"

"I'll check it out. You go on and head home."

"You're sure, Dev? I feel I should—"

"No offense, Barbara, but I might have a little better luck getting to the bottom of this. It wouldn't be the first time I've dealt with a runaway."

She nodded and said, "Okay, but keep me posted, and I mean it."

Eighteen

I watched Barbara pull out of the staff parking lot until her taillights disappeared. I turned and walked back to the kid named Taylor sitting on the steps in front of the cafeteria door. He looked nervous as I approached.

"You hear back from your mom yet?"

"No."

"Come on. I can give you a lift, you'll be home in five minutes."

"Oh, thanks, but I'll just wait."

His worn jacket looked about two sizes too large. The sleeves were draped over his hands, and I could just barely see his fingertips. One of his tennis shoes had a tear along the side. His jeans looked like they hadn't been washed in a month or two.

"You got a cellphone?"

"Yeah, I, I already told you I called my mom."

"Let me see it."

"What?"

"Just show me your cell. You don't have to give it to me. I just want to see it. I'm thinking of getting a new one, and I'm asking everyone what kind they have."

"It's not an iPhone, if that's what you're wondering."

"Mmm-mmm, okay, show it to me anyway, will you?"

He frowned but pulled it out of a jacket pocket and held it in his hand.

"Can you turn it on for me? I want to check the screen brightness. Mine is nice and bright, and I want to be sure whatever kind I get is the same way."

"Oh, well, umm, see the battery just went out. I gotta recharge it."

"Oh, so it must have gone off right after you left the message for your mom."

"Yeah." A guilty look washed over his face.

"Your name really Taylor?"

"Yeah," he said, looking up and sounding a little offended at my question.

"You living rough?"

"Huh?"

"Are you on your own? I'm guessing you don't have anywhere to stay. Maybe you ran away from home, maybe something went wrong. You were gonna spend the night in the school, weren't you?"

He focused on the sidewalk again, staring about a foot in front of him, and slowly nodded.

"Okay, tell you what. I got a spare bedroom at my place, and I was thinking of maybe cooking something when I got home. You're welcome to crash at my place tonight if you want."

He looked up and studied me for a moment.

"My name is Dev, Dev Haskell," I said, holding my hand out to shake.

"Taylor," he said, taking hold for a half-second and then letting go.

"Look, Taylor, it's starting to cool down at night. You stay out here for any length of time dressed like that, you're gonna catch a cold, or worse, maybe pneumonia. I got a guest room, and I'm guessing you haven't had much to eat lately. I'm gonna cook up a couple of pork chops and some boiled potatoes. I've got homemade chocolate chip cookies for dessert." At the mention of chocolate chip cookies, he looked up at me, nodded, and slowly got to his feet. It suddenly dawned on me how lean the kid was.

"You can crash at my place," I said as we walked toward my car. "But I gotta warn you. I got a golden retriever named Morton. He's liable to lick you to death."

"I like dogs," he said then stopped and looked at my black Crown Victoria Police Interceptor.

"You a cop?" he asked.

"What? Why would you ask… Oh, the car, no, I bought it at a police auction. The cops in this town are too smart to have a guy like me working for them."

It was a ten-minute drive home. Along the way, he started asking questions. "Where do you live?"

"About two blocks from the cathedral."

"You married?"

"I haven't found a woman patient enough to put up with me. I'm still looking. How about you? You got a girlfriend?"

He shook his head. "No, most everyone stays away from me. Girls are kind of afraid. The guys just give me a hard time."

I glanced over at him. He was either a runaway, or he was maybe from a family with a lot of problems. He seemed nice enough, but kids can be mean, and if he was being singled out at school, he could be a target. He'd be the guy a certain group would pick on.

"You know, I'm thinking, I got pork chops, or I've got chicken breasts. Which one are you hungry for?"

"The pork chops sounded pretty good. This is your place?" he asked as I pulled into my driveway.

"Yeah, all of it. And it seems like there's always something that has to be fixed," I said, opening the driver's door. "Come on in. I'll give you the cook's tour."

He climbed out of the car, took a careful look around, then followed me down the driveway and up the sidewalk to the front porch. I unlocked the front door and stepped inside. He closed the door behind him, and I locked it.

"Come on back to the kitchen. Let me get that dinner started, and then I'll give you the tour. You want something to drink? I got water or a couple of root beers."

"You gonna have anything?"

"Maybe just a water for me," I said, flicking on the kitchen light. "Help yourself to a root beer in the fridge. Let me just get out a couple of pans while you're doing that."

I pulled some pans out of the drawer below the oven and set them on a burner. I filled one pan with water, turned on the burner, and dumped in a number of small red potatoes.

"Pull out a stool and grab a seat while I get these pork chops going."

As he sat down, I grabbed three pork chops from the refrigerator, placed some oil in the pan and sprinkled lemon pepper on the chops. Taylor guzzled down almost the entire contents of the root beer bottle in the five minutes it took me to get the chops arranged. "Come on. I'll give you the quick tour. Bring the root beer or feel free to finish it and grab another one."

He drained the bottle and then opened the refrigerator door just as Morton appeared in the kitchen.

"Well, look who decided to join us. Taylor, meet Morton. Morton, this is Taylor."

Morton walked over, sniffed, and Taylor reached down and automatically gave him a good scratching behind the ears.

"Oh, man, Taylor. You just got a friend for life. That's what I do to him every morning. Come on. Let me show you around." We wandered through the first floor. I showed him the TV and told him how to work the remote. We headed upstairs. I pointed out my room. I showed him the guest room and the bathroom.

He eyed the shower in the bathroom, and I said, "It's going to be a while on those potatoes. You wanna grab a shower? I could toss those jeans and that t-shirt in the laundry."

"Yeah, maybe."

"Let me get something for you to change into and just bring the clothes down when you're out of the shower. I'll toss some clothes for you on the bed in the guest room. That sound okay to you?"

He gave me a nod. I went into my room, grabbed some sweat pants and a sweatshirt from a drawer, tossed them on the guest room bed, and went downstairs. Morton curled up on the floor in front of the bathroom door.

Taylor and Morton were downstairs a half-hour later. Taylor had the sweatpants rolled up on his ankles and the sleeves on the sweatshirt rolled back. He carried his clothes under his arm.

"Let's get that stuff in the washer, and then we can grab some dinner," I said. I opened the door to the laundry area and said, "There's the laundry detergent. Dump a cup of that into the washer, drop your clothes in, and push this button here. That's all there is to it. I'll get dinner ready. Sound okay?"

He nodded and pulled the detergent off the shelf. I stepped back into the kitchen and dished up dinner. The pork chops smelled wonderful, and Taylor hurried out of the laundry room as I set the plates on the kitchen counter.

"Dig in," I said as he pulled out a kitchen stool. He did just that while I made idle conversation for the next few minutes, and he inhaled his food. When his plate was clean, I said, "I cooked up three pork chops if you've got room for another one."

"Don't you want it?"

"No, I've had more than enough. But it would be a shame to let it go to waste."

"You sure?"

"Yeah, just a second, and I'll dish you up," I said, grabbing his empty plate. I placed the third pork chop on the plate, set it in front of him, and he attacked immediately. Three minutes later, the plate was clean. I took a plate filled with chocolate chip cookies from the cupboard, pulled off the cellophane, and set the plate in front of him. "Help yourself, man."

"You going to have any?"

"One of the problems with me is, if I eat one, I'm liable to eat that entire plate. You have as many as you want, and you'll be saving me from putting on more weight."

He didn't need any encouragement. Once the washer stopped, I tossed his clothes into the drier. We talked about nothing in particular. Taylor asked me questions about Morton, and we went upstairs to bed. I gave him a spare cord to charge his phone, and Morton followed Taylor into the guest room as if it was an every night occurrence.

Nineteen

I was up before my alarm went off. Morton wasn't in the room, and I presumed he was probably in the guest room with Taylor. I showered, shaved, got dressed, and headed down to the kitchen. I had a text message from Barbara asking about Taylor. I sent her a message back saying he'd spent the night at my house and didn't know much else other than he seemed like a nice kid.

I pulled his clothes out of the drier, folded the jeans and the t-shirt, went upstairs, and laid them on the floor in front of the guest room door. I'd finished the coffee, sent Louie a text message I would be in around noon, and was scanning YouTube for morning news when my phone rang. Barbara Wright.

"Good morning, Barbara."

"Give me an update," she said.

"Not too much to tell. He seems like a nice kid. He's still asleep upstairs in the guest room. I'm beginning to think he's not a runaway. He mentioned the girls at school stay away from him, and the guys give him a hard time. I'm thinking if he were a runaway, he'd probably have a pals house he could stay at. Just the way he talked about it, and he didn't say much, but the way he talked suggested this might be an ongoing situation. Maybe there's no father, or there's a drug or alcohol problem on the home front. I'll hopefully learn more, but I don't want to pressure the kid."

"The mother never called, never showed up?"

"I'm pretty sure he never contacted her. I had him show me his phone, and the battery was dead. I'm guessing it had been dead for a while. Hopefully, he recharged it when he went to bed. All he seems to have are the clothes on his back. I cooked him dinner last night. He ate two pork chops, about a dozen potatoes, and all the chocolate chip cookies."

"Shouldn't he be at school by now?"

"Yeah, maybe if things were normal, but they're not. I'm going to take him out and get some clothes, a couple pair of jeans and some shirts, maybe a haircut if he wants."

"I wonder if you shouldn't contact the school. I can give you the name of—"

"I thought about that, but I'm worried they may be required to alert child services, and then he'd end up in a facility or something."

"Mmm-mmm, possibly. I think they're probably required by law to contact child welfare or maybe even the police."

"I'd like to give it a few days, maybe get him stabilized, not that he's crazy or anything. But it might help him to be someplace that he doesn't have to worry about where he's going to sleep or where the next meal is coming from."

"Are you sure you want to do this?"

"Yeah, definitely. I washed his clothes last night. Unless he has things hidden somewhere, he's got a worn pair of jeans and a soiled t-shirt. He didn't say it specifically, but he's the kid at school everyone makes fun of. No friends, girls stay away, and the boys tease him. I think I can help this kid, Barbara."

I could hear her take a deep breath. "Well, all right. Please call me with any questions or concerns. I think what I'll do if you don't mind, is quietly poke around and see if I can find out anything. Did you get the last name?"

"No, but in fairness, I didn't ask for one. I just want him to get comfortable with me. Hopefully, I can begin to reduce some of the everyday stress he's dealing with. It's got to be pretty tough paying attention in school when you don't know where you're going to be sleeping that night or how you're going to get something to eat."

"I'm sure he's been living off of the school lunch program. That's probably been keeping him going."

"I didn't think of that, but it makes a lot of sense. He's very lean looking. Hey, I should ring off. I can hear some movement upstairs. Let's touch base later today. I'll give you a call."

"I'll give *you* a call this afternoon," she said and hung up. Twenty minutes later, Taylor and Morton arrived in the kitchen.

"So, how'd you two sleep?"

"I was out about thirty seconds after my head hit the pillow. That's the most comfortable bed I've ever been in."

Unfortunately, he probably wasn't kidding. "You mean Morton didn't take up all the room? He didn't try to steal the covers?"

"No, he was great."

Morton walked over for his morning head scratch. Once I was finished, I said, "Hey, Taylor, let Morton out the back door, and I'll get going on breakfast. Pancakes sound okay?"

"That would be awesome."

"All right, I can make you coffee if you drink it, or I think there's some orange juice in the fridge if you want to check."

He poured himself an orange juice and settled onto a stool at the kitchen counter while I mixed up the pancake batter. "Grab some plates out of the cupboard, Taylor, and the silverware is in that drawer," I said, pointing to the drawer.

I had my largest frying pan on the stove and poured enough batter into the pan for three pancakes. Once the pancakes were cooking, I leaned against the kitchen counter and said, "You up for one of my ideas?"

He got a troubled look on his face and said, "Maybe. What'd you have in mind?"

"You should be in school this morning. In fact," I glanced at the clock on the stove, "you're late."

"Wouldn't be the first time."

"I'm thinking we should use the morning, and let's do a little shopping. Maybe get you a couple pairs of jeans, some shirts, underwear. I think you could maybe use a decent jacket. After all, it is Minnesota, and it tends to begin to get chilly at this time of year."

"Well, see, I don't really have any money, Dev."

"Not a problem. My treat, you don't have to pay me back. But let's get you some decent clothes. Those guys that are giving you a hard time, maybe it'll be a subtle way to begin to tell them to get screwed."

He smiled at that.

I turned around and flipped the pancakes, not a moment too soon. A couple of minutes later, I placed the pancakes on a plate and handed it to Taylor. "Eat up. There's more if you want."

I poured three more pancakes into the pan. By the time they were ready, I placed two of them on Taylor's empty plate and kept one for myself. We sat and talked as I ate, and he devoured. He told me about the classes he was taking. I mentioned doing the two nights in detention in the cafeteria. I told him about Ramona and the other girls doing papers on Dennis's tattoo business. I didn't mention <u>To Kill A Mockingbird</u>.

"You're the guy that lined that up? I heard some kids talking about it. That is really cool. Everyone says so. I think they were going to go back there and take some pictures of the tattoo parlor. It had a pretty awesome name, but I can't recall what it is."

"Inkredible," I said.

"Yeah, that's the place."

"As a matter of fact, they're going back there tonight to talk to my pal. Are you in that class?"

He nodded and said, "Yeah, but I have it during a different hour than Ramona. She's one of the hot eleventh-grade girls. Believe me, she doesn't even know I exist."

"Well, what do you say we start to take care of that? Let's get the kitchen cleaned up, and we can head out to the Mall of America. You up for that?"

"Dev, that's really nice of you, but I, I can't pay you back. I told you. I don't have any money."

"I didn't ask you to pay me back in cash. Here's how you can pay me back. Let's get these clothes, and then, let's get you focused back on school. You're going to be living on the street for the rest of your life if you don't have an education. That's the only way out of the situation you're in, so let's do it. You can crash here as long as you follow the rules."

"What are the rules?"

"You just keep being the nice guy that you are. Oh, and one other thing."

"Yeah?"

"You gotta take Morton for a walk once in a while, but right now, let's get you some clothes to wear. Deal?"

He smiled, held out his hand to shake, and had a much more solid grip than last night.

Twenty

We drove out to the Mall of America. I'm not a shopper. Over the course of the next two hours, we went through a couple hundred shops. Taylor picked out two pairs of jeans, four shirts, two sweaters, six pairs of boxers, six t-shirts, a pair of casual shoes, a belt, and a jacket. It cost me close to four hundred bucks and was worth every cent and a lot more just to see the smile on his face.

He was wearing his new shoes, jeans, and a shirt on the way home from the mall. I took a slightly different route, turned onto Hamline Avenue, and said, "Hey, I'm not suggesting anything, but do you want to grab a haircut? We're going to pass a place that's really good."

"You think I need one?"

"I'm not judging. I'm just asking if you want one. It's your head."

"At a barbershop?"

"Yeah, a place called Schmidty's. I know the guy. No pressure, man. I'm just asking."

He nodded and said, "That would be great. I've never been to a barbershop before."

"You stick with me, Taylor. I'll show you the big time," I said, and we both laughed.

Fortunately, at half-past eleven, there was only one guy in the barbershop, and Schmidty was handing him a mirror to look at his finished product. Two minutes later, Taylor was seated in the barber's chair.

"So how do you want this done?" Schmidty asked.

As Taylor told him, Schmidty nodded and said, "No problem." He started cutting hair and said, "Dev, what have you been up to?"

"I remain the most boring guy in town."

"Yeah, right. Anything ever happen to that guy you were after, the one who knocked off the jewelry store and got all those diamonds?"

"Yeah, that wasn't a jewelry store. It was actually two jerks, and the guy they robbed was a diamond merchant about eighty years old. I grew up around the corner from him. Nice guy, I shoveled his sidewalk and cut his grass as a kid. He kept all his diamonds in these little envelopes and lined up the envelopes in shoe boxes. He worked out of a little office in a building in downtown Minneapolis. He thought the place was secure, but obviously, it wasn't. Those two clowns roughed him up and stole a couple of shoeboxes full of diamonds. I don't think they had any idea of the value. He ended up in the hospital for a day or two."

"And then he called you?"

"No, I heard about it from a cop pal. They'd run into a dead end, and I just happened to luck out and find the idiots who robbed him."

"Yeah, that's right," Schmidty said. He was shaving the sides of Taylor's head. It was beginning to look a lot like the haircut I got in basic training, so short you couldn't pinch the hair. "You broke one of their arms, right?"

"Half-right, I broke an arm on each of them. One of them came at me with an eighteen-inch wrecking bar. That kind of pissed me off."

Schmidty laughed and switched hair clippers. He cut a part along the side of Taylor's head. "Now, I'm going to trim these curls on top, okay?"

"Yeah, but not too much."

"I'll just take a little off. We wouldn't want to disappoint all the girls."

"Oh my God, Taylor, they'll be standing in line," I said.

"You better get extra locks for the door, son," Schmidty chuckled. He finished up about five minutes later and handed Taylor the mirror. "You take a look and make sure you like it. If you don't, you can just wait four or five weeks, and it will grow out."

Both Schmidty and I laughed. Taylor sat in the chair, grinning, seemingly mesmerized as he moved the mirror back and forth. "If you like, I could shave my signature in the back of your head," Schmidty said.

"Thanks, but I think it's fine just the way it is," Taylor said, not getting the joke.

"Okay, stay there for just a minute and let me take a picture," Schmidty said. He pulled out his cell phone and took two pictures and then undid the apron around Taylor. Taylor climbed out of the chair, and Schmidty brushed him off. "Okay, Taylor, you're good to go. Nice to meet you. Don't be a stranger and watch yourself around Dev, here. Trouble always seems to find him."

Taylor grinned, and we headed out the door. "You want some lunch?" I said as we climbed into my car.

"Actually, I can grab some at school. They serve until 1:00, and I can make my afternoon classes."

"Yeah, fine with me. I'll drop you off. You're free to stay at my place tonight."

"Okay, thanks."

"Good, is your phone working?"

"Yeah, I recharged it overnight."

"Call me with any problems. I should be home around five tonight. If you want to get there before that, give me a call, and I can pick you up." I pulled out my cellphone and handed it to him. "Call yourself on my cell, so I have your number, and we can set each other up as a contact. That way, we ever need to get a hold of one another, it's there." He punched in his number as I turned the corner. I knew better than to pull into the school parking lot. Instead, I just stopped at the curb, and he started to climb out.

"Hey, Taylor," I said before he closed the door, "do your best today, and you're welcome to stay at my place as long as you want. Okay?"

He smiled, nodded, and walked up the concrete steps toward the front door of the building. I noticed the stare he got from a couple of girls walking out to the parking lot. If Taylor noticed, he didn't let on. On the way home, I stopped at the CVS store and bought a couple of pens and some notebooks. I picked up Morton from home, and we headed down to the office. Louie was gone, and the coffee was on. I poured myself a cup and turned the burner off. Morton got comfortable on his pillow.

I settled in behind my desk and phoned Barbara. She answered on the second ring. "So, what's the latest?"

"Yeah, good afternoon back to you, Barbara."

"Sorry if I'm concerned about both of you. How is it going?"

"Things are going fine. We did a little shopping this morning. Got a haircut, and right now, he's in school. I dropped him off about forty-five minutes ago. He wanted to make his afternoon classes."

"Hmm-mmm. Any word on where he's from or what the family situation is?"

"No, and I don't intend to push it. I think he'll come around in time and begin to open up."

"So, what's the plan?"

"The plan is, he can stay with me as long as he wants. I told him if he doesn't want to spend the rest of his life on the street, he has to get an education."

"Stay as long as he wants? Dev, is that even legal?"

"It is, at least for the moment. The last thing he or we need is for Taylor to be focused on where he's going to sleep and how he can get his next meal. I want to get him feeling somewhat safe so he doesn't have to worry about the basics in life. Once that occurs, I suspect we may learn more about his family situation."

There was a long pause before she said, "Okay, so what can I do to help?"

"Well, don't mention what's going on to anyone. The last thing any of us need, especially Taylor, is some busybody involving themselves and thinking he'd be better off in some facility. Let's just take our time. Right now, he's safe and feels comfortable enough to want to go back to school."

"All right, please stay in touch, and mark your calendar for Tuesday and Thursday next week, detention."

"How could I forget?" I said.

"All right, thank you for the update. Let's talk tomorrow," Barbara said and disconnected.

I thought a long while about Taylor and called my friend Dennis.

"Inkredible," was how he answered the phone.

"Dennis, Dev Haskell."

"Twice in the same week. To what do I owe the pleasure?"

"Just wanted to say thanks for making the time to see Ramona and her girlfriends the other day. They told me about it last night, and they were just thrilled. I really owe you, man."

"Dev, thanks, but I really enjoyed myself. A great bunch of girls and they gave me some great ideas on new artwork. The type of images that will appeal to the younger market. As a matter of fact, they're coming back, I think tonight at some point."

"Yeah, they told me sometime around eight. That's when you close, isn't it?"

"Yeah, and Friday is usually a pretty quiet night, so it should work out just fine."

"Can I ask you for a favor?"

"Yeah, sure, man, I feel like I owe you."

"Hardly, but here's what I'd like to do…" I went on to explain Taylor's situation and finished up with, "So if we could chat with you for a couple of minutes and then leave once the girls arrive. You know, have them thinking this kid is really cool."

"Girls avoiding him and pain in the ass boys thinking they're hot shit. I remember those days all too well. Yeah, you bet. Come on down. I'll think of it as a kind of payback for those jerks that stole my clothes from the high school locker room."

"Yeah, we all have a story like that. Thanks, Dennis. I really appreciate it. I'll see you tonight."

"Looking forward to it, Dev."

Twenty-one

I was in the process of searching police department records online for Eli Cummings when I heard the stairs creaking and figured it was Louie heading up to the office. Unfortunately, when the office door opened and I looked up, a red-faced Fat Freddy Zimmerman waddled in. Behind him, huffing and puffing, came Tubby Gustafson. Both of them looked like they'd just run a marathon.

Fat Freddy's eyes were bulging, and his chest was heaving as he pulled back the client chair for Tubby. Tubby collapsed in the chair, pulled a handkerchief out from his suit coat, and mopped his brow. They both sat there, breathing heavily for a long minute or two before Tubby managed to gasp, "Damn it, Haskell."

"How nice of you to stop in, sir," I said and waited for the inevitable response about how I was totally worthless and would never amount to anything.

Tubby seemed to be staring at the floor, and as his breathing returned to a more or less controlled state, I wondered if he was maybe experiencing the beginnings of a heart attack.

"Sir, Mr. Gustafson. Are you all right, sir?"

"Just where in the hell did you get those?" Tubby groaned and pointed at the six paintings leaning against the wall behind me.

I had to turn for a moment because I didn't realize what he was pointing at. "Oh, those are some paintings I uncovered that were done by Eli Cummings, the man you asked me to find. Unfortunately, he was nowhere to be found. I've been combing through the police records as I speak," I said and spun the laptop around so Tubby could see the mugshot image of Eli Cummings from 2018.

Tubby glanced at my computer screen and shook his head. "I'm not interested in that damn thing," he groaned. "Where in the hell did you get those," he said, pointing to the three landscapes and three portrait images leaning against the wall.

"I believe I mentioned I had visited Cummings' last known address, sir. I was able to work out an agreement with the landlord and acquired those paintings. Unfortunately for the landlord, Cummings had fled the scene owing two months' rent."

Tubby shook his head. "Old, outdated information, just like that mugshot from two damn years ago. Worthless, completely worthless. I'm going to waste my time and ask, have you found him yet?"

"No, sir, not exactly."

"Not exactly? What, is he hiding under a bed somewhere, and you haven't pulled him out? Haskell, you pathetic moron, I told you to find him, damn it. That's all you had to do was find him. Of course, at no surprise, you've once again managed to fail miserably."

"Yes, sir, I understand that, and I'm trying my best to find him. It's just that he seems to have disappeared. I believe I suggested he may have left the country and—"

"Silencio!" he shouted then took a couple of deep breaths in an effort to calm himself. "He hasn't left the country, you one-watt idiot. He's somewhere in town. God almighty, why do I even bother? You're supposed to find him. That's all you had to do was find him. Is that so hard?"

"I'm trying to do that, sir, but it would seem he doesn't wish to be found. The police have no indication of where he might be. I can't find anyone who is associated with him. I've no knowledge of where he might spend his time. As I mentioned, he fled his apartment owing two months' rent."

"He fled after assaulting an individual I sent to deliver a message," Tubby said.

I could only imagine what the message was. "So, it would seem you've run into exactly the same difficulty as I have. I told you before he was a person of interest in some bank robberies, but no one knows where he is. I'm sorry, sir, but I'm going to need more time."

"Yet you found those paintings, didn't you?"

"I'm having them examined by a professional," I said.

"Let me save you the time. They're forgeries. There, problem solved. Now, if I may suggest, I think it would be wise to get back to work, find this individual, and fast!" Tubby shouted those last two words.

"Message received loud and clear, sir."

Tubby glanced up at the ceiling and mumbled, "Lord, give me strength. Fredrick, I'm waiting."

Fat Freddy jumped to his feet and pulled Tubby's chair back as Tubby groaned and stood. "Haskell, let me warn you. You are running out of valuable time. For your own good, I suggest you find Cummings and quickly."

He stared at the paintings again and mumbled, "Interesting," as he waddled toward the door. Fat Freddy smiled, nodded, and gave me the finger. He hurried to catch up with Tubby, slamming the door on the way out. I sat at my desk and listened to the stairs creak as they slowly made their way down to the main floor. A moment later, they appeared out on the sidewalk. Tubby continued to shake his head and apparently mumble as Fat Freddy ran ahead and opened the door. The black SUV rocked from side to side as Tubby oozed onto the seat and then slowly slid across to the far side of the vehicle.

Fat Freddy opened the driver's door and climbed in behind the wheel. I thought it amazing there was enough room for him with a steering wheel in the way, but the

SUV suddenly started up, pulled into the lane, and disappeared.

I looked down at the paintings leaning against the wall and thought for a moment. I pulled out my cellphone and pushed the contact number.

"Dinicci," was how Annette answered her phone.

"Hi Annette, this is Dev Haskell."

"Oh, hi Dev. What can I do for you?"

"Well, I'm wondering if you might have time to look at some paintings I've acquired."

"Acquired, you mean as in you purchased them?"

"No, actually, I paid a visit to the empty apartment Eli Cummings had been living in. Judging from the things left behind, he apparently departed in a hurry. I have six paintings, three versions of a portrait and three versions of a landscape."

"Oil paintings on canvas?"

"They're paintings, I'm not sure if they're oil or acrylic, and I think they're on canvas."

"Interesting, and they're works by Eli Cummings?"

"That's a presumption on my part. They were in his former apartment. There isn't a signature on them. Based on our luncheon conversation the other day, if I had to guess, I would say they're maybe a study of an existing work. I don't recognize either painting, but you might, and maybe they would alert you to a forgery or an attempted forgery."

"Yeah, I'd be very interested in seeing them. I can't make it tonight, but I could come over tomorrow morning first thing."

"That would be great, Annette, but tomorrow is Saturday. If you want to wait until Monday, that's fine with me."

"If you don't mind, I'd like to do tomorrow morning."

"Yeah, sure. Would sometime after nine be okay?"

"I'll be there, Dev, and thanks for the call," she said and hung up.

I heard a sudden creaking on the stairs and glanced out the window, hoping I wouldn't see Tubby Gustafson's SUV. Fortunately, Louie's faded orange Ford Fiesta was parked across the street. Louie stepped into the office a moment later. He was almost as red-faced as Tubby Gustafson.

He gave me the perfunctory wave, tossed his briefcase onto the picnic table, and settled into his desk chair. After a minute or two, he said, "Missed you this morning. Were you working or sleeping in someone's bed?"

"It's been an interesting twenty-four hours." I proceeded to fill him in on finding Taylor camped out in the school cloakroom, putting him up at my house, and taking him shopping this morning. "Then, just to remind me that no good deed goes unpunished, Tubby Gustafson and Fat Freddy showed up. You missed them by about twenty minutes."

"Perfect timing on my part. Hey, I'm thinking of capping off the day with a news briefing at The Spot. You interested?"

"Oh, man, I could use it, but I've got something lined up with Taylor. Afraid I'll have to take a rain check."

"Suit yourself," Louie said. "I think I'll head over there now. Are you in tomorrow?"

"Yeah, I've got someone coming in around nine."

"I'll probably be here. See you then," Louie said and headed out the door.

I sent a text message to Taylor, *'You need a ride?'*

I got an almost instant reply. *'Sitting on your front porch.'*

I decided to head home. I picked up Morton's leash and clicked it onto his collar. I was just about to head out the door when I glanced at the paintings and recalled Tubby staring at them and mumbling, "Interesting." I gathered up the paintings, and we left the office. Morton hopped in the back seat as I opened the trunk and laid the paintings inside.

Twenty-two

Taylor gave me a wave as I pulled into the drive-way. "Hey," I called, climbing out from behind the wheel. "I'm sorry. Have you been waiting long?"

"No, I just decided to walk down here after school. I checked it on my phone. It's two and a half miles."

Morton barked at the sound of Taylor's voice. I opened the rear door. He hopped out and made a b-line for Taylor sitting on the front porch." How'd school go?"

Taylor grinned. "It was different. Real different. A couple girls actually said hi to me, and a guy two lockers down nodded at me."

"That's great. Did you make it to that class where you have to write the paper?"

"Yeah, all the kids were talking about Ramona and her gang going to the tattoo place tonight."

"Yeah, Inkredible. Come on. Let's head inside. I got an idea we can discuss over dinner."

"Actually, I was thinking I should maybe take Morton for a walk if that's okay."

"Are you kidding? He'd love it. Take him for a couple of blocks, and I'll get dinner going while you guys are out."

Morton's tail was wagging back and forth as Taylor took hold of the leash. "See you guys in about twenty minutes," I called, and Taylor waved back.

I had chicken breasts and sliced red peppers frying up when they got back. "How did the walk go?" I asked as I tossed a biscuit Morton's way. He caught it in midair and hurried to a corner so he wouldn't have to share.

"Pretty good. He had a couple of favorite fire hydrants he wanted to show me. This is a pretty nice area you live in, lots of big old houses."

"Yeah, it was down on hard times back in the sixties and seventies, and a bunch of young couples moved in and started restoring the places themselves. I've met some of them, interesting folks. Why don't you wash up and set two places at the counter. Dinner will be ready in a couple of minutes. Check the fridge for something you want to drink. I'm just having a water."

"You sure I'm not stealing all the root beer from you?"

"No, not at all. In fact, it's better that you have it rather than me. We'll have to maybe do some grocery shopping tomorrow or Sunday. We'll load up for the next week's meals." I turned off the stove, dished up the chicken breasts and the roast peppers, and set a plate down in front of Taylor. I grabbed my plate and pulled out a stool.

We chatted for a couple of minutes. Taylor clearly enjoyed his afternoon at school. Halfway through the meal, I remembered the notebooks I got and said, "Hang on a second. I picked something up today." I hurried out to the front room and grabbed the bag then went back into the kitchen. "Not sure you can use these. It's more from my era, but I got you some notebooks and pens for homework or whatever. I suppose, in today's world, everything's on a computer."

"Oh, thanks, this is great, Dev. I can use these, honest. I always leave my computer in my locker at school because, well, I don't know where exactly I'll end up at night, and if it got stolen, I'd be in big trouble."

"You can bring it home here. I promise not to steal it."

"Yeah, I know you won't."

"Only because I probably couldn't figure out how to turn the thing on, let alone do anything on it. Now, you have any plans for tonight?"

He gave a sad smile and said, "No one wants to hang around with a guy like me."

"Well, I think it's time we start letting them know what they've been missing. You remember those girls going to Inkredible, the tattoo place."

"Yeah, Ramona Williams and her friends. I told you, everyone at school was talking about it."

"Right, so I talked to Dennis this afternoon. He's the owner of the place. I'm going to head down there in a bit and see him. I wondered if you might want to come along."

"But aren't the girls going to be down there?"

"We'll be down there before they will, and we'll leave when they arrive. Here's my thought, The girls will see you there and just might spread the word back at school that you're Mister Cool. You gotta work these angles, Taylor."

"Won't they think I'm following them?"

"No, because you're going to be Dennis's pal, and it'll look like a coincidence that they arrived just as you were leaving."

He seemed to think about that for a long moment, and then a smile spread across his face. "Yeah, let's do that."

We parked right in front of Inkredible and walked in. A female artist with sky blue hair was working a tattoo pen on a woman's leg. The two women were carrying on a casual conversation as the artist slowly worked her way up the leg. I glanced over, focused on the process for a brief moment, and had to look away. Taylor seemed to be fascinated and stared, or maybe he was just admiring the leg.

"Hey, Dev, long time no see," Dennis said, stepping through the beaded curtain hanging over the doorway. He was wearing cowboy boots, starched jeans with a crease, and a long sleeve shirt. The sleeves on the shirt were rolled up, exposing two muscled arms and a lot of artwork.

"Dennis, great to see you. This is my pal, Taylor. Taylor, this is Dennis Richards. He's the man in charge."

"Taylor, nice to meet you," Dennis said, shaking hands. "Why don't you guys come on back to my office, and we can chat."

We followed Dennis through the beaded curtain and down a hallway with framed images of tattoo artwork. "Grab a seat, fellas," Dennis said as he sat in the high-back leather chair behind his desk. The walls in the office were covered with more framed images of tattoo artwork.

"Dennis, did you do all this artwork?" I asked, looking around the room.

"Oh, some of it. It's what I loved to do. As a matter of fact, it's what actually got me into the business. But, being a business, and my business, I don't have the time to do artwork anymore. Now Taylor, Dev mentioned on the phone that you're in school with the girls that are coming down here tonight. What can you tell me about them?"

"Oh, well, I mean, we go to the same school, but I don't really know them. I just sort of know who they are, but we never talk or anything."

"You know this Ramona?"

"I know who she is, but that's all."

"Well, she seems pretty nice. I enjoyed talking with her. I guess she got the other three girls involved, and they'll be coming down tonight and asking me all sorts of questions. Dev, I guess it would be kind of like talking to a movie star for them," Dennis said and laughed.

"Yeah, a horror movie star."

"Some days, that's not far from the truth."

"So, Dennis, if you're not doing the artwork, who is? You said Ramona gave you a bunch of new ideas."

"Yeah, now I just have to find someone to come up with the sketches. Tough work, and on a normal day, we just don't have the time. It may not look like it now, but that's only because it's Friday night. We'll be jammed all day tomorrow with walk-ins. During the week, we have to schedule appointments. We're open until ten. Friday night is our slow night, and we close at eight, just to take a break. Don't get me wrong. That's not a complaint. I'm blessed to have the right kind of problems."

"What images did Ramona suggest?" Taylor asked.

"She had some pretty general ideas, but they were good, the usual, butterflies, dragons, lions, skulls, you know that kind of stuff. The key is the new design. I just have to try to find someone to come up with new designs."

"Would it be okay if I tried to come up with some designs for you?"

"You? Why are you interested in tattoos?"

"Not so much. I mean, I like them and all. I just don't think I want one. But I'd love to try to create some artwork for you. I've had some art lessons, and my uncle is a painter."

Dennis seemed to think about that for a moment then spun around in his desk chair and grabbed something off the credenza behind him. "Here's a sketch pad and some colored pencils. We call this 'Flash art.' The sheets in this tablet are eleven by fourteen. Figure maybe five or six images on a sheet. Sketch it out first and experiment on other paper. This paper is strictly for your final design. If I like your design, I'll pay you for it. Okay?"

"Yeah, okay. Thank you, Mister Richards. I'll get on this right away."

"You can call me Dennis, please. Now, be prepared. I'm going to turn some and maybe all your images down. It happens to all of us. Don't let that discourage you. It's happened to me a half-million times. It's part of the business. Got it?"

"Yes, sir."

Dennis smiled at that just as the woman with sky blue hair poked her head in the office and said, "Dennis, sorry to interrupt, but there are four girls out front to see you. They said they had an appointment."

"Okay. Tell them I'll be right out, Stacey. You have any questions, Taylor?"

"No, I'll get on this right away, Dennis. Thank you so much."

"Dev, you've been rather quiet. Any questions?"

"No, Dennis, thanks for the info and for taking the time to see us."

"My pleasure. Let me walk you guys out. I think it might be a good idea if we mention you'll be doing some design work, Taylor. Trust me, no one knows better than Dev and me about girls who don't want to be around us."

Taylor got a nervous look on his face. Dennis gave me a wink, and we walked out to the front room. The girls were seated on a bench along the front window. They looked up from their cell phones as Dennis continued chatting with us, and their eyes grew wide at the sight of Taylor.

"Once again, Taylor, thank you for taking the time and offering to help us. We'll be very interested in the new images you come up with. Dev, good to see you. We'll be in touch."

"Thanks, Dennis," Taylor said then nodded at the girls and said, "Hi."

I gave Dennis a long handshake and said, "Thanks so much, Dennis."

He smiled, turned toward the girls, and said, "Ladies, come on back and let's talk."

Outside, Taylor jumped up and down and pumped his arm. "Oh, Dev, that was so cool. Thank you. Thank you. Thank you."

"Yeah, it went a lot better than I could have hoped. You doing some sketches for Dennis, I couldn't have planned it any better. The girls were in shock, and I'm pretty sure the first thing they're going to do when they finish talking to Dennis is text a hundred of their closest friends and tell them just how cool you are."

As soon as we got home, Taylor excused himself and rushed upstairs to begin sketching. I let Morton out into the backyard, dished up a bowl of ice cream, and settled down in front of the TV. I thought for a moment and then pulled out my cellphone and called Gladys. I ended up leaving another message, my third. I clicked onto the Schitt's Creek series and lost myself in a world more insane than mine.

I let Morton out a little after ten, got the coffee ready for the morning, and we headed upstairs. I knocked on the guest room door.

"Hey, Taylor?"

"Yeah, Dev, Come on in."

He was seated at the small desk, sketching something out in one of the notebooks I'd picked up. "Oh, just working out some ideas here," he said and half-turned to face me.

"Good for you. How's it going?"

"Well, it's going. I'm in the early stages right now." Sheets of paper torn from the notebook were folded in half and scattered across the desk and on the floor.

"You want me to keep Morton in my room?"

"Oh, no, he's okay in here. Besides, he might give me some ideas."

"Okay, good luck. I've got to be up and out early tomorrow. I'm meeting someone at my office around nine. I don't know how long it's going to take. Help yourself to breakfast, clean up any mess, and if you decide to go anywhere, leave me a note. Okay?"

"Yeah, see you tomorrow at some time, and Dev, thanks for tonight. That was really awesome."

"Yeah, it was. Right about now you're probably the most popular guy in school."

That brought a smile to his face.

Twenty-three

I was up before my alarm went off. I did an extra careful job of shaving, and then, after my shower, applied a moisturizing cream to my face in anticipation of meeting with Annette Dinicci at my office. I grabbed a quick breakfast of peanut butter toast and two cups of coffee while I deleted virtually all of my emails. I debated getting Morton out of Taylor's room but decided to leave the two of them alone and headed down to the office.

I parked across the street, pulled the paintings out of my trunk, and hurried upstairs to the office. I was greeted by a partially opened door that had been kicked in sometime in the past twelve hours. The trim on the doorframe was shattered and lying on the floor. There was a large boot print on the door right next to the doorknob. A number of files and sheets of paper were scattered across the floor. Fortunately, my computer was still on my desk and looked to be in one piece.

As I set the paintings on Louie's picnic table, I wondered who in the hell would be stupid enough to break in here? It's not like there was anything of value, well, unless there was maybe something in a file. But that seemed rather doubtful. I noticed one of the hairdressers across the way staring at me. I gave a wave and walked toward her.

She unlocked the door as I approached. I'd completely forgotten her name, but fortunately, she wore a name tag. "Hi Rochelle," I said, hoping my reading her name tag wasn't too obvious.

"Hi, Dev. If you want your hair done or a pedicure, we're not open for another forty minutes."

"Not to worry. Hey, it looks like someone broke into our office last night. Did anything happen over here?"

" No nothing, thankfully. A break-in? Oh, God, that's not good. I know the doors were locked downstairs because I was the first one here this morning and had to unlock them when I arrived." She looked past me and saw the files and papers scattered across the floor. "Did they take anything?"

"Not really. They tossed some files around, but I can't tell if anything was stolen. With the exception of our coffee pot, we don't really have anything worth taking."

"I think everything's okay here, but I had better check our supply room just to be sure. You know, maybe talk to the insurance guys down on the first floor. They've got security cameras on the front door, and they could check their images. Maybe their camera picked up someone breaking into the building."

"That's where I was planning to go next," I lied. "Let me know if anything turns up missing on your end."

"If something was stolen out of here, they would have had to have a key to get in. I'll pass the word, and we'll keep an eye out. Hope nothing important was taken."

"Thanks, Rochelle. I'll keep you posted."

I pulled the door closed to our office then hurried downstairs to the insurance office. Bud Friehoff is the agent. The door to the office was open, but no one was seated at the receptionist's desk.

"Hello, is anyone home?" I called.

"Yeah, yeah. How can I... Oh, Dev," Bud said, stepping into the reception area. "What's up?"

"Someone broke into our office last night. Everything okay here?"

"Last night?" he asked and shook his head. "I'm not aware of any problem."

"They kicked in the door, rifled through some files but didn't touch the computer on my desk. There's really nothing up there worth stealing unless Louie was involved in some case I'm unaware of, but I think he would have told me."

"God, I don't think anything... well, wait a minute, follow me. Let's look at the security images. We'll be able to see if someone entered the building. Hopefully, we'll be able to get a look at someone heading up the stairs," he said. He led me down the hall to a dingy, windowless room with three computer screens. The screens images were black and white. One monitored the front door to the agency and the lower third of the staircase leading up to the second floor. The other two screens monitored the reception area and what appeared to be Bud's office.

"What time did you lock up last night?" he asked.

"Maybe a little before five."

"Okay, and the hairdressers close at eight on Friday, so let's start there. He typed in yesterday's date and 8:00 PM. The screen suddenly brought up an image and began to move forward. It took maybe thirty seconds to get to 8:23 PM. Bud stopped the screen as an image of Rochelle and another woman I recognized appeared on the screen.

"That's the hairdressers leaving for the night. They're usually the last ones to leave." He typed in something and said, "The scan will stop on any activity. A couple of minutes later, it stopped as a figure appeared at the foot of the stairs. The time on the screen read 12:56 AM.

"Oh, dear, not a nice looking person. Do you recognize him?"

I did, unfortunately, the bald thug with the blisters all over his face who worked for Tubby. He was the driver in the SUV the night Tubby was parked across the street from The Spot.

"Yeah, he works for one of my awful clients."

"Not those two fat guys I see around here occasionally?"

"Yeah, I'm afraid so. That would be Tubby Gustafson and Fat Freddy Zimmerman. This guy was driving the car for Gustafson the other night. I'm trying to remember his name, Larry, Lester, no wait, Lyle. Yeah, that was it. They called him Lyle."

"Tubby Gustafson, really… It looks like a bit of a blotchy face on this guy here. Hmm-mmm, I wonder if he'd be interested in some special health coverage? Let's see when he comes back down," he said and pushed a key on the keyboard. About five seconds later, another image froze on the screen. As Lyle came down the stairs, he appeared to be holding his right wrist and stared directly at the security camera. The time on the screen was 1:11 AM.

"Oh dear," Bud said, focusing in on Lyle and enlarging his face. "Dreadful, absolutely dreadful. Well, he was up there for no more than fifteen minutes. Any idea what he was after? He doesn't appear to be carrying anything. Looks like he might be in some pain."

"No idea what he would be looking for. It's not like we have anything of value up there. Just files, and if anyone wanted their file, all they'd have to do is ask, and we'd give it to them."

"Well, one other thing springs to mind. This gentleman was able to access the building seemingly without a problem. Apparently, he had a key. I'm going to call the landlord and request the locks to be changed on the front door."

"That's not a bad thought, Bud. I'll do the same. Is there a way you could print off those two images for me?"

"Not a problem at all. Good idea, give the police more to go on."

"Yeah, they'll hopefully have this guy by the end of the day," I said, and the printer fired up and spit out copies of both images.

"Good luck with this, Dev. I'll call the landlord in just a moment."

"Thanks, Bud. Listen, sorry to take up your time, much appreciated."

"You're going to report this to the police, aren't you?"

"Oh, absolutely," I said, having no intention of doing so. "I'll go back upstairs and call them right now."

"Excellent, nip this problem in the bud," he said and then laughed at his little joke.

'A little late to nip Tubby Gustafson in the bud,' I thought. "I'd better run. I've got someone coming in at nine. Thank you again for your time, Bud."

"Glad to be of service, Dev. You need any coverage, we're always here."

"Thanks, Bud. You stay safe," I said as I hurried out of the agency and up the stairs.

Lyle breaking into our office. I was ninety-nine percent sure there was nothing in the office that Lyle was interested in. I wasn't even sure he could read, which eliminated him searching my files. That left Tubby Gustafson, and there was nothing I could think of that Tubby would be interested in. So, it had to— Wait a minute. I stopped just outside the office door and thought about the six Eli Cummings paintings. That had to be it. Tubby had been shocked to see them yesterday. He'd stared at them, recognized them. It was the paintings. He'd sent idiot Lyle to get the damn paintings.

I hurried into the office and began picking up the files and papers. As I gathered them off the floor, I suddenly realized that all the files were mine. Nothing of Louie's was touched, which I guess was good in a way.

So Tubby's idiot breaks into our office and rifles through my files. He doesn't find the paintings and apparently doesn't find anything in the files. I pulled open the bottom drawer in my desk and opened the cigar box. My pistol in the sticky holster was still there. I checked the clip. It was still full and appeared untouched. I slipped the pistol into my belt and untucked my shirt to keep it hidden.

I stacked the files and loose documents on my desk then set the paintings back against the wall. I did a quick check of the closet and put some coffee on. I pulled the file drawer open, and there was the answer to what Lyle had found. The rat trap had been sprung, no doubt when he reached into the drawer. Hopefully, he broke some fingers. I was on my knees, nailing the door trim back in place when Annette came up the staircase.

"Good morning, Dev," she called as she headed up the stairs. I hit a nail the final time then stood and watched her as she climbed up the stairs. She was dressed in black jeans, a red blouse, and leopard print loafers. She carried a black briefcase in her right hand. "Getting ready to nail the door closed?" she joked.

"Actually, no. Someone broke into our office last night. They kicked the door open. Hey, thanks for coming down."

She quickened her pace, hurrying up the remaining steps. "What? Oh, God, I'm so sorry. I didn't mean to make a joke about that. Is everything okay? What did they steal? Thank God you weren't here. I mean, you weren't, were you?"

"No, it was sometime after midnight. We got a picture of the guy on the security cameras downstairs. You can see how he kicked in the door," I said, pulling the door closed and pointing to the boot print next to the doorknob.

"Oh dear, any idea what he was after?"

"I'm hoping you'll be able to tell me. Come on in," I said, opening the door and elaborately swinging my arm.

Twenty-four

nnette stepped in and looked around. "How about some coffee? I just put it on, and I can bring you up to date on what I know or at least suspect on this break-in."

"Yeah, okay, just black, please," she said, setting her briefcase down on Louie's picnic table. She glanced over at the paintings leaning against the wall and strolled toward them to get a closer look. "These are the works you want me to examine?"

"Yeah, here," I said, handing her a mug of coffee. "Grab a seat."

"Mmm-mmm, thanks," she said and took a sip. She continued to look at the paintings. "That landscape is called *'Planting Time.'* It's part of the William Bellows collection. Theoretically, these three could be initial works done prior to the final piece. Same thing with the portrait, the original artist was John Capell, and the portraits are of Elinore "Nora" Preston, wife of Minnesota Governor John Albert Johnson. Both of these paintings hang in museums. The landscape was, I think, done around nineteen-ten. The portrait was done in nineteen-seven. The originals auctioned for around fifty thousand, but that was ten years ago, so they'd probably go for half again as much in today's market."

"But these are forgeries, right?"

"Yes, most likely, but just a quick assessment, whoever did them knew what they were doing. I mean, the work is good. Interesting that there's no signature, but then if these were work-ups of the final piece, that would make sense."

"Grab a seat and let me tell you what I know and then if you wouldn't mind taking a closer look at them."

"Oh, I'd be happy to examine them. To say the least, I'm intrigued." She settled into the same chair Tubby Gustafson sat in yesterday. I sat in my desk chair and told her what I'd learned thus far on Eli Cummings. I describe the two-room dive he was living in, the portraits on the floor, and the landscapes hanging on nails. "Now, here's where it gets interesting. Tubby Gustafson was here just yesterday afternoon."

"Gustafson? What in the world did he want?"

"Remember? He has me looking for Eli Cummings. But he focused in on the paintings. I had them right where they are now. He literally lost his train of thought and wanted to know where I got the paintings."

"But if they were there against the wall, and he had someone break in here last night, why didn't they take the paintings?"

"Because the paintings weren't here. I just had a funny feeling and put them all in the trunk of my car.

Even this morning, when I saw the door had been kicked in, it didn't immediately dawn on me that whoever broke in here had been looking for the paintings. But now it makes perfect sense."

Annette finished her coffee and set the mug on my desk. "You have any more coffee?"

"Yeah, coming right up." As I refilled her mug, she went over to Louie's picnic table and opened her briefcase. She slipped on a pair of white latex gloves, laid a cloth over a portion of the picnic table, and arranged what looked like four glass squares on the cloth. She walked over, grabbed one of the portraits, and set it upside down on the glass squares.

"Here's your coffee," I said.

"Oh, just set it on the desk if you wouldn't mind," she replied, not looking at me but focused on the back of the painting. She pulled a magnifying glass from her briefcase and made an inspection of the wooden frame the canvas was attached to. She examined the tacks that held the canvas in place. After a few minutes, she stepped back, gave a quick smile, and sipped some coffee.

"So, what do you think?"

"Well, just a quick look would suggest it could certainly fool the unsuspecting. The nails are handmade, and if we ran some tests, they're probably in line with the dates of the original paintings. Something left in a jar or a drawer that you could use to attach the canvas, pretty standard for the day. The nails in each corner of the frame are most likely the same vintage. I would have to do an x-ray to verify that. The canvas looks to be aged. The thread count at first glance would seem to be correct. Again an x-ray would determine if there was another work beneath the portrait.

"You're making it sound like that may not be a fake."

"Isn't that the whole purpose, Dev? Now there are uncountable methods to make this appear legitimate. The canvas could be blank canvas from back in the first half of the last century that Cummings somehow acquired. It could be a newer canvas that he soaked in tea to make it appear aged. Honestly, he could have hung it out on a clothesline for a couple of months or set it under high intensity, incandescent lights. Just about anything is possible. At first glance, the wood on the frame appears to be aged, but again anything is possible. I'd like to look at all of these in my laboratory. Would you mind if I took them back there for a more complete examination?"

"No, not at all. As a matter of fact, after last night, that might be a pretty good idea."

"Let me take a look at one of those landscapes," she said. She carefully picked up the portrait she'd been examining and placed it next to the others then stepped back and examined the landscapes. Once she made a decision on which landscape to examine, she set it upside down on the glass blocks and went through the same process only much quicker. She turned the landscape right side up and stepped back, looking at it from a number of different angles.

She pulled some device that looked like a cellphone from her briefcase and turned it on then ran a light over a corner section of the painting. "Hmmm, not a hundred percent sure, but I think there might be another painting underneath this landscape. I'll know for sure when I get it back to the lab."

She set the scanner back in her briefcase and pulled out a thick white plastic. She promptly unfolded the thing, and it turned out to be a plastic bag, which she carefully slid the landscape painting into.

She pulled out five more of the folded plastic bags.

"You want me to give you a hand?" I asked, getting out of my chair.

"No offense, Dev. But I'd prefer if you didn't. Let me just bag these up, and we can place them in my car."

"Fine with me," I said, settled back in my chair, and watched over the next five minutes as she bagged each one of the paintings. When she was finished, she said, "Okay, you can help me carry these out to the car. We'll be taking them one at a time."

"I just stacked them one on top of another and carried them up here this morning. I mean, they spent the night in the trunk of my car and were banging off one another while I was driving."

"That's exactly why we're going to carry them carefully one at a time. Think of it this way, Dev. If these are originals, and I haven't determined they aren't, you're looking at maybe a quarter million, maybe even half a million dollars. Be a shame to ruin that because you wanted to skip a couple of trips up and down the stairs.”

“Good point. I didn’t think of it that way. Any special way to carry them?”

“Yes, don’t grab them. Place the panting between the palms of your hands. Carry it with the back of the canvas facing you.”

“Do I have to hold my breath or anything?”

“Ha-ha-ha, you’re so not funny. Come on. Let’s go.”

She took her car keys, pointed them at the window, and clicked on the fob. The lights on her car flashed. I followed her down the stairs and across the street to her car, a burgundy Chevy Suburban. The rear door was unlocked, and she held the painting in one hand and raised the door. In the back of the car was a rack with sponge covered spaces to slide the paintings into.

Once she slid her painting in, she turned toward me and said, “Let me set this in the rack.” She took the painting from me, carefully slid it into the rack, and we headed back into the building, repeating the process two more times. We had just finished with the last two paintings, and she’d locked the Suburban when a faded orange Ford Fiesta groaned past us and pulled to the curb.

“Oh, perfect timing now that the work is done,” I said.

Louie climbed out of his car a moment later and waved. “You two coming or going?”

"Just finished putting a half-million bucks worth of artwork into Annette's car."

Based on the look he gave us, he wasn't sure what to say.

"I'm taking them to the lab for an examination. We'll see if they're originals," Annette said.

Louie nodded and said, "Are you leaving now?"

"I could use a couple of minutes of meaningful conversation after what I've had to put up with over the past hour," she said, looking at me.

"You don't have to tell me," Louie said, and we headed back up to the office.

Louie noticed the repair job on the door frame as he got to the top of the stairs. "What the hell happened here?"

I went on to give him the details over a cup of coffee, finishing up with the two images of Lyle on the stairs.

"Whoa, not a very happy looking guy," Louie said and handed the pictures to Annette. She seemed to shiver when she glanced at them and quickly slid them back across the desk to me.

"Yeah, I'll be taking it up with Tubby later today."

"What are you going to tell him?"

"I think I'm going to tell him that someone stole the paintings from me and all the information I had on Eli Cummings."

"But if this Lyle character was here and couldn't find the paintings…"

"Well, that just means some jerk beat him to it. Either that or maybe Tubby will think Lyle's holding back on him. They can search here and my place for all I care. They won't find anything."

"Good luck with that. Let me know when you talk with Tubby. It may be a good time to work from home," Louie said.

"It'll be later today."

"Gee, Tubby Gustafson, and I thought I worked in a crazy world with art forgeries," Annette said.

"Hey, once again, Annette. Thanks for all you've done so far," I said.

"You're welcome, and if you'll excuse me, I'm more than a little anxious to start in on a closer examination. I'll keep you posted. I'm maybe eighty-five percent sure they're forgeries, but very good forgeries. If I can prove one, the rest will fall into place. Just now, my thought is either Eli Cummings, the artist, had six people lined up to purchase them, or he was going to offer them first come, first serve to maybe a dozen folks."

"But wouldn't word get out that some guy purchased the painting and the other two people who purchased the same painting would tell him that his was fake?"

"They may have purchased thinking it was an original. The seller tells them, if word gets out, the painting could be confiscated and returned to the rightful owner, maybe a private party or a museum. They'd keep their mouth shut in order to keep the painting. Wouldn't be the first time that ruse worked. Okay, I'm out of here, fellas. Dev, thanks again."

"Thank you, Annette. Keep me posted," I called as she headed out the door. I watched out the window as she crossed the street and climbed into her car. "Louie, thanks for putting me in touch with her. She's a really nice lady."

"Yeah, she is. Aren't you still involved with Glad Ass?"

"I don't know. I can't get her to answer any of my phone calls. Just because I was twenty minutes late going to her house for dinner."

"I'm sure that poor woman has a lot more to complain about. That might be escape music you hear playing in the back of your head."

"Yeah, I'm starting to think that way. Hey, I should head home and check in on Taylor. See if he's up yet."

"Funny, sounds like it might be payback time for all the stuff you did to your folks."

"No, he's way nicer and a lot smarter than I ever was. I'll see you Monday. What's your schedule?"

"I'll be here all day. I don't have a court appearance until Tuesday."

"Well, enjoy your day and don't forget to lock up when you leave."

"You think it's gonna make a difference?"

"Probably not. I think I might call a guy and have a new doorframe and door installed. God forbid we'd ever have a time when there was something important in here."

"See you Monday," Louie said as I headed out the door carrying the two images of Lyle on the staircase. I closed the door behind me and got the distinct impression, if you knocked hard enough, even if it was locked the door would swing open.

Twenty-five

I drove home, let myself in the front door, and walked into the kitchen. Surprisingly, it was clean. The backdoor was locked, and Morton wasn't pawing at the door. I walked out to the front room and called, "Taylor?"

"Yeah, Dev, I'm up here."

As I climbed the stairs, Morton peeked around the corner.

"So much for barking when someone comes into the house, Morton," I said and gave him a rub behind the ears.

Morton headed back into the guest room and curled up on the floor next to the desk. Taylor was seated at the desk, working with the colored pencils Dennis had given him. He was drawing on a page from the tablet. A couple of pages sat off to the side with a half-dozen colored images arranged on the top sheet. The images looked pretty good, two different snakes, three butterflies, a flag with fireworks. One of the images looked like a portrait of Morton. At the moment, Taylor appeared to be working on an image that looked like a compass.

"Wow, you cranked these out already?"

"Yeah, I was up until about two last night. Morton woke me this morning, and I let him out."

"Did you feed him?"

"Yeah, and then we went for a long walk. He led me through the neighborhood, and we stopped at all his favorite haunts."

"Trees and fire hydrants?"

"You got it. How'd your meeting go?"

"Oh, fine," I said, not going into any detail on the break-in. "A nice woman I was put in touch with is going to help me with something I'm working on. You interested in breaking for lunch?"

"To tell you the truth, if you don't mind, I'd like to keep working. I'm kind of on a roll."

"Not a problem. Can I make a sandwich and bring it up to you?"

"Oh, man, that would be great."

"Okay. You keep working."

"Thanks, Dev," he called as I headed back downstairs.

I grilled a couple of Swiss cheese and ham sandwiches and took one up to Taylor. The compass image now had a clock with Roman numerals behind it and what looked like a black crow flying above. I set the grilled ham and cheese on top of the chest of drawers out of Morton's reach.

"Wow, that image is coming along nicely."

"Oh, thanks, you like it?"

"I like all of them. They look great. You've got some real talent."

"Thanks. I guess it runs in the family. I want to crank out a bunch of images for Dennis. You think you could give me a ride back down to Inkredible sometime on Monday?"

"Yeah, absolutely. Let me know when you're finished, and I'll give him a call and set up an appointment."

That brought a smile to his face, and he said, "Thanks, Dev. And thanks for helping me. I didn't know where I was going to go."

"It's been my pleasure, Taylor, and I mean that. When you feel up to it, you can tell me about you. You're a good guy."

"Thanks," he said and went back to drawing.

I headed back down to the kitchen and attacked my sandwich. Once I finished, I washed the pan and set the plate in the dishwasher. I grabbed my keys and headed to the front door.

"Hey, Taylor. I'm heading out to another meeting. I'll be back sometime later this afternoon."

"Okay, good luck," he called back.

I climbed in the car and headed to Tubby Gustafson's. It didn't seem to make any sense to call and ask for an appointment. He'd just tell me how stupid I was, then he'd look to the sky, shake his head and ask, 'Why do I bother?' It would be interesting to see what he said when I showed him the two images of Lyle from Bud

Friehoff's security cameras. On the drive over, I worked on formulating my story.

I pulled in front of the iron gate leading into Tubby Gustafson's lair, a brick mansion surrounded by an eight-foot high brick wall and a security camera every other foot. I turned my car off, climbed out, and walked over to the intercom mounted on the wall next to the closed gate. I pushed the button labeled 'contact,' a green light flashed on, and a moment later, a voice growled, "What is it?"

Nice way to welcome guests. I was tempted to say I was there collecting signatures for a petition. Instead, I said, "Hi, my name is Dev Haskell, and I'm here to see Tub— err, Mr. Gustafson."

"I can see who you are," was the reply, followed by a click on the intercom, and the green light switched back to red. Maybe a minute later, the voice came back on and asked, "What's this about?"

"Mister Gustafson asked me to find someone."

"You can give me the information, and I'll make sure he—"

"I would like to give Mr. Gustafson the information personally. If he's indisposed, he's more than welcome to come down to my office sometime next week. I'll be out of the office until after—"

"For God's sake, take a breath," the voice growled, and the intercom light went back to red again. A moment later, the iron gate began to open slowly. I hurried back behind the wheel of my Crown Vic, fired up the engine, and slowly drove into the compound.

I followed the circular drive toward the parking area. As usual, there were two armed individuals standing in the shade on either side of the front door. When they saw my car, one of them immediately stepped into the house. I parked next to an antique red pickup truck with collector license plates. I grabbed the two pictures of Lyle that were resting on the passenger seat and stepped out of the car.

Two more thugs stepped out of Tubby's mansion, which made four goons in front of the house. They were spread out with hands resting at their waist, theoretically hiding their weapons while at the same time indicating they were all armed. One of them stepped off the front porch and headed toward me. I recognized him and his little goatee but couldn't recall his name.

"Every time you show up, it seems to create a problem, Haskell. Now you're driving around town in a cop car. Assume the position," he said.

I turned around, spread my legs, and leaned over the trunk of my car. He patted me down, pulled out the blue sticky holster with my pistol from my waistband, and said, "It never fails. You can grab this on your way out. Let's go. You can follow me."

I followed him to the front porch. While I was searched for a second time, I scanned the group of thugs for Lyle but didn't see him. I was eventually deemed acceptable and allowed to enter Tubby's palace. One of the thugs opened the door for me and I stepped inside. I recognized the guy with glasses reading in a chair. He set his comic book down and stood.

"You're here to see Mr. Gustafson?" he asked.

"Yeah, Squiggy, how are things going?"

He pushed his bifocals up on his nose and said, "You know how it is," and whispered, "same shit different day."

"Yeah, tell me about it."

He waved me forward, and as I approached, he picked up a black and yellow wand. I'd been through this uncountable times and assumed the position, this time standing with my legs spread and my arms out at shoulder height. He ran the wand back and forth over me. Fortunately, I passed inspection.

"Follow me. He's working in his office," he said, turned, and headed across the black and white marble floor toward the hallway. Fortunately, we passed by the small door beneath the staircase where I had to go during the COVID-19 pandemic and headed down the hall.

Tubby's office was the third door on the left at the end of the hall. Squiggy knocked on the door, and Tubby suddenly growled, "Get in here."

"Haskell to see you, sir," Squiggy said as he opened the door and stepped inside.

"Get over here and sit down, Haskell," Tubby said. He was seated at his desk wearing a white shirt with a striped tie. For the first time in a long time, there weren't any women standing over him, taking his blood pressure, or giving him a massage.

He laid his pen down and watched me approach. Once I sat down in the black leather chair, he exhaled loudly and shook his head. "I presume you're here with some form of disappointing news. What a shame, I was beginning to enjoy the day."

I reached into my back pocket and pulled out the two images of Lyle. I unfolded the paper and placed them on Tubby's desk. He picked up a pencil, turned it upside down, and using the eraser, dragged the top paper toward him.

He looked at the image for a moment then, still using the pencil, slid it off to the side and examined the second sheet. When he was finished, he looked up at me and said, "So?"

"So, he stole all the information I had accumulated on Eli Cummings. The files, the photos, paintings, the list of addresses where he might be staying, it's all gone. Stolen," I lied. "It would appear your friend Lyle took all of it."

"But he said he didn't find… Umm, find the time to meet with you, Haskell. He was working on another problem."

"Well, sir, you can see the time and date marked on the images. He kicked in the door to my office and took everything. So, I'm back to square one. If you'd care to share any information you might have I—"

"I told you before, Haskell. I don't have any information. That was your job, and once again, you've managed to fail."

"Okay. If that's what happened, I'll start over, but the trail is just that much colder."

"Any other day brighteners?" Tubby growled.

"Just trying to be upfront with you, sir, and give you current information."

"Right now, the best thing you could do for me would be to get the hell out of my sight, Haskell."

I nodded, stood, and for the first time, noticed the newly framed painting hanging on the wall above the fireplace. "Say, is that William Bellows *'Planting Time?'*" I asked, looking at the same painting as the three copies we'd placed in Annette's car. Once again I wondered about Tubby's connection to Eli Cummings.

Tubby's face grew red, and he jumped to his feet. "Get out of my damn office, you Moron!" he screamed. It was suddenly apparent, that along with the starched white shirt and striped tie, he was wearing red boxer shorts and no trousers. There didn't seem to be anything positive to be gained by making a comment, and I hurried toward the door.

As I opened the door, I turned and said, "Thank you for your time, Mr. Gustafson," just as a blonde woman climbed out from beneath his desk.

Squiggy was hurrying down the hallway as I closed the door behind me. "Everything okay?" he asked.

"Yeah, fine. We had a short conversation. I have the feeling I was interrupting something," I said and made tracks for the front door just as Squiggy's cellphone played a reveille bugle call. He stopped and pulled the phone out of his pocket as I hurried toward the front door. I let myself out of the mansion and headed toward my car.

"Hey, Haskell, you dumb shit. Forget something," the guy with the little goatee called. He was holding my blue sticky holster.

"Oh yeah, thanks. I was just about to look for you."

"Yeah, sure you were."

"There you are, you worthless piece—"

I turned and stared at Lyle, storming toward me. All four fingers on his right hand were encased in shiny metal finger splints with blue sponge between the splint and his fingers, reminding me of the rat trap from my file drawer. I started to back up and thought about running, but Squiggy suddenly poked his head out of the front door and shouted, "Hey, Lyle, the boss wants to see you. Now."

"Be there in a minute. I just need to deal with—"

"He said now, dude, and he didn't sound happy."

Lyle stopped and snarled something I couldn't understand.

Fat Freddy suddenly shoved Squiggy out of the way and said, "Lyle, get the hell in here."

At the sound of Fat Freddy's voice, everyone seemed to focus somewhere else and quickly made a path for Lyle to head into the mansion.

"Just what in the hell do you think you're—" Fat Freddy started to say, but whatever followed was cut off once Lyle stepped inside and Freddy slammed the door closed.

"Oh, sounds like the shit is about to hit the fan," the guy with the goatee said and handed me my sticky holster. "Might be a good idea to get the hell out of here."

I didn't need any additional encouragement.

Twenty-six

On the way home, I must have checked the rear-view mirror at least a dozen times to see if I was being followed. I drove around my block twice just to be sure before I pulled into the driveway.

I hurried into the house, looked out the front window for a minute or two just to be sure, and then called upstairs, "Taylor?"

"Yeah, Dev, we're up here."

I climbed the stairs and popped my head in the guest room. Taylor was still working away at the desk. It looked like there were at least a half-dozen sheets of paper filled with color sketches of tattoos. Morton was curled up on the floor next to the desk. He opened his eyes then stood, stretched, and walked over to me. I gave him a long scratch behind the ears and said, "Have you been working all this time?"

"Yeah, pretty much. I took a couple of breaks, and we went for a walk."

"Great. Hey, sorry I interrupted. Anything I can get you, a root beer or something?"

"No, I'm fine. I'm going to knock off once I finish this one. Probably another forty-five minutes, and I'll be done."

"You hungry for anything special for dinner?"

"Whatever you have is fine with me."

"Careful what you wish for. Okay, I'll leave you to it. Morton, you want to come with me?"

Morton walked back over to the desk, slowly turned around, and curled up on the floor again.

I went downstairs, looked out the window once more to make sure Fat Freddy, or worse, Lyle, wasn't out front, then headed into the kitchen. I turned on my laptop and Googled the *'Planting Time'* painting. The image that came up looked exactly like the painting that had been hanging on Tubby's wall and the three in Annette's car.

I phoned Annette. I was just getting ready to leave a message when she answered, "Dinicci."

"Hi Annette, Dev Haskell."

"Hi, Dev."

"You find out anything on those paintings?"

"Yes and no. I'm still working my way through them. I have two left to look at. The four I have examined are all forgeries but very good forgeries. One of them appears to have been painted over a previous canvas. Thus far, all the canvases and frames have been altered to appear old."

"Interesting. I wonder what he intended to do with them."

"My guess is he planned to sell them to interested parties and then warn them that if they made the acquisition public, there was a chance law enforcement would be involved and return the painting to a rightful owner."

"Would that actually work?"

"Oh, you'd be surprised. The price people pay for a forgery is a lot of money, but far less than the actual value of the original. Which makes the price of a forgery so appealing, everyone thinks they're getting a deal. There are a lot of people who think they deserve a classic painting. Thinking it's an original, they'll store the forgery in a vault where it won't see the light of day for years, decades even."

"Maybe not so amazing based on my afternoon."

"Oh?"

I went on to tell her about my meeting with Tubby Gustafson and the *'Planting Time'* painting hanging in his office. "Your mention of storing the painting in a vault, maybe explains Tubby's reaction to my comment. I mentioned William Bellows and *'Planting Time'*, and he went crazy."

"Based on the way Mr. Gustafson responded, Dev, it would suggest to me that the painting is a forgery he paid a lot of money for, always intending to keep quiet about his acquisition. But you recognizing the work just blew that out of the water."

"I wonder if he actually knows it's a forgery. And then the next question would be, was he somehow involved in the sale of other forgeries?" I asked.

"Could be," Annette said. "But then why get so upset when you identified the painting? Why not just say it's a copy and laugh it off? That would seem to put everything to rest."

"If he paid a high price for it and found out later it was forged, that may be why he wants me to find Cummings."

"An awful lot of craziness," Annette said. "Say, I'm going to finish up here later this afternoon. Could I talk you into joining me for dinner tonight? Nothing fancy, I've got a stew going in the crockpot."

"Oh, that sounds great. I could bring— Oh, wait. I better take a pass. I've actually got a guest." I told her about Taylor then said, "Tell you what, why don't you join us tonight? Bring the crockpot over. I'll do up some potatoes and a dessert. I'll walk up the street and grab a bottle of wine. Besides, Taylor's been working on some artwork, and I'd love to have you take a look and give him some encouragement. He's really been working hard."

"You know, Dev, that sounds great. You name the time."

"How does 5:30 sound? We can have a glass of wine before dinner. I'd love for you to meet Taylor."

"Thanks, Dev, looking forward to it. I'll see you then."

I called upstairs to Taylor and told him I would be back in fifteen minutes. I walked up the street to Solo Vino. I decided two bottles of a Pinot might be a better idea than just one. I stopped at the bakery in the next block, bought a dessert, and then hurried back home. I set everything on the kitchen counter and headed upstairs.

"Hey Taylor, I've got a friend coming over for dinner. Actually, she's bringing dinner, a stew. She's an arty type, and if you want, you could show her your work."

"Yeah, sure. I should be finished up here in just a bit. I'm starting to run out of steam."

"Well, you've got a couple of hours before she arrives. Grab a nap if you feel like it."

"I just might do that," he said.

I went back downstairs and did some light cleaning. I grabbed a half-dozen items I'd piled on the dining room table and stuffed them in a closet. I was getting things ready in the kitchen when my phone rang. "Dev Haskell," I answered without looking at the caller ID.

"So, you decided not to call?" Gladys said.

"Gladys, hi, are you okay? It's been days since—"

"Your phone works both ways, Dev. You can make calls as well as receive them."

"Didn't you get any of my messages? I called you a number of times, and I sent you text messages."

She ignored my question and said, "I'm going to order a dinner, and if you're not busy you're welcome to come over."

"Oh, thanks, I wish I could, but actually, I'm having someone over, two people as a matter of fact."

"Oh, well, pardon me if I'm interrupting your social calendar."

"No, it's not that. It's just that I've already invited the woman, and she's bringing dinner, a stew. She's helping me on a forgery case," I quickly added.

"Yeah, sure she is. Well, I'm sure you'll enjoy your-self."

I thought for half a moment about inviting Gladys and immediately decided that would be a recipe for disaster. Taylor didn't need to be put in that situation, nor did Annette. "Hello, Gladys, are you still there?"

"I just wanted to be sure you heard this," she said and then hung up.

If I'd had any doubts about not inviting her, she'd just erased them. I guess I was supposed to call her back immediately and beg forgiveness. Instead, I decided to set the dining room table.

Taylor stepped into the kitchen around 5:00. He was dressed in one of his new shirts and a new pair of jeans. Morton was right behind him. Taylor let him out in the backyard and set about making a peanut butter sandwich.

"My friend Annette is going to be here in about thirty minutes with dinner."

"Yeah, I know. I just needed something to tide me over until then," he said and proceeded to stuff half the sandwich into his mouth.

Actually, that seemed to make sense, and I grabbed a spoon and scooped up a spoonful of peanut butter for me. "You know, it might be a good idea to take the tag off the back of those jeans," I said.

He reached behind him and pulled the tag off the back pocket. It said, 'Slim Fit 29W 30L'. "Mmm, thanks for pointing it out. Been a while since I had a new pair of jeans," he laughed.

I gave him a little smile and took another spoonful of peanut butter.

Twenty-seven

I had begun boiling the potatoes, and I had the red peppers going on low heat. Annette knocked on the door promptly at 5:30. She was carrying the crock-pot in a round, green carrying case. "Dinner has arrived," she said as I opened the front door.

"Oh, here, let me take that from you."

"Relax, I got it. You just lead the way back to the kitchen."

I did just that and pointed to a spot on the kitchen counter. "Set it down there, and you can plug it into that outlet. Can I talk you into a glass of wine?"

"You just did. Yeah, I'd love one."

"Hi, I'm Annette," she said, holding her hand out to Taylor.

"Taylor, pleased to meet you," he said taking her hand.

"Dev told me you're staying here for a while."

"As long as he wants," I said, twisting the cap off the wine bottle and filling Annette's glass.

She unzipped the top of the case and pulled the crockpot out. The wonderful aroma of stew began to fill the room.

"Oh, that smells delicious," I said.

Taylor's stomach growled, and we all laughed.

Morton was suddenly scratching at the back door. "I guess he must have smelled the stew," Taylor said and let Morton into the kitchen.

"High praise," Annette said as I handed her the glass of wine. "Thanks, Dev. Now, Taylor, Dev mentioned you're working on an art project, but he didn't give me any details. Tell me about it."

Taylor went on to describe our meeting with Dennis. He didn't mention Ramona Williams or the other girls who were waiting to interview Dennis when we left.

"And you've already created some of these images?"

"Yeah, I pretty much worked non-stop on them over the last day and a half, ever since we got home from Inkredible."

"Would you be willing to show them to me?"

Taylor nodded vigorously and said, "I'll run upstairs and get them."

"Oh, he seems like a really nice kid," Annette said, as Taylor literally ran up the stairs.

"Yeah, I don't know much about him, other than he appears to have been living rough. Wait until you see his sketches. They're pretty good."

"You're a really decent guy for helping him, Dev," she said and placed her hand on top of mine for just a moment. We heard Taylor hurrying back down the stairs. Annette reached for her wineglass and took a sip.

Taylor stepped back into the kitchen, carefully carrying the various sheets with the images.

"Set those over there, away from the wine glasses," Annette said, pointing to a distant section of the kitchen counter.

Taylor spread out the sheets, one next to the other for a total of eight. Each sheet had six images.

"Oh my," Annette said and moved alongside Taylor. "You did all these since last night?"

"Yeah, and then today. You're looking at a lot of hours."

"Where did you learn to draw like this? Did you take lessons?"

"I never had a TV or a computer, so I had time to practice a lot. A guy I knew gave me some lessons."

"These are exceptional, Taylor. How old are you?"

"I turned seventeen last spring."

"I'm very impressed. Tell me about them."

Taylor gave a brief description of each image. Occasionally, he mentioned some idea that he'd had that didn't work as well as he thought, and he had to redo the image. "So once I had a sketch I was happy with, I would add it to one of these sheets. There might be a half-dozen or more workups before I felt comfortable enough to add it on here. Dennis was pretty adamant that this paper stock was only for the final version."

Annette nodded and said, "I'm very impressed. I mean that. Have you thought about a price?"

"A price?"

"A price per image, anywhere from fifteen to maybe a hundred dollars. That's the market."

"I was just going to give them to Dennis. He said he'd pay me, but I think he was just being nice."

"Don't sell yourself short. Maybe discuss it with him. I'm sure he would be expecting to pay for these. They're very good. I would like to make one suggestion."

"Yeah, sure."

"If I were you, I would think about adding some lower back tattoos. Lacy designs, butterflies, hearts, eyes, use your imagination, just like you did on these. You're familiar with lower back designs?"

"Not really."

"Mmm, popular with us ladies. Okay, here," she said, turning her back to him and untucking her blouse. "Now don't let Dev see this," she said, bending over. "I drew the design years ago and had it done. As far as I know, I'm the only one with my blue hummingbird design. That might be another angle you'd want to consider. You could offer unique, one of a kind designs," she said, turning back to face me and tucking the back of her blouse in as she talked. "Hey, we can talk more about this over dinner, but I had better dish up that stew."

We chatted over dinner. Taylor had two helpings of stew, which made Annette happy. "Oh, he is such a wonderful kid," she said when he'd gone into the kitchen to dish up his second helping of stew. "Kid is probably the wrong term. He's a very nice young man."

"Yeah, I'm afraid he's had to grow up a lot faster than most."

"There's no family around?"

"We haven't had that conversation yet. I didn't want to pressure him. I want him to feel safe and comfortable here, and then we can talk."

"But what if there's family out there looking for him right now?"

"If they're looking for him, he hasn't made any effort to connect with them. I'm pretty sure there's something in the background. I just don't know what, yet."

"Maybe there is but maybe not. I won't push you, Dev, but you should have that conversation sooner rather than later."

Taylor came back into the dining room, all smiles, carrying another plate full of stew, roast potatoes, and red peppers.

"Remember to save some room for dessert, Taylor."

"Not to worry, I won't let any dessert go to waste."

I cleared the table while Annette and Taylor continued to discuss the art world. I dished up three slices of cheesecake and brought them into the dining room. I think I was on my second bite when Taylor set his fork down on the empty dessert plate.

"All finished?" I asked.

"Yeah, would you mind if I excused myself? I'd like to go upstairs and begin working on those lower back designs Annette mentioned."

"Go ahead, get back to work," I said and chuckled.

"It was really nice to meet you, Annette. Thanks for the encouragement and the ideas."

"You be sure to let me know how it all works out," she said.

Taylor nodded and hurried upstairs.

I refilled our wine glasses, and we sat and talked. Actually, Annette did most of the talking, interrogating me about Taylor, wanting to know his background. "Dev, you don't even know his last name? You at least have to find out the basics, if for no other reason than there might be family out there looking for him. Make the effort. Those aren't just good sketches. They're incredible. I'll be honest. They're some of the very best I've ever seen. You need to find out."

"Yeah, I know, Annette, but I don't want to pressure him. He's only been here a couple of nights. I want him to feel comfortable before I start giving him the third degree."

"What about school?"

"He's going to school. In fact, that's where we first met. He was hiding in the school so he'd have a safe place to sleep. Which, by the way, was on the floor in a cloakroom. I think the only time he had food was probably lunch at school. He didn't have any real friends. He told me the boys gave him a hard time, and none of the girls would talk to him. We went out the other day, got him some decent jeans, a couple of shirts, and a haircut. Now all of a sudden, some guy said hi to him, and a couple of girls looked like they might be interested. Things are starting to go well for him, and I don't want to risk screwing that up."

"Okay, I get that, and it's important. Now, can I give you an update on the paintings?"

"Yeah, please."

"I would label them all as forgeries. That said, they're all very good. The question still is, were they practice works? Was someone preparing for a final forged masterpiece, if you will, or do they represent multiple markets? I honestly have no idea. I wish you had a line on Eli Cummings."

"Yeah, me too."

"Any word from Mr. Gustafson regarding his *'Planting Time'*?"

"Not a word, which is probably a good thing. The less I hear from that guy, the better."

She smiled at that and said, "Believe me, I understand. Now, I don't want you to take this personally, but I'm going to go home."

"You know you don't have to do that."

She smiled and said, "Thank you. I know that, and I'd love to stay the night. But I think, under the circumstances, it might be better for all involved if I'm home tonight." She raised her eyes up toward the second floor.

"Let me know how things go for Taylor with the tattoo designs."

"I'll be sure to do that," I said. We kissed at the dining room table. At her direction, I put the remainder of the stew in a large plastic container and set it in the refrigerator. I washed and dried her crockpot, placed it in the carrying case, and walked her to the door.

"Thanks for a wonderful night, Dev. We'll talk tomorrow. Do you want me to return those paintings to you?"

"The Eli Cummings forgeries? Is it a problem if you hang onto them?"

"No, not at all."

"Good, if you wouldn't mind holding them for a bit longer, at least until I get our office secured. I want them to stay somewhere safe."

"Not a problem."

"Thank you for a delicious dinner," I said.

"Mmm-mmm, you're very welcome. Now, I'm taking a rain check on spending the night."

"I'm counting on it," I said and walked her out to her car. I got another quick kiss, this time on the cheek. I stood on the sidewalk and watched until her taillights disappeared. I went back inside, cleared the dining room table, and cleaned up the kitchen. I settled in front of the TV, watched a couple of episodes of a mystery series, and went upstairs.

Taylor was at the desk busily sketching out more designs. Morton was curled up on the floor, comfortable and sound asleep. I said good night and went to bed.

Twenty-eight

It was Sunday morning, and I could sleep in late, so naturally, I was wide awake just a little after six. I showered, shaved, threw on some jeans, and headed downstairs. I poured myself a cup of coffee, turned on my laptop, and noticed my cellphone on the kitchen counter. Apparently, I'd set it there when Annette arrived last night. I turned it on to see if I should charge it and noticed I had two voice messages.

"First message, left at four thirty-one AM," the recording said and delivered my message. "Yeah, Dev, surprise, surprise, it's Gladys. Against my better judgement, I decided to stop over last night. I thought we needed to talk. Boy, was I wrong. I watched the show as you kissed, groped, and grabbed that woman out on the street. I drove home and decided this just isn't working out. So I packed everything of yours I could find, put it in a box, and left it in front of your car in the driveway." Click.

I replayed the message just to make sure I heard it correctly. Then walked out onto the front porch as I listened to the message again. A cardboard box rested in front of my car. A paint roller hung over the edge of the box. I could see what looked like my St. Paul Saint's sweatshirt and baseball cap lying on top of whatever else was in the box. I walked down the front steps, across the lawn, and picked up the box.

I pressed '7' on my phone to delete the message and listen to the second one. "Next message, left at four thirty-three AM."

"Yeah, Dev, hey, sorry, I forgot to tell you, screw you!" Gladys screamed those last two words and disconnected. I carried the box inside, set it on the floor next to the front door, and headed back to the kitchen. It was too early to phone her, so I fooled around on my computer, trying to decide what I was going to say when I called her.

Morton came downstairs maybe an hour later, and I let him out. I got his food and water dish ready and let him back in. I fooled around on the computer for another hour and a half and phoned Gladys just before ten.

"Hello," was how she answered the phone. In all the times I'd called her, I'd never heard her answer the phone like that.

"Hi, Gladys, got your message this morning, actually, both messages. I'm wondering if I could stop over for a minute tonight."

Long pause. "What time were you thinking?"

"Whatever time works for you, maybe around four this afternoon if you're not busy."

"That will work. I'll see you then." Click

I heard Taylor turn on the shower just before noon. I waited until he was out of the shower then fried up some bacon, scrambled some eggs, and made some toast.

"Mmm, whatever you're cooking smells really good," he called, coming down the stairs a few minutes later. I set the plate on the kitchen counter and poured him an orange juice. Morton wandered over to Taylor and got his head scratched.

"Dig in, Taylor. Were you up working late last night?"

"Yeah, really late, but I think I got some nice designs laid out. You want to see them after breakfast?"

"Yeah, I'd love to."

"I really like that Annette lady. She's very nice. How long have you known her?"

"Just a little more than a week. Louie, my office mate, introduced us. She works for an insurance company in the fraud division. She's looking at some paintings I acquired, checking their authenticity."

"Authenticity?" he said and shoveled in another forkful of eggs.

"Yeah, they're forgeries of a landscape and a portrait, and we suspect they were going to be sold as originals. They could go for a hundred grand each. In my business, I occasionally have to deal with an unsavory individual, and one of them got me involved in this painting situation."

"He wants you to sell the forgeries?"

"No, he wants me to find the artist who painted them. They're very good, by the way."

"What's going to happen once you find the artist?" Taylor asked and pushed the half-finished breakfast plate away.

"Well, first of all, I don't know if I'll even be able to find him. So far, I've come up empty-handed. If I do find him, I think what I'll probably do is tell him my client is looking for him, and he'd better leave town. My client is not a very nice person."

"You're not going to call the police?"

"I suppose I could do that, but as far as I know, no crime has actually been committed yet, so they really couldn't make an arrest. If they did arrest him, I don't think the guy would be safe in jail. My sometimes client is a guy named Tubby Gustafson. He's not a nice person. He's a criminal, and with his connections, even if the guy was locked up in jail, he wouldn't be safe. I'm afraid it's a pretty sad commentary on our society. You're finished with that breakfast? You still have half of it left."

"I'm not really that hungry."

"Taylor, you were starving five minutes ago. What's wrong?"

"Nothing. I guess I was just thinking about working, doing more drawings."

"Oh, yeah, let me see what you worked on last night. Give me just a minute to clean up the kitchen."

"Yeah, okay. Thanks again for all you've done for me, Dev. I really appreciate it."

"Thank you, Taylor. You know you've done a lot for me, too. You reminded me about what's important."

"Well, thanks again," Taylor said and headed upstairs. I cleaned up the breakfast dishes. I ate the bacon Taylor left on his plate and gave the scrambled eggs to Morton. I was about to go upstairs when my phone rang, Barbara Wright.

"Hi, Barbara," was how I answered.

"Oh, well, at least now I know you're alive."

"I was going to give you a call later today. Yesterday was kind of crazy." I went on to tell her about the office break-in and then having Annette over as a dinner guest. As long as she provided dinner.

"That's a scam if I ever heard of one. How is Taylor doing?"

"Incredible, the guy really has a talent for art." I went on to tell her about all the work he'd put into the images for Dennis and how impressed Annette was with his talent. "Seriously, she was really impressed, and she knows what she's talking about. She works with museums, auction houses, and collectors all around the country." We talked for another twenty minutes, and I promised to call her with an update tomorrow. No sooner had I disconnected than the phone rang again, Annette.

"Hi, Annette."

"Hi, Dev, I just wanted to thank you for a really wonderful evening. I've been thinking about Taylor all morning."

"Oh? Is that good or bad?"

"It's good, very good. There's a school for really gifted kids over in Minneapolis. It's for eleventh and twelfth-grade students, a boarding school called the Art Academy. The emphasis is on art, but they study all subjects, graduate from an accredited high school, and it's a doorway into some of the most prestigious art schools in the nation."

"Interesting. Of course, my first question would be, what does it cost?"

"It's twenty thousand per year, but I happen to know they have a very well-endowed scholarship program that could cover the cost."

"Define 'could.'"

She went on to explain in detail the requirements, not the least of which were letters of recommendation.

"That sounds wonderful, unfortunately, a recommendation from me and even one from Dennis Richards would probably do more harm than good."

"You're probably right, however, not to brag, but one from me would carry quite a bit of weight, and I could line up one or two more with a couple of phone calls. We could set up a meeting, introduce Taylor to these people, show them his work…"

"By his work, you mean the tattoos?"

"Dev, trust me, for someone to crank out all those images in that amount of time, it's beyond impressive. The whole purpose of this school is to get young, talented individuals focused on the future. I think it would be perfect for Taylor."

"You know, as you're telling me all this, it sounds like it could be just the thing for him, not to mention a roof over his head and a path forward."

"Exactly what I'm thinking."

"Let me put him on the line and—"

"No, Dev. I'd like to present this to him in person, over here at my place."

"Okay, I'll call you back. Is there a time you'd want us over there?"

"Whatever works for you and Taylor. I'm here all day. Just let me know when you can make it. Let me give you my address," she said, and I wrote it down on a note pad.

"Okay, I'll get back to you in a bit," I said and disconnected.

Twenty-nine

I hurried out of the kitchen, calling, "Taylor. Hey Taylor." I kept calling as I ran up the stairs. I opened the door to the guest room, and Morton jumped off the bed. I didn't see Taylor, not that there was anywhere he could hide. Then I noticed that the desk was cleaned off, and all the tattoo sketches were gone. The jeans and shirts, all the clothes we got yesterday morning, were gone. "Taylor," I called, stepping out of the room. I checked my bedroom, the spare room, and the bathroom. I picked up speed with every empty room. I hurried back downstairs, checked the den and the front room. I yelled down the basement stairs and looked out in the backyard. He was gone.

I pulled my phone out, called and ended up leaving a message. "Taylor, it's Dev. Call me. Please." I grabbed my car keys and hurried out to my car. I backed out of the driveway to the sound of a major horn blast. A guy swerved into the oncoming lane to avoid smashing into me, gave me the finger, and shouted some expletive I couldn't hear.

I pulled to the curb and thought for a moment. It couldn't have been more than thirty minutes since he'd headed upstairs. He was on foot. Where could he be? And why did he leave?

The why part could wait. Right now, I needed to find him. I drove up the street and back down. I criss-crossed all the neighborhood streets. I drove over to the school. I walked around the building, tugging on each door, but they were all locked.

I drove down to Inkredible and talked to Dennis. I told him about all the work Taylor had done, and he promised to call me if Taylor showed up. I drove through downtown, peeked inside a bunch of coffee shops, and still came up empty-handed.

I phoned Annette and explained the situation.

"Why would he do this?" she asked.

"If I knew that, I'd probably know where he went. I don't know. I don't get it. Now I'm just really worried about him."

"What did you say that made him run away?"

"What? I didn't say anything."

"Did you mention the Art Academy?"

"No, I never had a chance. In fact, that was what I was going to tell him about, but he was gone." I started to choke up, my voice rose, and tears were welling up in my eyes.

"Dev, Dev, listen to me. I want you to come over here."

I cleared my throat and got back to a semblance of normal. "But I've got to find him. Night is coming on, it's going to be dark soon, and I don't want him out on the street."

"That's why you need to come over here. Two heads are better than one. We'll find him." She gave me her address again. I made another spin through downtown, drove past the Salvation Army and Catholic Charities shelters, and then headed out towards Annette's.

She lived just out of town off Highway 10 on a cul de sac called Sunflower circle. Her two-story home had a stone front, an attached three-car garage, and what appeared to be a work building in the back of the lot— apparently checking art forgeries paid pretty well. I pulled into her driveway and climbed out of my car. She opened her front door before I was even halfway up the sidewalk. "How are you doing, Dev? Come on in. Look, we're going to find him. Now, have you called the police?"

I shook my head. "They can't do anything until it's been more than twenty-four hours. Taylor's only been gone since just a little after the noon hour. I had two phone calls. Yours and another woman, Barbara Wright. She runs the group at the high school giving homework help to kids. I got off the phone with you, ran upstairs to tell him the news about the Art Academy, and he was gone."

"And you don't know why?"

I shook my head. "No, he was eating breakfast, said he wanted to do some more design work, and went upstairs. That's the last I saw of him."

I followed Annette into her kitchen. She filled a mug with coffee and handed it to me. "Here, I just put the pot on. You'll need it. We may be at this for a while."

"Thanks," I said, and drank some coffee.

"Now, back up for a minute. You said he was eating breakfast and wanted to work some more." "Yeah, he slept in until almost noon. Said he'd been working late. You remember how excited he was about doing those new designs."

"The lower back designs."

"Yeah. So he was up late working on those. Comes down for breakfast about noon and then doesn't finish his breakfast and heads back upstairs. I get two phone calls, you and Barbara, and the next thing I know, he's gone. I didn't even hear him leave."

"He didn't finish breakfast?"

"No, all of a sudden, he pushed the plate away and went upstairs to work."

"What'd you serve him?"

"Annette, what does it matter? He's gone."

"Dev, this is the kid who had two helpings of stew, inhaled that slice of cheesecake in about sixty seconds. He was eating like someone who's been hungry, seriously hungry, often. He isn't going to take a pass on food because he's still subconsciously thinking he doesn't know where the next meal is coming from. Now, all of a sudden, he pushes his plate away?"

"Yeah, scrambled eggs, toast, and bacon, about six slices of bacon. In fact, when he was coming down for breakfast, he said, 'Whatever it is it smells really good,' then all of a sudden, he isn't hungry."

"Did you guys argue or anything?"

"No, nothing like that. In fact, he said he really liked you. Wondered how long I knew you, that sort of thing."

"What did you tell him?"

"What'd I tell him? I said we met maybe a week ago. That you were helping me in a forgery case…"

"What is it, Dev?"

"I told him you were helping me in a forgery case. That Tubby Gustafson wanted me to find the guy who did the paintings. Then I said if I found the guy, I would tell him to leave town so Tubby wouldn't find him. That's when he pushed his plate away and thanked me for all I'd done for him. I told him he'd done more for me, made me remember what was important. The next thing I know, he's gone."

"Don't worry. We're going to find him. You mentioned Mr. Gustafson. Did you mention Eli Cummings?"

"Cummings? No, I'm pretty sure I didn't. In fact, I know I didn't. I just said 'the painter' or 'artist' or something."

Annette shook her head. "Strange, there has to be some connection. I wonder what it is. Well, we can't worry about that now. Finding him is the top priority.

Did he have any friends at school? Maybe he's landed at one of their homes?"

I shook my head. "No, he was really a loner at school. The girls stayed away from him, and up until Friday, the boys pretty much gave him a hard time. He didn't have any friends."

"Well, he could go to the shopping malls, but they close down around nine. Does he have any money?"

"Not that I'm aware of. I don't think he could get a hotel room if that's what you're thinking. I don't think he has a driver's license, and I'm pretty sure he doesn't have any credit cards."

"Did he mention anything about a church?"

"No, never."

"Does he have a key to your house?"

"No, I meant to get him one. I just haven't done it yet."

She walked over to her computer and started typing. "I'm going to draw up two lists, one for each of us. We can check these places and see if he's there or maybe he's been there. You don't happen to have a picture of him, do you?"

"No, I don't. I wish I knew his last name. We could at least have a shot at contacting a relative or someone."

Annette hit a key on the keyboard, and the printer fired up. A moment later, the printer spit out two pieces of paper. She grabbed one and handed it to me. "Okay, so that's your list of places to check out. Don't just drive past. Go inside and ask someone, look around. I'll do the same. Let's plan on calling one another every ninety minutes or so just to check in."

"Oh, Annette, thanks so much. You don't have to do this."

"You're right. I don't. But I want to, so I'm going to help you try to find Taylor. You just keep your head on straight. This is what we're focused on. Oh, and Dev, stop beating yourself up. You haven't done anything wrong. Now let's get going. It's going to be dark in a couple more hours."

I looked over the list she'd handed me. I'd already been to three of them, but it made sense to check again with night coming on. There were a couple of places I'd never heard of. "Annette, thanks for all your help. I really mean it."

"We're going to find him, Dev. Don't worry."

"I'll feel a lot better once we do. Okay, I'm going to hit all these places."

"I'll be right behind you. I'm just going to shut things down here and lock up. Don't forget we're going to touch base with one another every ninety minutes."

"Yeah, I got it. I'll let myself out. Talk to you in ninety minutes," I said and hurried out the door to my car.

Thirty

The first four places were a bust. They were all overnight homeless shelters, first come, first serve. I described Taylor to the people monitoring the doors. No one had seen him, and I was pretty sure they were telling me the truth. Annette phoned me just as I was pulling in front of a place run by Catholic Charities.

"Yeah, Annette, any luck?"

"No, I was about to ask you the same thing."

"A big blank. I'm pretty sure the people I spoke with were being straight with me. No one has seen him."

"Same on this end. I'm thinking you may want to check your place just in case he's had a change of heart. God, if only it would be that easy."

"That's a good idea. It never occurred to me. I just pulled in front of St. Francis. I'll talk to them, then check the house just in case he's there."

"Your turn to call next time," she said and disconnected.

I climbed out of the car and walked into the St. Francis Residence. There were probably twenty or thirty chairs in the two front rooms. All the chairs were occupied by a rough-looking group of folks. Not that they were necessarily dangerous, but a lot of beards, worn clothing, unkempt hair. A couple of folks had carts in front of them, no doubt holding all their worldly possessions. Two or three people were talking to themselves. One guy was wrapped in a quilt.

Some guy was handing out paper cups of steaming coffee. As he finished and I approached him, he said, "Hi, are you one of the volunteers for tonight? Just head down the hallway and knock on the door marked office. They'll take your name and—"

"Actually, no, I'm not a volunteer. I'm here looking for someone."

"You're with the police?"

"No. I found this kid the other day, about seventeen, nice kid. His name is Taylor. His hair is close cut on the sides and curly on top. He was staying at my place here in town, and he left. I just want to make sure he's okay, and I've got a guest room for him if he wants."

He looked me over for a moment, not sure if I was telling the truth or not. Eventually, he shook his head and said, "No, I haven't seen anyone like that. He may show up later, although as you can see, we're already full for the night. Unfortunately, we'd have to turn him away."

I pulled out my business card and handed it to him. "If he does show up, all he has to do is get in touch with me, and I'll gladly come down and pick him up. I just want him to be safe."

He glanced at my card. "You're a detective?"

"I'm a private investigator."

"What's he done?"

"Done? He hasn't done anything. I'm not looking for him because he did anything. I just want to find him and make sure he's safe. Let him know he can stay at my place for as long as he wants, no strings attached."

He looked me up and down, and I got the distinct impression he didn't believe a word of what I'd just told him. "Oh, I'll be sure to tell him," he said and placed the card in his pocket.

"Thank you," I said.

"It would probably be best if you left, detective."

There was no point in arguing or trying to explain. The guy's mind was made up. I made a mental note not to hand out any more business cards. I climbed back in my car and drove home. Morton was standing on the couch, looking out the front window as I pulled up. He barked a couple of times and disappeared, no doubt waiting for me at the front door.

I unlocked the door and stepped inside. Morton jumped a couple of times until I got him calmed down. We walked back to the kitchen, and I let him out the back door. Just in case, I walked back to the staircase and called Taylor's name. The house remained eerily quiet. I heard Morton scratching at the backdoor, and I hurried into the kitchen to let him back inside.

I tossed a biscuit Morton's way. He grabbed it in midair and devoured it in three quick bites. I thought for a minute and decided it might be a good idea to have Morton along just in case I had to look for Taylor in a crowd. Who better to find Taylor than Morton? I wrote Taylor's name, my name and phone number on about a dozen pages in a pocket notebook and shoved it into my jeans.

"Come on, Morton. Let's go for a ride."

At the sound of the word ride, Morton's head snapped up, and his tail began to wag back and forth. I turned the kitchen lights on and hurried upstairs. I turned on a light in the guest room and then wrote a note to Taylor in the event he returned. *'Taylor, out looking for you. Hope you are all right. Please phone me. Dev'*

I clipped the leash onto Morton's collar, and we went out the door. I locked the door then stuck the note to Taylor between the door and the doorframe. We climbed into the car and headed out to the next place on our list, a county-run facility. There was a line of at least a hundred people waiting to be let inside. Morton and I walked to the head of the line and pulled on the door. It was locked.

"You thinking we're all stupid?" The guy at the head of the line said, "I been standing here for going on three hours. Be best if you got your privileged ass all the way to the back of this line and wait your damn turn just like the rest of us."

"I'm not looking to stay. I'm looking for a kid, wondering if maybe they've seen—"

"What's her name?"

"Not a girl, it's a boy. He's seventeen, about this tall," I said, indicating Taylor's height by holding my hand up.

"And just why do you want this boy?"

"I've got a place for him to stay. He can stay as long as he wants. I just want to make sure he's all right and safe."

"Yeah, sure, I bet that's all you want. Like I said before, end of the line. Your dog can stay here, but you gotta get your ass all the way back to the end."

Just then, someone appeared on the other side of the door and unlocked it. "I ain't fooling around, mister. Best you get your ass to the back and wait your damn turn."

The guy on the other side of the door pulled it open. "Okay, Walter, first again, come on in. Sorry, I'm afraid we can't allow any pets," he said, looking at Morgan. Walter stood behind him, gave me the finger, and mouthed something I couldn't translate.

"I'm not looking to spend the night. I'm looking for a young boy, maybe seventeen. His name is Taylor."

The guy shook his head and said, "Sorry, haven't seen him. We're just opening up for the night now. You might want to check the line. We only have room for sixty people, and there's at least twice as many waiting to get in tonight. Come on in, Maddie, good to see you. Vivian, good evening. Oh, sir, I'm sorry it looks like you've been drinking. We don't allow that here," he said and gently pulled the man out of the line and off to the side.

"Wish I could help you," the guy said and signaled more people in the door. I pulled out the pocket notebook, tore out a sheet, and handed it to him.

"Dev Haskell, I think I've heard of you," he said and waved four more people in.

"Don't believe what you hear. I'm really a pretty nice guy."

He smiled at that. "If I see him, I'll give you a call. Good luck," he said and continued to wave people in. Morton and I walked down the line of folks waiting to get inside. No one caught Morton's attention. At the end of the line, the guy who'd been denied access sat on a stone wall finishing what was left in a half-pint bottle.

I climbed back in my car and called Annette.

"Any luck," was how she answered.

"No, thus far I've talked to a guy who I'm sure tossed my card as soon as I left thinking I was a cop. Another guy waiting in a line told me to move to the back of the line and gave me the finger. It's been a big fat zero on my end. How about you?"

"Pretty much the same result, although everyone I've been talking to could not have been nicer. Unfortunately, no one has seen Taylor."

"Well, I'm going to keep at it. Annette, feel free to knock off whenever you want. You've done way more than anyone could have expected, and I really do appreciate the effort. God, for all I know, maybe he did have cash or a credit card, and right now, he's on a flight down to Florida or out to California."

"I doubt that, Dev. We're probably within five minutes of him. The question is where?"

"Yeah, well, nothing for me to do but keep looking. Go ahead and feel free to take off whenever you want."

"I'm going to check a couple more places, and I'll give you a call when I'm finished," Annette. She phoned me about forty minutes later and said she was heading home. I couldn't blame her, and I thanked her profusely. We promised to touch base in the morning and disconnected.

Thirty-one

In case I had any doubts, and I didn't, the downtown changed drastically once darkness set in. You'd want to keep an eye on just about everyone out on the street. The other thing I found interesting, and at the same time disappointing, was the number of young girls. They definitely weren't women, and a number of them were pushing a baby stroller with a child after 11:00 at night. My immediate thought was neither the girls nor the babies had a snowball's chance in hell.

My phone rang just before midnight. I was on my third cup of coffee from a twenty-four-hour joint. Since I figured it would be Annette, I didn't bother to check who was calling.

"Hi Annette, you decide to come back out?"

"Oh, how absolutely charming," Gladys said. "Well, at least now I can put a name to the slut you were groping last night or is this someone completely new?"

"No, wait, Gladys, you got it wrong. I'm out driving. I'm working a case actually, looking for someone."

"Yeah, sure you are, Dev. You were going to come over this afternoon at four. I understand you may be busy, although God only knows what you're doing at four in the afternoon on a Sunday, but you've pretty much answered all my questions. You go ahead and keep doing whatever in the hell you're doing. I'm sure it's important."

"Hold on, Gladys. See, I've been helping this kid who—"

"Oh, a child from a previous relationship? Well, no real surprise there. But then why even bother to mention it to me? You stood me up this afternoon, and now you decide to drop that bomb on me. We are so done, Dev Haskell. Do not ever call me again. Ever!" She shouted and disconnected.

Nothing like dealing with someone who's understanding. I kept driving around, looking at people. Occasionally, I slowed down, thinking I might have spotted Taylor, but that never turned out to be the case. Through it all, I kept replaying Gladys' most recent phone call. To be honest, it didn't really bother me, and in no time, I began to feel as if a weight had been lifted from my shoulders. Based on her order to never call her again, all that did was provide me with more time to search for Taylor tomorrow.

It was close to three in the morning when I pulled into the driveway. Morton was asleep in the back seat, and I gently woke him. I had an outside hope that Taylor might be waiting for us inside but no such luck. The note I'd placed between the door and the doorframe remained untouched. I shoved the note in my pocket and unlocked the door.

Morton wandered in and slowly made his way upstairs. I walked into the kitchen, got the coffee ready for morning, and headed up to my bedroom. Morton was in the guest room, staring at the empty bed. He gave a little whine and looked over at me.

"Yeah, I know what you're thinking Morton. I'm missing him too. Lets go to bed." Despite all the coffee I'd been drinking, I think I was asleep as soon as my head hit the pillow. I must not have moved for the rest of the night because I woke in exactly the same position just minutes before my alarm was set to go off.

I checked my phone just in case someone had called with a Taylor sighting. No such luck. I showered, shaved, pulled on my jeans and a clean shirt, and headed downstairs. I couldn't google Taylor because I only had his first name, but I tried anyway. I sent Louie a text message giving him a quick update on Taylor and told him I would be out all day searching for the kid. I sent Annette a text and told her I didn't have any luck but to call me anyway. I sent Barbara a text message and asked her to call me.

Morton drifted downstairs a little later. I gave him an exceptionally long head scratch since we both seemed to be in the same frame of mind, missing Taylor. I let him out into the backyard and got his food and water ready.

My phone rang a couple of minutes later. Based on my call from Gladys last night, I checked to see who it was. Unfortunately, it was Tubby Gustafson.

"Good morning, Mr. Gustafson."

"Save the happy act for someone who cares, Haskell. What do you have?"

"What do I have? A headache. I was out until three this morning searching and didn't come up with any- thing. I've looked all over town, but he seems to have simply disappeared. I don't know where else to look, but I'm determined to find him. I can't believe he left town. It's not like he's got any transportation."

"Transportation? You Moron, I told you he stole Lyle's car."

"Lyle's car? I don't think he even knows how to drive, let alone have a license. How did he steal Lyle's car?"

"When he attacked him with that bowl of hot grease or whatever it was, that's when he grabbed his car keys and stole the car."

"How in the hell did Taylor attack Lyle? When? Where? Why?"

"Haskell, what in the hell are you talking about?"

It suddenly dawned on me I was on the wrong page. I'd been so focused on Taylor that I'd completely forgot- ten about Tubby Gustafson and Eli Cummings.

"Haskell, get your worthless ass over here now. I want to see you within the next thirty minutes. Do you understand me?"

"I do, sir, but I'm afraid I'm involved in something else at the moment. As soon as I get this matter cleaned up, I'd be happy to—"

"Listen to me, you worthless piece of— Let me put it this way, Haskell. Either you get over here now, or I'll put a price on your head that will cause you to spend the rest of what few days remain in some wretched hole in the ground."

"But sir, if I could— Hello? Hello, Mr. Gustafson?"

Tubby hung up. I let Morton in and encouraged him to finish breakfast quickly. Ten minutes later, we were driving down to my office. I opened the bottom drawer on my desk and grabbed the sticky holster with my pistol from the cigar box. I stuck the holster in my belt, left a quick note for Louie, and we hurried out the door.

I pulled into Annette's driveway twenty minutes later. She answered the door wearing a white bathrobe and fuzzy pink slippers. "You here for breakfast?"

"You have enough to spare?"

"Come on in," she said and headed back into her kitchen.

As she poured me a mug of coffee, she said, "So if you're here, I'm guessing there isn't any good news."

"A major league screw-up on my part. I got an irate call from Tubby Gustafson earlier this morning. He asked me what I had concerning the investigation I'm supposed to be doing to find Eli Cummings. Since I was dealing with about three hours of sleep, my mind had me thinking he was talking about Taylor."

"What?"

"Yeah, I told him I was out till three in the morning looking for him. He told me Eli stole a thug's car. I said he couldn't drive, thinking Taylor again. Anyway, it got to the point where he said, if I didn't get over to his place in thirty minutes, I would be dead."

"Well, I'm sure he didn't actually mean that."

"Are you kidding? Annette, this isn't some nice guy we're talking about. This is Tubby Gustafson. Believe me. He doesn't kid around like that."

"So, what did he say when you went over there?"

"That's the whole point. I didn't go over there. I don't believe it. I'm going to have to go into hiding just like Taylor. Everything just keeps getting crazier and crazier."

Annette shook her head. "Well, no offense, but if you want to continue to try and find Taylor, you're going to have to deal with Mr. Gustafson first."

"You're talking about mission impossible here, Annette. No one tells Tubby what to do. No one tells Tubby no. If they do, it's just about the last thing that will come out of their mouth. I'm telling you, the guy is an absolute nutcase."

"Yeah, and he's your client."

"Believe me, that's not by design."

"Well, you're going to have to deal with it, Dev. I mean, I wish I could help, but obviously, I can't. The sooner you deal with this, the better off it's going to go for you. He still needs someone to find Eli Cummings, and that's your strong card."

Unfortunately, Annette seemed to be making sense. I pulled out my phone and made the call.

"What?" Tubby answered.

"I'm on my way over to see you. Stuck in traffic at the moment," I added in an attempt to buy a little more time.

"You'd better get your worthless ass over here and fast, if you know what's good for you, Haskell," Tubby said and disconnected.

I turned off my phone and shoved it back in my pocket.

"There, now was that so bad? What did he say?" Annette asked.

"He just told me to drive carefully."

"See, things are already starting to look better. Call me when you're finished talking to Mr. Gustafson. You know, it may make sense to ask him if he has any idea where Taylor might be. You know, with his, ummm, background, he just may have an idea where a kid like Taylor might be hiding."

"I'll be sure to ask him." I said, dreading the thought of having to deal with Tubby.

"You did the right thing, Dev. You'll see, he'll prob-ably welcome you with open arms," she said and gave me a little peck on the cheek.

Open arms, yeah, only to strangle me.

Thirty-two

I hurried out of Annette's house and sped toward Tubby's palace. Every time the wheels turned, I seemed to dread the meeting just a little bit more. The drive seemed to go all too quickly, and before I knew it, I was climbing out of my car and pressing the button on the intercom at Tubby's front gate.

"Well, Haskell, back for more. Good luck with that," the voice answered, laughed, and the gate suddenly began to open.

Great, apparently, everyone had been alerted to my pending arrival. They'd probably set up some way to tape my beheading and use it as a warning to anyone who even thought of crossing Tubby in the future.

I climbed behind the wheel and drove up the circular drive to the parking area. The usual two thugs were leaning against the house, enjoying the shade on the front porch. By the time I parked, placed my pistol in the glove compartment, and climbed out of the car, one of them was next to my car.

"You must be a glutton for punishment, Haskell. Suit yourself. Assume the position," he said.

I leaned over the trunk of my car, and he patted me down, twice. "Okay, you're good to go," he said.

I walked over to the front door, where his partner patted me down. "Lucky you. You get to go inside," he said and laughed.

He opened the door, and I stepped inside. Squiggy was reading a comic book. Probably the same one he was reading the last time I was here. He looked at me, shook his head, and pushed his bifocals up the bridge of his nose. He stood, grabbed the black and yellow wand, and I assumed the normal position with my legs spread and my arms out at shoulder height.

"Okay, you're good to go. You know, Haskell, I'd normally tell you this is your lucky day, but you know better than that. Follow me," he said and set off across the entryway. He was knocking on Tubby's office door a moment later.

"It's about damn time. Send him in here," Tubby growled as Squiggy opened the door.

"Good luck," Squiggy half-whispered as I hurried past and headed into Tubby's office.

I'd seen Tubby in this situation before, his massage hour. He was stretched out on a table that must have had steel I-beams for legs to support his massive weight. Dimpled flab from his stomach and sides hung over the edge of the table. Thankfully, a white towel covered his large, flabby rear end. His eyes were closed, and his pitted nose, the size of a baked potato, was red. No doubt due to the exertion caused by the two Asian women massaging his hairy shoulders. Both women were clad in black lace thongs and, at no surprise, latex gloves.

"Damn it, Haskell, you've set my schedule back by a full hour," Tubby said, keeping his eyes closed. "So where in the hell is he?"

"You mean Cummings, sir?"

The redness from his nose suddenly seemed to infect his cheeks. Still keeping his eyes closed, he growled, "Just why in the hell would you be here if it wasn't to give me an update on Cummings? You seem to have plenty of time to run around town at all hours of the night, no doubt enjoying yourself. So, where is he?"

"I don't know, sir. I'm continuing to search, but if you'll recall, after Lyle's break-in, I was forced to start back at square one."

"Oh, yes, now I remember." He looked up at one of the women. "Bao, if you would be so kind as to provide Mr. Haskell with a taste of what he's been missing."

The smaller of the two women bowed toward Tubby lying on the table. Her partner said something in a language I couldn't understand, and they both giggled as she approached. She was a demure woman, well-endowed, with dark brown eyes. I couldn't help but stare. She raised her eyebrows and smiled as she stepped in front of me and bowed politely. She reached out and gave my shoulders a little rub just before she spun around, raising one of her gorgeous legs, and connected her heel with my nose.

I sailed over an end table next to the leather couch and landed on the floor. Pretty little Bao strutted over. As I rose on all fours, she kicked me in the ribs, flipping me over onto my back.

"That will be enough for now, Bao," Tubby said, raising his shoulders and fat head. "Let me warn you, Haskell. Don't you dare bleed on my rug. Now get the hell out of my sight and do not come back until you have that worthless piece of shit, Cummings, in your possession. Do I make myself clear?"

I attempted to focus on Tubby, but with the room spinning, it was difficult.

"Well, do I?" Tubby shouted.

"Yeah, I mean, yes, sir," I said and began to crawl toward what I thought was the door.

"Haskell, once again, you're headed in the wrong direction. Bao, lead him the hell out of here," Tubby said. I was still attempting to focus when someone, I presumed Bao, grabbed me by the hair and led me toward the door. I attempted to crawl fast enough to keep up. She suddenly jumped on my back, laughed and slapped the back of my head as I crawled forward. She hopped off, opened the door, and then kicked me hard in the rear, knocking me into the hallway. The door slammed closed behind me.

"All finished?" Squiggy asked a minute or two later. I was sitting on the floor, leaning against the wall with my head tilted back. He didn't comment on my bloody face. "Here, let me help you up," he said and extended a hand. He led me down the hall, across the entryway, and out the front door.

"How did it go," one of the thugs leaning against the front of the house asked, and both of them laughed.

I ignored them and slowly headed to my car. I pulled out of the parking place and cautiously drove toward the front gate. As I approached, the gate slowly opened. I pulled out onto the street and drove home. I parked in my driveway and, for the first time, looked at myself in the rearview mirror.

My face was covered with blood, some of it still dripping off my chin. My nose was swollen to almost twice its normal size and now seemed to be situated at about a forty-five-degree angle. I gently placed both hands on either side, added pressure, then forced the bridge more or less back into position, letting out a scream as I did. The flow of blood picked up its pace, and I tilted my head back and sat there behind the wheel for a good half-hour, breathing through my mouth.

When I phoned Annette ninety minutes later, the first thing she said was, "Dev, you sound like you have a cold. How did your meeting go?"

"Not to worry. I didn't learn anything I didn't already know."

"Meaning?"

"Meaning Tubby is an awful person, and I shouldn't have wasted my time going there."

"What happened?"

"I'd just as soon not go into it right now. I'm going to go check out the high school, and hopefully, I'll see Taylor there."

"Is there anything I can do to help?"

"Oh, thanks for offering, Annette, but I'm pretty much out of options."

"Oh, Dev, I wish there was something I could do for you."

"Yeah, so do I. Look, if anything changes, you'll be the first person I call. Thanks for all your help and support thus far, and I mean it. You've been great."

"Well, thanks, that's kind of you to say. You're sure I can't—"

"Yeah, thanks, hopefully, Taylor is at the high school. I'd better get going. I'll chat with you later." I ran inside, changed shirts, and carefully patted a wet washcloth on my face.

My head continued to throb as I drove over to the high school. I parked in the parking lot and pulled out a pair of binoculars from the glove compartment. At 2:46, the doors to the school flew open, and a mob of teenagers blasted out of the building, anxious to flee the scene. I searched the crowd through my binoculars for the next ten minutes but never saw anyone who resembled Taylor.

I attracted more than a little attention looking through binoculars with two pieces of rolled toilet paper stuffed up my swollen nose. I focused my swollen, black eyes on the second surge of kids coming out of the building when there was a knock on the driver's window. I turned and looked at a police officer then quickly glanced the other way and saw his partner standing at a discrete distance in a position that suggested he was ready to draw and fire.

I lowered my window and said, "Can I help you, officer?"

"Yes, sir. You can keep your hands where I can see them and step out of your car."

"I was just looking for a friend and—"

"Please, sir, I'd like to do this the easy way. It would appear you might like to avoid another contentious discussion," he said and made a general nod toward my nose and eyes.

"Yeah, sure, I'm getting out. I'm going to place these binoculars on the passenger seat if that's all right."

"Yeah, but nice and slow, okay."

I followed his instructions and slowly set the binoculars on the passenger seat.

"Thank you," he said, opening my door. "Now, if you'll step out and assume the position."

How many people got told that twice in the same day? I stepped out of my car, placed my hands on the hood, and spread my legs. When he was finished patting me down, he cuffed my hands behind my back, pulled the wallet from my pocket, and led me into the back seat of his patrol car. There were only about two hundred kids standing around. A couple of them were chanting, "Lock him up!" to the collective laughs of the crowd. If Taylor had been anywhere in the vicinity, I was certain that, by now, he had headed in the opposite direction.

Both officers settled into the front seat, and the one who cuffed me said, "Care to explain what, exactly, you were doing here."

"I'm looking for a kid I found living rough. He'd been staying at my place for a couple of nights, and then he just up and disappeared yesterday. I wanted to find him and tell him he could continue to stay at my place."

"And he goes to school here?"

"Yeah, in fact, this is where I met him. I'm a volunteer with the detention group that meets here on Tuesday and Thursday evenings. He was going to try to spend the night in the school, and I've got a guest room, so I offered it to him."

"What's the boy's name?"

"Taylor."

"Does he happen to have a last name?"

"He does, but I never asked what it was. I just wanted him to feel safe in my house."

"And why wouldn't he feel safe?"

"Oh wait, I know where you're going with this. No, that's not the deal. I'm not into young boys or young girls for that matter."

"You had a gun in your glove compartment," the cop who'd been standing off to the side said.

"Yeah, I'm a private investigator, licensed to carry."

"I didn't find your license in the glove compartment, and it's not in your wallet, Mr. Haskell."

"Yeah, it's, umm, probably at my office. I've been meaning to put it in my glove compartment. I guess it slipped my mind."

A car full of boys drove past. All of them were laughing and giving me the finger.

"Looks like you had a bit of a disagreement recently. I'm guessing maybe this morning. You want to tell us about it?" the guy in the passenger seat asked.

"Nothing to tell, really. I just slipped on the stairs. Looks a lot worse than it is."

They both nodded in a way that suggested my excuse confirmed any suspicions they may have had.

"You could call my pal with the department, Lieutenant Aaron LaZelle. He'll vouch for me. I just had dinner with him last week. I know most of the people in his division. I've worked with a number of them."

"Yeah, he's a little busy right now. There's been a shooting. We're going to take you downtown, Mr. Haskell and get all this sorted out."

"Oh, come on, fellas. You don't have to do that. I'm sure if you gave Aaron a call, he'd vouch for me. It would only take a minute and save you a lot of trouble. If he's busy, just about any of the detectives would tell you I'm good."

The guy behind the wheel looked at his partner and nodded. The partner pulled out a cellphone and pushed a button. "Yeah, sorry to bother you," he said. "We've got someone out here at Central High School. His name is Devlin Haskell. He's a P.I. No. We got a call from someone at the school. He was parked in the parking lot checking out kids with a pair of binoculars. Told us you could vouch for him. Mmm-hmm. Yeah, we can do that. Okay, thanks, appreciate the help."

"Did he vouch for me?"

"Actually no, that was Detective Sergeant Norris Manning. He suggested it would be a good idea if we brought you in."

"Manning? That guy hates me. Can't you talk to Lieutenant LaZelle? I'm telling you, we're good friends. We've known one another for years. We used to play hockey together."

"We already told you, LaZelle is busy. I'm sure once he's back at the station, he can put in a good word, and you'll be free to go. Until then, Mr. Hassle, you'll be a guest of the city," he said.

The cop behind the wheel turned on the ignition, and we headed out of the parking lot.

Thirty-three

I waited another three hours in the holding cell. Some guy was passed out on the concrete floor, snoring. Two individuals kept arguing back and forth about which one was supposed to 'deal with' whoever was in a back room. Another guy kept giving me the eye. I think he was looking for something I had that he might want. Apparently, he decided I really didn't have anything worth taking. Finally, a cop walked over to the cell and called my name, "Hassle, Devlin Hassle?"

Why bother to make a correction? I stood and walked over toward him. "Yeah, that's me," I said through the bars.

"Okay, the L.T. wants you up in homicide. If you'll turn around, I'll cuff you."

"What? Cuff me? You gotta be kidding."

"Well, while you take your time to determine whether or not I'm kidding, I can attend to the thousand other things I have to do and come back tomorrow morning. So, if you want to go up there, you better turn around. Either that or you can choose to spend time with your new friends down here. Don't matter much to me. It's your choice."

I immediately saw his point and turned around. He cuffed my hands behind my back and called to another guard who came over and unlocked the door. As I stepped out, the guy who'd been giving me the eye stood and hurried over.

"Hey, I want whatever this dumb ass is getting."

"Then you'll have to wait your turn," the guard said and led me away.

We took the elevator up three or four floors and then walked down a hall. The guard wore an ID around his neck. He held the card in front of the keypad, and the door lock buzzed. He pushed the door open, grabbed my arm, and led me into the homicide section.

I'd worked in one capacity or another with just about everyone in the room. As we headed toward Aaron's office, I heard a couple of laughs. Someone shouted, "It's about time," and a couple guys started clapping.

We stopped at Aaron's door, and the guard knocked on the doorframe. Aaron was on a phone call. He waved his hand, indicating we should enter, and then moved his hand back and forth, signaling to take the handcuffs off. Once the guard did that, Aaron placed his hand over the receiver and said, "Thanks, Tony."

"You bet, L.T., good luck," Tony said and left.

Aaron pointed to a chair in front of his desk. I sat down and waited until he finished his phone call.

"Thanks for getting me out of that holding cell," I said once he hung up.

"What the hell were you doing? Looking at under-age girls through a pair of binoculars? And what the hell happened to your nose?"

I went on to tell him about the demure little girl in a thong who knocked the hell out me at Tubby Gustafson's, then brought him up to date on Taylor disappearing.

"And so I thought maybe he went to school. That's where he was getting fed. I think it was probably about the only stable place in his life. Well, until he moved in with me."

"Yeah, and after three days, he fled that scene. I have to give him some credit for being smart." Aaron said.

"Very funny, not. I was just trying to help the kid. When I met him, he was hiding in the school, so he'd have a safe place to sleep. All he had were the clothes on his back. Apparently, the boys were teasing him. All the girls were either afraid of him or didn't want to be seen with him. I just felt sorry for the kid. He's a nice guy, Aaron. A really nice guy."

"No idea where he went?"

I shook my head and said, "None whatsoever."

"Well, it happens, Dev. If you had a full name, we could check him out. Unfortunately, we'll add him to the list of kids that are cast adrift."

"He's really talented. We were going to try to get him into an artistic boarding school on a scholarship. I just can't figure out where he went or why."

"To be honest, Dev, that's not so unusual."

"Yeah, tell me about it. Driving around last night, seeing all the kids at eleven or twelve at night walking the streets. More than a few of them were pushing strollers. The deck is stacked against them, and they don't have a snowball's chance in hell."

Aaron nodded and said, "Where did you leave your car?"

"In the parking lot over at the high school. Hopefully, it's still in one piece."

"Well, you haven't been charged, so let's go down, grab your possessions, and I'll give you a lift over to the school."

"Oh, you don't have to—"

"You got a better idea?"

"Well, now that you mention it, no, not really."

"Yeah, so let's go."

"You know, Aaron. None of this would have happened if your Detective Manning had vouched for me."

"Manning? What's he got to do with anything?"

"Those two guys that arrested me, I told them to check with you. They called. Apparently, Manning answered, and well, the rest is history. Just letting you know. Not only did he waste the two officers' time, but also the guys who processed me in, not to mention the guy who brought me up here. Now you've been kind enough to offer me a ride. You start counting the time involved, all so Manning could play his little dirty trick on me. I'm telling you, Aaron, that Manning hates my guts."

"Maybe you should work a little harder at being nice to him." It took a good twenty minutes, but I finally got my cellphone, wallet, car keys, and my gun and sticky holster back.

On the way to the high school, I said, "So, did I hear correctly, you were involved in a shooting this afternoon?"

"No, who told you that?"

"I thought I heard something about you and a shooting."

"Another bank robbery by those two clowns, whoever in the hell they are."

"Are these the two idiots robbing banks, but they never get very much money?"

"Yeah, they're still out there. We can't seem to get a handle on them. For the first time, one of them fired his weapon today. Fortunately, he fired into the ceiling and not at someone."

"How much money did they get?"

"That's to be determined, probably not more than a grand, maybe fifteen hundred at the most."

"Split between two guys?"

"Yeah. Once they're caught, and they will be sooner or later, but once they're caught, they're going to end up doing seven to ten years. It doesn't make any sense."

Aaron pulled into the high school parking lot and headed for the only car at the far end, my Police Interceptor.

"I can't believe you're still driving that thing," he said, pulling alongside.

"I like it."

"It can't possibly work for anything undercover."

"Yeah, there is that." As he put his car in park, I noticed someone had spray-painted the word 'OINK' in red along the side of my car. "Oh, will you look at that. This just caps off the worst day I've had in a long time, a really long time."

"Welcome to the club, Dev. Get out and make sure it starts before I take off."

"Thanks for the ride, Aaron. I owe you big time."

"Yeah, you do. Now, get out. I gotta get back to work."

I climbed out, gave him a wave, then pressed the fob. The locks popped up, and I climbed in behind the wheel. I placed the key in the ignition, fired up the engine, and gave Aaron a thumbs-up.

He nodded and sped out of the parking lot.

Thirty-four

My cellphone rang as I watched Aaron's car speed off. "Hey, Annette."

"Well, you're finally answering. Didn't you get any of my messages?"

"I haven't had a chance to check. I just got my phone back."

"Just got it back?" she said. "Did you lose it?"

"Let just say it's been a pretty lousy day."

"Well, I might be able to make it a little bit better."

"Oh?"

"Maybe join us down here at Inkredible. Taylor's here. He's got some interesting news, and oh, by the way, Dennis liked all his sketches, and he's going to buy the whole batch."

"You're kidding. Are you down there now?"

"Yeah, we're in Dennis' office. Hurry up and get down here."

"I'm on my way," I said and sped out of the parking lot. I made it down to Inkredible in record time, parked right in front, and hurried inside.

The blue-haired woman from the other day was applying ink to a guy's shoulder. She stared at me for a long moment then said, "They're in his office. You can go on back." I hurried through the beaded curtain and down the hall to Dennis' office.

Taylor's sheets of images, there were ten of them, were all pinned on the bulletin board. Taylor and Annette were sitting in two leather chairs in front of Dennis's desk. Taylor had a big grin on his face. Dennis was seated at his desk. He had his business checkbook out and was in the process of signing a check for the amount of nine hundred dollars. I did some quick math in my head, and that figured out to fifteen bucks per image.

Dennis looked up as I stepped in the door. "Oh, my God. What the hell happened to you?" he said.

That caused Taylor and Annette to turn around in their chairs and stare.

"Oh, Dev," Annette said.

Taylor just sat there wide-eyed, too shocked to say anything.

"Yeah, it's been kind of a crazy day," I said.

"Can I get you an ice pack or something?" Dennis asked.

"No, thanks. I'm okay. It looks a lot worse than it is. Nine hundred bucks, congratulations, Taylor. That's fantastic."

Taylor just nodded and continued to stare.

"Here, grab a seat, Dev," Dennis said. He picked up two stacks of files from the leather couch, set them on top of two other stacks, and indicated that I should sit down.

"Dev, what the hell happened?" Annette asked.

"Relax, I'm fine. We can get into it later. So, Dennis, you liked the tattoo images Taylor did?"

"I love them. This will be huge. I can't tell you how many people we have stopping in on a regular basis to see what's new. Taylor's promised to keep these exclusive to Inkredible and work up another batch over the next few weeks."

Dennis rolled his desk chair across the floor to a water cooler. He filled a paper cup with water and rolled back to his desk. He pulled open a desk drawer, took out a bottle of ibuprofen, shook out two tablets and handed them to me.

"Thanks, Dennis, but really I'm okay."

"Yeah, sure. Take them anyway. It will make all of us feel better."

Annette chuckled, Taylor smiled, and a good deal of stress seemed to leave the room.

Once I downed the tablets, Dennis said, "Okay, now level with us. How many guys were there?"

I shook my head and said, "I went to Tubby Gustafson's and—"

"Oh, no," Annette said. "His gangsters did that?"

"Not exactly." I went on to tell them about Tubby and the demure woman who kicked the crap out of me.

"At least your nose looks halfway decent," Dennis said. "Well, I mean except for being black and blue and all swollen. Be interesting to see how bad it looks once the swelling goes down.”

“Yeah, I appreciate your concern, Dennis.”

“I’m sorry I made you so worried about me,” Taylor said. “My uncle never seemed to care, and I figured you would just be the same. I, I’m not used to anyone caring.”

“Yeah, I was really worried about you,” I said.

“We both were,” Annette added.

“I didn’t mean to cause you any problems, honest.”

“Why did you run off?” I asked.

“Well, you were telling me about having to deal with Mr. Gustafson and how mean he was, and I was afraid, if he found out you were letting me stay with you, it would just get you in deeper trouble.”

“Tubby Gustafson? Look, I agree he’s an awful person. But he wouldn’t care. Believe me, Tubby only cares about himself.”

“Well, yeah, that’s just it.”

“Dev doesn’t know, Taylor,” Annette said.

“Know what?” I asked.

“Go ahead and tell him. It’s okay,” Annette said.

“Tell me what?” I looked at Annette and then Dennis. Taylor was staring at the floor.

“Well, umm, see, Eli Cummings, the guy you’ve been looking for, he’s, umm, he’s my uncle. That’s who I’ve been living with, well, for as long as I can remember.”

"And by the way, he's gained one hell of a lot of artistic experience," Dennis said. He picked up his pen, wrote Taylor Cummings on the *Pay to the order of* line on the check, then made a show of tearing it out of the checkbook and waving it back and forth a few times before handing it to Taylor.

Taylor took the check and said, "Thank you." He turned toward me, handed me the check, and said, "Here, Dev. I really owe you."

"No way, pal. You earned it fair and square. It's yours to keep. I might suggest we put it in your bank account, you know, for safe-keeping."

"I don't have a bank account."

"Well then it's time we opened one up for you, but the money is all yours. You more than earned it."

Taylor grinned, nodded, folded the check in half, and put it in his pocket.

"Taylor, I meant what I told you," Dennis said. "I'd like to see more work from you. Say, in a month, if you could come up with maybe thirty more designs, that would be really great."

"Yeah, I can do that."

"Good, I'll be looking forward to it. Dev, Annette, I'd love to chat, but I've got an appointment coming in shortly. Thanks for coming down and bringing Taylor. And Taylor, you listen to these two. They only want what's best for you, and you can't do any better than that."

Taylor nodded, and we all stood. Annette and Taylor headed out of the office. Dennis grabbed my arm just as I started to leave. "Dev, that kid is really talented, and it sounds like he's been handed a shit life so far. You hang in there for him. He needs you more than either of you know."

"Thanks, Dennis, not to worry, and thanks for giving him the win. Never enough of that in life."

"Well, he's been a win for me, too. I'll make that money back within the week once I get those images out there, and after that, it's all pure profit. Now get the hell out," he said and grinned.

"Boys," Annette said out on the sidewalk, "I think Taylor's first sale, a major one at that, calls for a celebration. Dinner at my house tonight. Show up around 6:00, if that works."

"Works for me," I said. "Taylor, you got anything going."

He shook his head.

"We'll be there with bells on. What can we bring?"

"Just yourselves," she said and crossed the street to her car. We headed toward my car, and Taylor saw the 'OINK' spray-painted along the side.

"When did that happen?" he said.

"Oh, earlier today. Another long story," I said as a distant roar came down the street toward us. About a dozen guys on motorcycles stopped and backed their bikes against the curb. They were wearing black leather vests. Two or three stared at my black and blue face. A couple of them nodded at us, and they all headed into Inkredible. Everyone sported tattoos on their arms, and God only knew where else.

"I think that's a reminder that it's time for us to leave."

"They must be the appointment that Dennis was talking about," Taylor said.

"Maybe he'll have them look at your designs."

We climbed in the car and headed home. Neither one of us said anything during the ten-minute drive. Morton was on the couch, looking out the window when I pulled into the driveway. He just watched as I got out of the car, but as soon as Taylor appeared, he started barking and jumping.

He met us at the front door and went for Taylor. His tail wagged and bounced off the open door. Taylor gave him a good scratch behind the ears, and Morton licked Taylor's face. Once Morton calmed down, I said, "You want to grab a shower before we head over to Annette's?"

"Would that be okay?"

"Yeah, if you feel like it. It's up to you."

"I kinda left both bags with my clothes in the back of her car."

"Make sure we grab them tonight, and Taylor, you're welcome to stay here as long as you want. No pressure, I'd love to have you here."

"Thanks, Dev. I'm sorry for what happened."

"Let's promise one another, if there's something that's bothering us, we'll talk about it in the future. Okay? That goes for both of us, you and me."

"Yeah," he said and held out his hand to shake. He headed upstairs to his room, and I went into the kitchen. A moment later, I heard the shower running upstairs.

I couldn't remember who, but someone had left a double-sided makeup mirror in the house. I hurried up to my bedroom, pulled the mirror out of the back of my closet, flipped it to the magnified side, and looked at my face. Not pretty. The area around my eyes was black and swollen. The whites of my eyes were bloodshot. My swollen nose was black and blue, and then there was the matter of dried blood around my nostrils.

Taylor was out of the shower a half-hour later. I got undressed and headed into the shower. I was out ten minutes later and feeling better. I dressed in black jeans and a black shirt just in case I started to bleed again.

I went down to the kitchen, grabbed a bottle of wine, and set it at the front door, so I wouldn't forget it. I let Morton out for a bit, called upstairs to Taylor twenty minutes later, and we headed out the door to Annette's.

"How'd that shower feel?" I asked in an attempt to start up some conversation.

"It felt fine, great actually."

"You mind if I ask you where you went? We looked all over town, but no one had seen you."

He gave a little laugh and said, "Well, actually, I was right behind you."

"Behind me," I said and glanced over at him. "What do you mean? I was driving all over town."

"Yeah, and I was right behind your house in that backyard with the treehouse."

"So, all that time, you were maybe fifty feet from the house?"

"Yeah, pretty much. After you came back this morning, I waited a bit until you left again. Then I went onto the front porch. I read your note, and I was waiting. Annette pulled up, and we talked for awhile. She figured if you were still looking for me, you'd maybe go to Inkredible."

"Why didn't you just call me?"

"I forgot my phone in my room."

That made me laugh.

"What's so funny?"

"Oh, nothing, except it sounds like something I'd do."

Thirty-five

We pulled into Annette's driveway. I grabbed the bottle of wine from the back seat, and we headed for her front door. She opened the door before we were halfway there and waved.

"Hi, you two, right on time. Come on in," she said and held the door for us as we stepped into the house. "I've got dinner going. Come on back to the kitchen."

"Here, this is for you. Open it tonight or save it for another night," I said and handed her the bottle of wine.

"Oh, thank you. I've got a wine open, so if you don't mind, I'll just put this in the rack."

We followed her out to the kitchen. The closer we got, the better it smelled. The table was set for three, complete with a pair of candles and a view of a gorgeous backyard. Off to the left was a one-story structure, clearly not a garage and too large to be a shed where lawnmowers and snow shovels might be stored.

"Who's that?" Taylor asked as a couple walked along the far edge of the backyard and waved.

Annette waved back and said, "Oh, they're my neighbors. There's a five-mile walking path back there that's absolutely gorgeous. Maybe a mile from here, there's a large park area, and the path weaves all through that area and then gradually circles back. It's really lovely and very relaxing. Just the local people know about it, so it's never crowded. Sometimes I've done the entire five miles and never run into anyone else. Dev, can I talk you into a glass of wine?"

"You don't need to talk me into it. I'd love one."

"Taylor, I've got root beer, orange soda, or diet Coke."

"I'll take the root beer," he said. "You don't have to get me a glass."

She got the root beer out of the refrigerator and then poured two glasses of wine. We chatted for maybe ten minutes, and then Taylor asked her about the painting in her living room.

"Oh, well, come on out, and I'll tell you about it."

We walked out to the living room. I guessed I'd never noticed it on the two previous times I'd been to her house. The painting featured a weathered red barn and was in a gilt frame. The roof on the barn appeared to be tin, and in front of the barn were a half-dozen large rolls of hay.

"It's awesome," Taylor said.

Annette smiled. "Thank you. It's my folk's place. It's where I grew up out in Western Minnesota. I painted that one summer for a college project. The memories of the place grow fonder with every year," she laughed. "Lots of work growing up. My folks had six hundred acres. A small dairy herd, plus pigs and sheep. There was nothing but a lot of work, all day, every day."

"Do your folks still live there?" I asked.

"No, thankfully. They'd both be dead from heart attacks. No, my brother and his family took it over maybe ten years ago. He's got five boys, so all the work pretty much keeps them out of trouble. My folks moved into town. They spend their winters in Florida now, taking a well-deserved vacation every year."

"I love your textured work," Taylor said and indicated the weathered siding on the barn.

"Thanks, I'd read a book on the technique and was fortunate enough to be able to produce that over the summer. It won me a scholarship, which thrilled my father and didn't surprise my mother. In a lot of ways, it's the reason I was able to approach art as a business with my father's blessing. I always say, if it wasn't for this painting, I'd be up at 4:00 AM tomorrow morning milking cows."

Taylor smiled at that, and a timer went off in the kitchen.

"Oh, dinner time, homemade lasagna, hope you're hungry," Annette said and hurried back into the kitchen. I followed right behind her while Taylor remained in the living room, studying the painting for a few more minutes.

Once Annette had dinner dished up and on the table, she called Taylor. He came in, finishing a quick sketch in a little pocket notebook.

As he sat down, Annette asked, "Mind if I take a look?"

He passed the notebook over to her, and she studied it for a moment. "Interesting, very good. If you'd like, I have some blank canvas and paints out in my studio. You're welcome to take them or use the studio if you would prefer."

"Really?" he asked and then looked over at me.

"Hey, I'm not involved. You two seem to know what you're talking about. You work it out, and I'll adjust to whatever you decide," I said then took a large forkful of lasagna and shoved it into my mouth.

I took my time eating while Annette and Taylor discussed painting methods and styles. I was amazed at the knowledge Taylor seemed to have. Annette kept talking as she cleared the table. She dished up three slices of apple pie, sat down, and then looked at me and said, "Have you had a chance to discuss the school with Taylor?"

Taylor looked at me and said, "School?"

"Let me preface this conversation by saying this is not an attempt to get you out of my house. I'll say it again. You're welcome to stay as long as you want. Okay?"

Taylor got a confused look on his face, but he nodded.

"Good, go ahead, Annette. You know all about this place."

"All right, so here's the deal…" She went on to tell him about the Art Academy. How it was a boarding school for eleventh and twelfth-grade students and that it opened the door to a number of different opportunities.

"On top of that, based on just the little bit of work I've seen you create, namely the images for Dennis, I think you would be a natural, and I firmly believe that, if you're interested, we could get you a full-ride scholarship."

"And this is a boarding school?"

"Yes, you'd live there year-round, study primarily art but also standard high school subjects. You would graduate with a certified high school diploma but, in addition, you would be on the fast track for a number of colleges. In fact, if you work and apply yourself, the colleges will seek you out."

"Do you think I could get into the place?"

"I know you could, and with my recommendation and the recommendation of two other people I've already talked to, yes. I don't think you'd have a problem. What we would need would be samples of your work."

"What do you think, Dev?"

"I think you should take a look at it and you decide. If you want to do it, I'm behind you. Either way, I support you a hundred percent."

That brought a smile to his face.

"After dinner, let me take you out to my studio. You can take a look around. I'll give you a couple of canvases and some oils. You decide if you want to work in the studio or at Dev's house. Is that okay with both of you?" she asked.

Taylor nodded excitedly, and I said, "Whatever Taylor decides."

Thirty-six

We waited for Taylor to finish a second piece of apple pie before we cleared the dishes, and Annette loaded the dishwasher. She poured another glass of wine for both of us, and we chatted for a bit before heading out to her studio. She unlocked the door and turned off the alarm as we stepped inside.

There was a large room with a poured concrete floor and glass paneling over about a third of the roof. A wooden easel was positioned beneath the glass panels. A blank canvas rested on the easel. A small table with wheels was next to the easel with all sorts of paint tubes, two palettes, a can of turpentine, brushes, and a stack of rags.

"This is where I work," Annette said. "The problem is that, I'm so busy with my day job, I don't have the time to do what I love."

"That's life, isn't it?" I said.

Taylor was looking over toward the far wall where a light booth was positioned. The lights were off in the booth, but the six paintings I'd gotten from Eli Cummings place, three landscapes and three portrait paintings, were lined up in the booth. I'd completely forgotten I'd given them to Annette to examine.

"Where did you get those?" Taylor asked Annette as he walked over to the booth.

"Actually, I gave them to her. I got them from Eli's landlord. They were in the apartment, and he—"

"Yeah, I know they were there. I painted them."

"You painted them? I just presumed your uncle did."

"No, he did one of each, and I liked them so much I did these. At first, he was pretty mad because he'd treated the canvas and the frames to look old. Once he saw the paintings, he pretty much dialed down."

"You did them?" Annette asked. "Taylor, the work is really good. I don't mean to question you, but are you sure these are the ones you created?"

"Oh, yeah, if you check them out, I used a Hansa yellow pigment and acrylic paint. My uncle said that could be detected."

Annette had a shocked look on her face. "Really, Taylor? I mean all the work on these—"

"Oh yeah, honest. I worked long and hard on them. The few times my uncle got his act together, he could be a demanding instructor. Tell you what. If you could give me maybe sixty minutes, I could do a rough up for you. It's kind of like having to memorize a speech or a poem. You never forget what you did."

"Actually, I would be very interested in that. Dev, are you on any type of schedule?"

"No, I've got all night if you want," I said and raised my eyebrows.

Annette shook her head and said, "Taylor, would you mind if I look over your shoulder?"

"No, not at all."

"Let me do my part and refill our wine glasses," I said. "Taylor, you want another root beer?"

"No, thanks, Dev, I'd better cut back on the sugar intake for a bit."

"Let me run into the laundry room. I'll grab a smock for you," Annette said and hurried back into the house.

Taylor took one of the paintings and set it on the table with all the tubes of paint.

"You okay doing this?" I asked.

"Yeah, not a problem. But are you okay with me doing this?"

"Absolutely, Taylor, you never cease to amaze me."

Annette was back with a white smock a moment later. Taylor pulled off his shirt, slipped the smock on, and said something technical to Annette that went right over my head. I grabbed both wine glasses and went into the house. I filled the wine glasses, ate a thin slice of apple pie, and went back out to the studio.

Taylor was mixing up a paint concoction on the wooden palate and explaining to Annette what he was doing. Annette took the wine glass from me and said, "Thanks," without even looking at me. They may as well have been speaking Latin, for all I could understand. After the better part of thirty minutes, I made up some bogus excuse and headed back into the house. I settled into a comfortable leather recliner in her den and turned on the TV.

The smell of bacon woke me in the morning. I moved the recliner into the upright position and blinked a half-dozen times. Taylor was snoring softly on the couch as I tiptoed out and into the kitchen.

"Hey, good morning."

Annette had her back to me, standing at the stove. She jumped at the sound of my voice. "Oh, Dev, I didn't expect you up for another hour. Can I interest you in a cup of coffee?"

"Yeah, please."

She filled a cup and slid it across the kitchen counter.

"What time did you two finish things up last night?"

"Late. Very late," she said.

"You learn anything?"

"Oh, Dev, the talent Taylor has is nothing short of amazing. He worked for maybe two hours on the landscape. God, it felt like two minutes watching his technique, just incredible. There's no doubt in my mind that he created every one of those paintings out there. He has to go to the Art Academy. I could tell he loved what he was doing."

"He's that good?"

"The term 'good' doesn't do him justice. I've sent text messages to my friends. One of them is on the board of the Art Academy. Hopefully, they can come over this afternoon. I'd like them to see Taylor's work and maybe meet him. Would you mind if he stays here today? I've got two bags of new clothes that he left in my car. He can get cleaned up, meet these women, and we could have him enrolled in a week or two if everything works."

"Really?"

"Dev, the talent he has is amazing. Talk about a natural. Seriously, it's the chance of a lifetime for him. He deserves a break."

"Amen to that. It works for me if you're okay with it and if it's what Taylor wants to do."

"Good. My thought is we let him sleep in. I'll dish up your breakfast in just a minute, and we'll see how things go this afternoon. Hopefully, the women won't have a conflict."

"Sounds like a plan," I said and pulled out a kitchen stool and sat down. Annette handed me a placemat and some silverware, topped up my cup of coffee, and dished up a breakfast plate for me.

"You're not having any?" I asked.

"I thought I might wait for Taylor."

I glanced at the clock on the stove. It was a few minutes after seven. "You might be waiting until noon."

She seemed to think about that and then placed two pieces of bread in the toaster, apparently some form of a compromise.

I finished my eggs and bacon and had another cup of coffee. "Something comes to mind on this school option," I said.

"That's not sounding too positive."

"Forewarned is forearmed. I'm with you on the school. I think it would be an incredible opportunity for Taylor. Here's my concern. If his uncle is his legal guardian, could he shut it down? Forbid it?"

"I don't know. To be honest, I never thought of that. Why would he? I mean—"

"I don't know that he would. I'm just thinking out loud and want to be prepared that, in the event he tries something, we're prepared to deal with it. I'll talk to Louie this morning and get some information. My first thought is, based on the life Taylor has been forced to live over the past few years, any rights the uncle might have would be negated simply based on past lifestyle. He seems anything but responsible."

"Oh God, do you think he could screw this up? It's a once in a lifetime opportunity."

"Don't you worry about it. I'll check it out. I'm sure we'll be okay. I just want to have all the 't's' crossed and 'i's' dotted so that, in the event he does try something, we can shut it down."

She nodded and said, "That makes a lot of sense."

"Of course it does. It's my idea. I'd better hurry home. I have to let Morton out."

"Once I get this afternoon nailed down, I'll let you know."

"Okay, thank you again for dinner and for helping Taylor."

"It's my pleasure, Dev. Thank you. Now go on, off with you before Morton has a surprise waiting for you."

Thirty-seven

Morton wasn't at the front window when I pulled into my driveway. I hurried out of the car and into the house. I headed back to the kitchen, but Morton wasn't in there. I thought about heading upstairs and decided against it. Letting Morton wake up under his own power was a much better idea.

I put on a pot of coffee, turned on my laptop, and sent Louie an email. *'Louie, can you save me some time today? I have a question about legal guardian rights regarding Taylor. Thanks, Dev'*

Louie replied five minutes later, *'No problemo.'*

It was another half-hour before Morton wandered down to the kitchen. He did his normal morning stretch in the doorway and headed over to me for his head scratch. He seemed to be looking around the room, no doubt searching for Taylor. I let him out into the back-yard, filled his food and water dish, and poured myself a coffee. We headed down to the office a half-hour later. Louie wasn't in yet, so I made enough coffee for two mugs.

Louie pulled in across the street just as the coffee was ready. I poured a mug for him and set it on his picnic table. I poured myself a mug and settled into my desk chair just as the staircase began to creak. Red-faced Louie stepped in a moment later, stopped, and stared at me.

"What in the hell happened to you?" he asked.

"It looks worse than it is."

"Mmm-mmm," he said and gave me a thumbs-up. He set his briefcase on the picnic table and settled into his desk chair. After maybe a half-dozen sips of coffee, he said, "Tell me about the nose."

"Against my better judgement, I paid Tubby Gustafson a visit yesterday morning." I went on to give him the details about a woman half my size assaulting me.

He shook his head and said, "So who's having trouble with their legal guardian rights?"

"Sorry if my text message was misleading. No one is having any trouble. I just wanted to be prepared in case a problem arose." I went on to explain Taylor's potential opportunity at the Art Academy and my fear of Eli's involvement.

Louie shook his head. "That's not going to be a problem. No employment, running out on his rent, missing for days if not weeks at a time. You can testify to Taylor having to live rough. You and Taylor have got a pretty strong case that things have worked out much better for the boy with his Uncle Eli out of the picture. You might want to get a statement from his landlord regarding the failure to pay rent."

"Is there anyway we could get a ruling in advance?"

Louie seemed to think about that for a brief moment and then shook his head. "I don't think so. My sense would be just to leave this alone. Did you tell me the other day that Tubby Gustafson was after Eli?"

"Yeah, something to do with painting forgeries," I said and then wondered if, after what we learned last night, that might extend to Taylor as well. The last thing the kid needed was involvement with someone like Tubby.

"Gustafson just might eliminate the problem for you," Louie said and chuckled. "So, if you're asking this, I'm guessing Taylor has turned up."

"Yeah, everything's good. Annette worked with him on some artwork, and she's come up with this Art Academy idea. She thinks he'd qualify for a scholarship and already has a couple of women lined up to write letters of recommendation. Hopefully, Taylor's meeting with them at Annette's this afternoon."

"Good. He deserves a break."

I went on to tell Louie about Taylor doing all the mockups for Dennis at Inkredible. "Dennis wrote him a check for nine hundred bucks. As a matter of fact, if there's time after meeting these women at Annette's, I want to get him to the bank and open an account. Otherwise, he's going to end up running around with the check still in his pocket and either lose it or cash the thing somewhere and blow all the cash."

My phone rang. "Annette, everything all right?"

"Oh, yes, just heard from my friends. They'll be over here this afternoon to meet Taylor."

"That's great. Do you want me there?"

"Actually, Dev. Don't take this the wrong way, but no. One look at those black eyes and that nose, and why take the chance they'll think you're somehow tied up with Mr. Gustafson?"

The more I thought about that, it made perfect sense. "That's probably the wise decision. Let me know how it goes and if there's anything I can do. Give me a call when you're finished, and I'll come out and pick up Taylor."

"I will, Dev. Keep your fingers crossed," she said and hung up.

"Everything all right?" Louie asked.

"Yeah, they're all meeting at Annette's this afternoon. She seemed to think my showing up looking the way I do wouldn't be the best idea."

Louie nodded and said, "I'm afraid I have to agree with her."

The file Tubby had tossed out of his SUV the other night at The Spot still sat on the far corner of my desk. I slid it over, opened it, and stared at the image of Eli Cummings for a moment. Thankfully, other than dark hair, I couldn't see any physical similarities between Eli and his nephew Taylor. I read through the list of addresses in the file. The dingy unit I'd been to over on the east side was on the list, but there was another address after it.

"I've got some things to check out. Shouldn't take more than a couple of hours. You around all day?" I asked.

"I'll be here until happy hour over at The Spot," Louie said without looking up.

"Okay, catch you later." I clipped the leash onto Morton's collar, and we headed out the door. We did a quick walk around the block, and I put Morton in the backseat. My first stop was the hardware store. I purchased a can of high-gloss black spray paint. I went out to the parking lot and covered up the red 'OINK' some idiot had sprayed on my car yesterday afternoon.

It didn't completely eliminate it, but you pretty much had to know it was there to see it. I tossed the empty can in the dumpster, waved at the two hardware store guys watching me, and drove off.

The first address was a two-story gray stucco structure down on Daly street. It appeared to have originally had wooden siding and was probably covered with stucco back in the 1950's. There were three doorbells next to the door. I rang the first one and waited. After a long minute, I rang the second doorbell. No one answered. I rang the third and was about to head back to my car when a redheaded woman answered the door. She looked to be in her fifties. I guessed her weight at maybe ninety pounds.

"Yeah? If you're selling something, I ain't buying."

"I'm not selling anything. I'm looking for a guy who lived here. I opened the file and showed her the image of Eli Cummings."

She shook her head and said, "Is he the guy that did that to you?"

"No, this is from a little fender bender."

"Yeah, sure it is," she said and closed the door. I heard the lock snap a moment later.

I climbed back in my car, hoping things would improve. They didn't. I went through the next five places on the list rather quickly but only because no one was home in the first four.

At the fifth place, what I thought was the most recent address, another woman answered the door. "Are you my eleven-thirty?" she asked then seemed to stagger a step or two to regain her footing.

"No, sorry, wondering if you may have seen this man," I said, showing her Eli's photo. "Old pal of mine, I'm trying to find him."

She shook her head. "No, I ain't seen him. But you look kinda familiar. You the guy left without paying me the other night?"

"No, that wasn't me."

"You sure?"

"Thanks for your time," I said and hurried back to my car. I glanced at her as I drove off. She was still talking, apparently to herself. I drove over to the Minneapolis Art Institute on a whim and showed Eli's photo to the two people at the front desk, a woman and a man. Both of them looked from the photo to my nose and then back to the photo.

"He kind of looks familiar, but on any given day, we maybe get a hundred folks coming in here. More on the weekends. What's his name?"

"Cummings, Eli Cummings," I said.

The guy got a strange look on his face and pulled a file from a rack on their desk. Hang on just a moment," he said, opening the file. He began to run through a list, moving his index finger down the list as he read. He stopped about two-thirds of the way down.

"You said, Eli Cummings?"

I nodded and said, "Yes."

"He's on our list," he said and passed the list over to the woman. "We're supposed to call security if he attempts to enter. Did he do that to you?" he asked, nodding at my nose.

"No, had a bit of a car accident. You haven't seen him here?"

They both shook their head.

"Why do they want you to call security?"

"They never tell us. It could be anything from doing damage to an object to purse snatching. I've been here for over two years, and I've only had to call once. As soon as I called, the guy hurried out of the building."

"Well, thanks for your help. Hopefully, things will remain quiet for you," I said and headed back to my car.

Thirty-eight

y phone rang just as I was about to start the car. Barbara Wright calling.

"Hi Barbara, I'm sorry. I was so busy yesterday afternoon I forgot to call you. Taylor is back, and all is well."

"Oh, thank God. Now, I can move on to worrying about something else. Where did he go?"

"Well, I searched all over town until about three in the morning. After maybe four hours of fitful sleep, I resumed my search. It turns out he was up in a treehouse in the yard right behind me, not more than fifty feet from my place."

"But he's back, and everything is all right?"

"Yes, everything is fine, thankfully."

"Oh, that's good news. You can fill me in on all the details tonight at detention."

With everything going on, I'd completely forgotten about detention. "Yeah, about that. I think I'd better take a pass on it tonight."

"Why? What happened? Is Taylor—"

"Everything is fine. I was doing some work around the house, working on a new beam in the basement, and thought I had it in place. It slipped and more or less landed on my nose."

"Eeew, are you all right?"

"Yeah, I'm fine, but my nose is swollen and black and blue, and I've got two black eyes. I'm afraid it may send the wrong message to the kids if they see me looking like this."

"Mmm-mmm, you're probably right. Well, the important thing is that you're okay. Sounds like you're lucky you didn't break your neck."

"Yeah, that's what I was thinking. I'm sorry to miss out on tonight. I really enjoyed it last week."

"Plenty of time for more of that. You just get better. Please give me a call tomorrow on Taylor. I want to be sure he's okay. If there's another problem with him, don't hesitate to call."

"Thanks, Barbara. I'll keep you posted."

Thirty-nine

I didn't make it back to the office until the middle of the afternoon. Louie was at his picnic table, wolfing down the remnants of a BBQ sandwich. Based on the two Styrofoam trays, he was finishing up the second sandwich. As I walked in he nodded hello, picked up the last bits of meat from the second tray, tilted his head back, and dropped the meat into his mouth. Once he swallowed, he proceeded to lick his fingertips.

"Must have been pretty good," I said and settled in at my desk.

"Delicious. How'd things go for you?"

"My time would have been better spent napping at my desk. What a waste. I got more responses regarding my nose than anybody having seen Eli Cummings."

"At least the guy seems to be keeping a low profile."

"It would be better if he'd fled the city with the idea of never coming back."

"You going to tell Gustafson?"

"I hadn't planned to, but now that you mention it, that's not a bad idea."

I pulled out my phone and dialed Tubby's number. "Haskell," a voice answered. "You calling to try and get a rematch with that ninety-two-pound little girl who kicked your ass?"

"I'm calling to talk to Mr. Gustafson."

"Let me just check and see if he can't come up with something better to do," the voice said and put me on hold.

"Haskell?" Tubby shouted into the phone a moment later.

"Just checking in, sir. I was out and about searching for Eli Cummings."

"You sound dreadful. Do you have a cold? Is it contagious?" Tubby said, waited a moment, and then laughed until it morphed into a barking cough.

"I went through the entire list of addresses you provided the other night. No one recognized Cummings' photo. There was no indication he'd been at any of the places."

"Damn it. He has to be somewhere. He can't just disappear."

"You mentioned he ran off with Lyle's car last week."

"What difference does that make. I don't give a damn about Lyle's car."

"If you could get me a description of the vehicle and a license number, I might be able to get a BOLO, Be On The Lookout, on the vehicle and—"

"I know what the hell a BOLO is, Haskell."

"Well, if you could get me that information or have Lyle call me, it might be just the thing that would help me find Cummings."

"Haskell, so help me. All right, I'll have him get in touch."

"The sooner, the better, because—" Click. Tubby had disconnected.

"A conversation with your favorite pal?" Louie asked, not looking up from his computer.

"Not even close to a pal, my favorite, or a conversation. I'm just trying to find this idiot Eli Cummings. I want to warn him that Tubby is looking to kill him, so he gets the hell out of town. Then, hopefully, I can get Tubby off my back."

Louie looked up and shook his head. "You're a more patient man than I am."

"What would you do?"

"Oh, probably the same thing you're trying to do. But fortunately, I don't have to do it."

"You know I've been thinking—" My phone rang, Annette.

"Hi, Annette, everything okay?"

"More than okay. The girls just left. They're going to submit letters of recommendation for Taylor. One of the things he'll have to do is submit a painting as an example of his work."

"Are you thinking one of those landscapes or the three portraits of that woman?"

"Yes, as a matter of fact, that was my idea, but he said no."

"Does he have a plan?"

"He does. Why don't you join us for dinner tonight, and we can go over it?"

"I can do that. What would you like me to bring?"

"Just yourself. If you feel you have to bring something, bring a bottle of wine."

"Red or white?" I asked.

"You choose, no pressure. Any time after five will work and feel free to bring Morton."

"Morton? Are you sure?"

Morton raised his head at the sound of his name.

"Very sure. We can take him for a walk."

"Looking forward to it. I'll see you then," I said and disconnected.

I chatted with Louie for a bit, put Morton in the car, and we drove home. As soon as we stepped into the house, I headed into the kitchen and let Morton out the backdoor. I walked up the street on foot to Solo Vino, got two bottles of a California sauvignon blanc, and headed home. I set the wine in the freezer, hurried upstairs, and climbed into the shower. I put on a wrinkled shirt and jeans, pulled the wine out of the freezer, and drove over to Annette's. It was rush hour, and the drive took a good thirty-five minutes.

We rang the doorbell, and Annette answered a few seconds later.

"Oh, good, you brought Morton. Taylor mentioned him a couple of times, and I thought he could maybe use a break. He's in the den going over all sorts of Art Academy scholarship information."

"Did everything go okay?" I asked, handing her the wine bottles.

She smiled and said, "Could not have gone better. He knocked their socks off, to use an idiom."

"Don't get too technical with me before I have a glass of wine."

"Let me take care of that. You remember where the den is."

"Right around the corner?"

"Yes. I'll join you in a bit."

Morton followed me into the den. Taylor was stretched out in the middle of the floor with all sorts of papers scattered around him along with his laptop. He was typing away and appeared to be filling out an application. As he looked up, Morton bounded toward him and began licking his face.

"Hey, Morton. How's it going? Did you miss me? I missed you, boy. Good to see you. Good to see you," Taylor said, sitting up and scratching Morton behind the ears. Morton's tail waved back and forth as he took in all the attention.

"So, Annette said things went pretty well this afternoon."

"Yeah, I think so. Two nice ladies. They asked a lot of questions, and I was able to show them the pieces I'd done out in the studio plus the one I started last night."

"They liked them?"

"Seemed to. At least they didn't say they disliked them. They want me to do a painting and submit it for review."

"Can you use one of those paintings out there?"

"No, and I wouldn't want to anyway. I've got an idea for one, but I wanted to run it past you."

"Yeah, sure. Let me warn you. Art critique is not my strong suit, not that it ever stopped me. What'd you have in mind?"

"I'd like to do a portrait."

"Okay, that sounds good. Who are you thinking of?"

"I was thinking of you, Dev."

"Me?"

"Yeah. Think you'd be up for it?"

"Well, umm, I mean that's really nice of you, Taylor. Don't get me wrong. I'm honored, but wouldn't someone else be better? Annette's gorgeous. What about that woman tattoo artist at Inkredible? She was attractive."

He shook his head and said, "No, Dev. I want to do you."

"Well, thank you, I'm honored. That's really kind of you. But for starters, this nose and my black eyes, I mean who would want to—"

"That's a big part of what I want to capture, Dev. Almost all portraits are of people in the best of clothes. They've shaved, their hair is done. They're wearing fancy jewelry. You're more like a street guy. The kind of person who would never have a portrait of himself. I think you would be perfect."

"Mmm-mmm, I don't know, Taylor."

"No offense, Dev. But you're right. You don't know. I have to submit a painting. I don't want it to be like the hundred other paintings they get, a vase of flowers, a pretty woman, some rich guy in a suit. I want it to be memorable, unique. You with that nose and the black eyes, you'd be perfect."

"You're really serious?"

"You bet I am. We could start tomorrow. I'll adjust to whatever fits your schedule. Annette said we can use her studio. She's already gone out and got the canvas. She's got a few hundred tubes of oil paint and a ton of brushes out there."

"Okay, I guess you talked me into it. How can I refuse?"

"Oh, thanks, man. That's just great. I really appreciate it."

"I'm honored that you want to do this."

"Everything okay in here?" Annette asked. She stood in the doorway, holding two glasses of wine.

"Yeah, Dev agreed to the portrait," Taylor said.

"Oh, so you both knew?" I said and gave Annette the evil eye.

She grinned. "I think it's a wonderful idea, Dev. Taylor had a good point, it will really stand out. I've seen the submissions over the past few years. They're all excellent work but of a type. Lovely landscapes, models, parents. A painting of you in your current state would really be unique."

"Maybe I should call and thank the person who did this."

"Yeah, who was that, by the way?" Annette asked and took a sip of wine.

"Oh please, I'd just as soon not go there. Okay, I'd like to propose a toast to this soon to be magnificent work of art. I'll take two copies, dartboard size," I said and raised my wine glass.

Everyone laughed, and we headed into the kitchen for dinner. Annette gave me a peck on the cheek and whispered, "Congratulations. Wanting to do a portrait of you is very high praise from Taylor."

Forty

Taylor and I were due out at Annette's at 9:00. I was up before the alarm went off. After my shower, I pulled a clean shirt and a pair of jeans from the closet. I only had one clean t-shirt, but since I was wearing a shirt, it would be okay. I woke Taylor up at a quarter to eight and had breakfast dished up by the time he came downstairs. We pulled into Annette's driveway promptly at nine.

I stopped for a mug of coffee in her kitchen, and we headed out to the studio. The blank canvas was on the easel, and all sorts of paint tubes were laid out on the table next to the easel. Taylor pulled a drawer open and set his laptop inside.

"I've got to meet with someone this morning. Anything you two need before I leave?" Annette asked.

"I'm good," I said.

"Thanks for laying everything out, Annette," Taylor said.

"My pleasure. More paints in the drawers and over on the workbench. Help yourself to whatever you need.

Dev, I'll leave the coffee on in the kitchen. Help yourself," she said and left.

"What should I do, just stand here?" I asked.

Taylor shook his head and said, "No, I want you to sit in this chair." He pulled over a wooden chair that looked to be about a hundred years old. The chair was oak with a pressed back and had probably been a dining chair originally.

He positioned the chair just below the glass panels in the roof and said, "I want you to sit backward in the chair and just looked relaxed." He stepped back and looked at me. "Maybe take off that shirt before you sit down."

"You sure? The t-shirt I have on isn't exactly what—"

"It will be perfect, Dev. Whatever it is."

"Okay," I said and unbuttoned my shirt. I walked over, and set the shirt in the light booth. I sat down on the chair, rested my forearms on the pressed oak back, and leaned forward.

"Oh, that's great, Dev," Taylor said, admiring my t-shirt emblazoned with the line 'I pee in pools.'

"I think it would probably be better if I wore my shirt. Don't you?"

"Are you kidding? This is perfect, definitely setting you apart from all the usual stuff."

"You sure, Taylor. I can—"

My phone rang. The call came across as an unknown number. I took the call anyway. "Haskell Investigations."

"Quit trying to sound important, Haskell."

"Who's this?"

"It's me, Lyle. Tub— er Mr. Gustafson told me to call you. Said you needed a description of my car."

"Yeah, I'm going to try to get a BOLO out there on it. That means Be On The—"

"I know what the hell a BOLO is, dumb shit."

"Mmm-mm could have had me fooled. So what's the make and model?"

"It's a red 2012 Chevy Chevelle SS sitting on staggered Forgiato Veccio 22's. It's got a chrome breather sticking out of the hood."

"Would you care to translate?" I asked.

"I knew you wouldn't get it. The model is a Chevrolet Chevelle SS," he said very slowly so I would understand. The tires, there's four of them, Haskell, and they're round. The chrome rims are Forgiato Veccio 22's. There's a chrome breather on the hood that makes the engine sound like a beast and a double white racing stripe, each one six inches wide that runs from the front of the hood to the windshield and from the rear window to the edge of the trunk."

"Sounds delightful," I said, meaning anything but. "What's the license plate?"

He seemed to chuckle for a second. "I snuck a personalized plate past the powers that be. The license number is 3JOH22A," he said and laughed.

"What do you mean you snuck it past? Is that someone's password?"

"Look in a mirror to get it, Haskell."

Why did I think Lyle would make any sense? "I'll see if I can get a BOLO out there on this. You'll be the first person I call if anything comes up, Lyle," I lied. "What an idiot," I said once I'd disconnected.

"One of your clients?" Taylor asked.

"No, just a guy who works for a client. A real jerk. So how do you want me to sit?" I said, moving the subject away from the car Taylor's uncle was supposed to have stolen.

"Just the way you were— arms resting on top of the back of the chair. Lean forward a little, you know, like you're talking to pals on a sunny afternoon, and there's nothing bugging you. Yeah, there you go. Maybe don't lean quite that far."

I straightened up a little.

"Yeah, perfect," he said and grabbed a brush.

I took two breaks over the next three hours. I refilled my coffee mug twice and used the bathroom the second time. I grabbed a quick look both times I walked past to retake my seat. Taylor was definitely making progress.

Annette popped back into the studio just after the noon hour. She stood behind Taylor and studied the portrait for a moment. "I'm thinking of making a quick lunch, Taylor. Are you at a stopping point?"

"Yeah, don't make anything too fancy. I just want to take a short break."

"Perfect. I've got sandwich makings on the kitchen counter. Come in whenever you're ready."

"Dev, you can go in now if you want. I've just got a little touch-up to do. It'll take me maybe ten minutes. You go ahead."

I didn't have to be told twice and hurried out the door to catch up with Annette.

"How's it going in there?" she asked.

"You tell me. You were looking over his shoulder. I'm just sitting there chatting away."

"He really is talented," she said. "Oh, I'm praying he gets this scholarship."

"Yeah, you and me both." My phone rang, Dennis Richards. "Hello, Dennis," was how I answered.

"Hi, Dev. How's the head feeling today?"

"Not a bother, thanks for asking. What's up?"

"Actually, I was calling for Taylor. I've got a group of customers who want him to design a logo for their organization."

"Really?"

"Yeah, and they're willing to pay him."

"Hang on a minute, and I'll put him on," I said and hurried back out to the studio. "Hey, Taylor," I said, stepping into the studio. "Phone call for you."

"For me?"

"Yeah, Dennis at Inkredible."

"Really?" he said, setting his brush down and taking my phone. While he talked with Dennis, I looked at the painting. It was far better than anything I'd ever be able to do, and it was still in the early stage. Taylor chatted for a couple of minutes, passed on his phone number, then disconnected and handed the phone back to me.

"What'd he want?" I asked.

"Just what he told you," he smiled. "I'm going to design a logo for some guys. They're going to call later this afternoon. Hope that's okay. I told him to go ahead and give them my phone number."

"Yeah, that's okay. You thinking of working on the painting some more this afternoon?"

"If we could work until around three, I can get all I need from you. I can take a couple of pictures with my phone and put them up on my computer. That way, you won't have to sit there on that chair and get any crazier than you already are."

"That sounds like a pretty good plan," I said.

We had a quick twenty-minute lunch and were back in the studio. I quickly ran out of things to say and just sat there while Taylor worked. At one point, I dozed off and suddenly jerked myself awake.

"Okay, Dev, let me take some pictures of you with my phone." He took five pictures, emailed them to himself, then said, "You're free to go if you want."

"Yeah, I'll head to the office. Are you going to stay here?"

"Annette offered to give me a ride in around five or six if that's okay."

"That will work great. Would you mind if I invited her for dinner? I feel like we owe her big time for letting you use all this stuff and for lining up a chance at that scholarship."

"No, I wouldn't mind. In fact, I'd like that."

"Okay, keep up the good work," I said, standing behind him and looking at the painting. "You know, what if you eliminated the black eyes and made my nose look normal?"

"Yeah, and that would eliminate the whole sense of what I'm trying to accomplish."

"Okay, okay, just a thought. Good luck," I said and headed out of the studio.

I talked to Annette for a brief moment, trapped her into coming over for dinner, and headed to the office.

Forty-one

I parked behind Louie's faded orange Ford Fiesta. "Perfect timing," he said as I stepped into the office. "Twenty minutes earlier and you would have had the pleasure of Tubby Gustafson."

"You talked to Tubby?"

"No, thankfully, I saw them coming out of the building, him and that fatty guy. I drove past and went around the block, waited until I was sure they had left and then parked and hurried in."

"God, I wonder what he wants," I said, sitting down at my desk.

I thought for a moment and then phoned Aaron LaZelle. Surprisingly, he answered.

"Yeah, Dev. What's up?"

"I'm wondering if you can put out a BOLO on a stolen car."

"Who would steal your car?"

"No one with any sense. Fortunately, this isn't about my car." I went on to explain how Eli Cummings was suspected of stealing Lyle's car.

"And this Lyle character is one of Gustafson's thugs?"

"Yeah, in fact, it was Tubby who wanted the BOLO out there, well, and this Lyle idiot too, I guess."

"So why didn't they contact us? This Lyle character has supposedly been without a set of wheels, and he's just getting around to having you contact us now? My first thought is there might be some difficulty with the title, you know, as in a stolen vehicle. He has you making the call. Did you see the vehicle being stolen?"

"No, I didn't."

"And how did you get the information, the description, and the personalized license plate number?"

"Lyle called me with it. Tubby made him call me."

"Are you sensing a pattern here, Dev? Why would we want to waste our time if the supposed owner of the vehicle can't be bothered to spend five minutes informing us of the theft."

"Aaron, they told me the car was stolen by Eli Cummings. I've passed the information on to you. Do with it what you will."

"Okay, I'll put it out there. Hopefully we can get him before he hit's another branch bank. How's everything else going, Dev?"

"I remain the most boring person in town."

"Keep it that way, Dev. I gotta run," he said and hung up.

Louie looked over at me but didn't say anything. I puttered around the office for a bit then phoned La

Grolla, the restaurant across the street from my house, and placed a takeout order. Thirty minutes later, I had just set the three Styrofoam trays on the kitchen counter. No sooner had I let Morton into the backyard when there was a knock on the front door.

Annette and Taylor gave me a wave as I approached the door, and I let them in. "Come on back to the kitchen. I've got dinner going. Get you a glass of wine, Annette?"

"Yeah, if you're having one. I brought a little something for Morton," she said and handed me a brown paper lunch bag. "It's a ham bone."

"Oh, he'll love you. Let me call him in, and you can give it to him."

I let Morton back into the kitchen. His tail began to wave at the sight of Annette and Taylor. He got a head scratch from Taylor, and then Annette presented the ham bone to him. He grabbed it and hurried off to a corner so he wouldn't have to share.

I opened the refrigerator and pulled out a bottle of white wine. "Taylor, you want a root beer?"

"Yeah, please."

I served up the beverages, and we settled in at the kitchen counter. Annette looked at the white plastic bag with the three styrofoam trays and said, "Dev, is that the dinner you're working on?"

Taylor laughed.

"Yes, it is. I had to go to three different places before I found Styrofoam trays."

"Actually, this works out just fine. I've got an early morning meeting. Tell me if this will be okay. We'll have the dinner you worked so hard on, and then I'll take Taylor back to my place and he can spend the night there. You won't have to bring him out early. He can wake up and continue working. And I'll get to my meeting."

"What about school tomorrow?" I asked.

Taylor made a face and said, "Well, I am working, and I hope to finish up your portrait tomorrow. I want to submit it as soon as possible."

"If he gets accepted, he could begin the second quarter in just a week or two," Annette said.

"Or, you could spend the night here and go to your meeting," I suggested.

She smiled and said, "Ahh, no, Dev."

We decided that, under the circumstances, Taylor could go back to Annette's and hopefully finish up the portrait.

I served up the dinner, which amounted to passing Annette and Taylor a styrofoam tray. It wasn't even seven, and they were out the door heading back to Annette's house. I put the silverware and the wine glasses in the dishwasher and headed down to The Spot. There were only a few people in the place. Louie was on his usual stool reading a newspaper.

"Hey, Dev, I feel like it's been about a year since you've been in here. Where's Morton?"

"At home in the middle of a love affair with a ham bone."

Mike stepped up and said, "You having a beer tonight, Dev?"

"Yeah, I think that would be perfect and another of whatever Louie is having. Let me just grab some cash from the ATM."

"Don't bother. We had a break-in last night. Someone tried to get into the ATM and screwed it up. One of their repair people is scheduled for tomorrow, but until then, I'm afraid it's out of order."

"What'd they do to it?" Louie asked.

"I was told over the phone, but it wasn't making sense. Technical jargon," Mike said. "Whoever it was came in through a window in the back."

"I'll cover Dev's beer," Louie said.

"Actually, I'm glad you're here, Dev. I'm more than a little worried about security tonight. Would you ever consider spending the night here? Free drinks, and I'll pay you."

"When you say the night, what exactly are you talking about?"

"I'm going to shut down at midnight, sooner if we're empty. I was planning to spend the night here, but I'll be dragging tomorrow and can't get anyone to cover for me. If you were here, I could be back around 6:30 or 7:00 tomorrow morning. Like I said, I'll pay you. I just can't leave that ATM unguarded. If someone breaks in, we're liable for the cash and any damage. You could just sack out in one of the booths."

"Yeah, okay, I guess. I'll head home around nine, let Morton out, and come back down."

"Great, let me get you that free beer. Louie, your drink is free tonight, too."

"That's nice of you to do, Dev," Louie said.

"No big deal. Taylor's at Annette's. I'd just be watching TV at home, so might as well get paid for the time."

"Plus the free drinks," Louie said and drained the glass in front of him.

"Yeah, well, I'll be having just the one."

I actually stopped after two beers, which surprised both Mike and Louie, and me too, come to think of it.

I went home and let Morton out then headed back down to The Spot. I hurried up to the office, grabbed my pistol in the sticky holster, and joined Louie. Dennis Richards popped in for a beer. He and Louie left a little after ten. The last two guys headed out just before eleven, and Mike locked the doors. He went home a half-hour later. I watched a movie on one of the TVs mounted above the bar then stretched out in the corner booth sometime after one in the morning.

Forty-two

I woke to the sound of a loud thump. At first, I thought maybe Morton had fallen out of bed, but then I got my bearings and realized I was still in The Spot. I slowly pulled my feet into the booth and sat up. I kept my head down and cautiously peeked around the corner of the booth.

"Okay, yeah, wrap it around good and tight, then pull this out," a fat guy shouted.

I was looking at two guys I didn't recognize. One wore a Chicago Cubs baseball cap and looked to be wrapping a chain around the ATM. He stood and walked backward out the side door, laying the chain along the floor.

The other guy was fat, with curly blonde hair and a black shirt. The shirt had an image of flames all around the bottom of it. By the looks of things, they were going to pull the ATM off its base then probably toss it in the back of their pickup and deal with it somewhere else.

"You got it wrapped around there tight?" the fat guy called out the door.

A moment later, I heard an engine start-up, and the chain slowly raised up off the floor as it grew taut. The fat guy yelled, "Give it some gas."

The chain seemed to grow even more taut. The ATM groaned for a brief moment before the chain fell to the floor, and the fat guy yelled, "What the hell happened?"

That seemed to be my cue. I pulled my pistol as I stepped out of the booth and shouted, "Hey, what the hell do you think you're doing?"

The fat guy took one look at me, holding my pistol, and ran out the door. By the time I hurried around two tables and made it to the door, the pickup was turning the corner and racing up the street toward the Interstate. I stepped out the door. The pickup's rear bumper was on the sidewalk. The chain was still wrapped around it, and the license plate for the pickup truck was still attached to the bumper.

* * *

"So, a fat guy with curly blonde hair wearing a black shirt with flames around the bottom," the officer said. We were seated at the bar, and he was taking notes. His partner had a camera out and was taking pictures of the chain wrapped around the ATM.

"Yeah, I'm guessing the same guys that broke in here last night. They came in through a back window and tried to break into the ATM. Mike should be down here shortly, and he can give you the info on that. He'll probably have the case file number. At least now you know who the pickup belongs to," I said and nodded at the rear bumper with the license plate.

"Hopefully, unless they stole that pickup."

"Have you had a lot of these happening? People stealing the entire ATM?"

"This wouldn't be the first time. The things are designed to be tamper-resistant. So usually, we're dealing with someone who doesn't really know what they're doing. They think it's going to be easy. The truth is, it's not, and they simply become determined they're not going away empty-handed. I'd say they forget, but the truth is they probably never knew there's a tracking device on all ATM's. Not to mention a red dye that will explode if the unit is forced open. We had a case last summer where three guys successfully stole an ATM but eventually were ID'd on security cameras and arrested. All three were covered with the red dye."

It was maybe a half-hour before sunrise when the side door opened, and Mike stepped in. He looked like someone who'd just been pulled out of a deep sleep. "What the hell happened?" he asked, staring at the pickup bumper and the chain.

"I'm guessing the same guys as before. Only this time, they left a calling card. Their bumper and the license plate," I said.

The police took my information. They talked with Mike for a bit, gathered up the chain and the license plate, and left. They promised to send someone over later in the day for the bumper.

"Dev, I'm so glad you were here. How in the hell did they get in?"

"I'm not sure. I dozed off for a minute in the corner booth and heard them in here. There were only two of them, so I was able to fight them off and chase them out the door. They took off but fortunately left the bumper. Hopefully, the cops will be paying them a visit shortly."

We chatted for a while. Mike put on the coffee and made me a sausage pizza for breakfast. After breakfast, I headed home, showered, and got dressed. Morton wandered into the kitchen an hour later. He did his usual stretch by the door and then came over for his morning behind the ear scratch. I let him outside, filled his food and water dish, and let him back into the kitchen. We were down at the office before nine. I noticed a handyman truck parked alongside The Spot but decided it would be better for all involved if I stayed away.

Louie showed up an hour later. I watched him park out on the street and had his coffee waiting for him when he finally made it up the flight of stairs. I filled him in on my early morning visitors at The Spot, and then Louie left for a court appearance. I drifted off to sleep at my desk and was out for a good long while before my phone rang and woke me. Taylor was calling.

"Hey, good morning, Taylor."

"Dev, it's almost two in the afternoon."

"Oh, yeah, sorry about that. I was so involved in this case, I guess I lost track of time. How's it going?"

"Pretty good. I've finished your portrait."

"Really, that fast?"

"Yeah, Annette looked at it, said I would be a shoo-in. I like it, and I'm worried that if I do any fine tuning, it will only serve to screw it up."

"Makes sense to me. You want me to pick you up?"

"Yeah, if you wouldn't mind. This morning, I got a call from those guys who want me to design their logo. I've got some ideas, and I wanted to sketch them out with the colored pencils and show it to them on that special paper Dennis gave me."

"You want me to bring it out to you?"

"No, if you could pick me up, I'll work on it at your place. They're going to stop by later tonight around eight. I was wondering if we could maybe stop at a bank on the way home. I've still got Dennis's check, and I'd like to open a bank account and deposit it."

"Yeah, sure. That's a good idea. I'll head out to you in just a minute. Is Annette there?"

"No, she had another meeting to go to."

"Okay, write her a note and leave it in her kitchen so she knows what's up, and you can call her later to-night. You want to be sure to stay on her good side for all the help she's given you."

"Yeah, okay, I'll see you when you get here."

Forty-three

Taylor was looking out the window when I pulled into Annette's driveway. He waved and opened the front door as I walked up the sidewalk.

"Do I get to take a look at the painting?"

"Yeah, sure, it's in the kitchen," he said and headed in that direction.

The painting was on the kitchen counter, leaning against the wall. Despite my two black eyes and my black and blue nose, I had to say it looked great.

"Taylor, I got to tell you, that is one hell of a great painting. I'm not just saying that because it's me. You really did a wonderful job."

"You like it?"

"No, I love it. I'm not kidding you. Me, the chair, the way the background fades, it's really good. Glad you eliminated the words on my t-shirt. What did Annette say?"

"She said she really liked it, and she was surprised I could do it that fast."

"Yeah, well, unlike me, she actually knows what she's talking about."

Taylor set his note to Annette on the kitchen counter and carried his painting out to the car. I opened the trunk, and he carefully set the painting in the trunk.

"You still want to open up that bank account?"

"Yeah, if you wouldn't mind."

"Not at all. It'll only take a couple of minutes. I know just the place."

We drove back into town and headed up Grand Ave to the aptly named Grand Bank. I pulled into the parking lot, turned off the car, and asked, "Do you have the check and an ID?"

Taylor reached into his back pocket and pulled out his wallet. He reached inside and pulled out the nine hundred dollar check from Dennis Richards and a photo ID from school.

"Good, that's all they'll need. Let's get you set up," I said, and we walked into the bank through the back door. Two tellers were just off to the right behind a black granite counter. The teller stations were maybe six or eight feet apart.

I called, "Hi, Deb," and gave a quick wave to the blonde teller. She waved and took a bite out of a candy bar as we headed to a cubicle.

Pat, one of the bank officers, was seated at his desk, working on his computer. He looked up, smiled, and said, "Hi, Dev, what can I do for you?"

"Pat, this is my friend Taylor Cummings. He would like to open an account."

"Sure, take a seat guys. Savings or checking?" he asked Taylor.

"Savings," Taylor said and then looked at me.

"Yeah, that's probably the best for right now," I said.

Pat reached into a drawer and pulled out a sheaf of papers. "Okay, just fill out this top sheet, and we'll get it set up."

Taylor began filling out the form and stopped just after he entered his name. "Can I use your address?" he asked, looking over at me.

"Yeah, that's where you're living," I said and gave him my address with the zip code.

He filled in some more info and paused, "I'm not exactly sure of my birthdate. It's either April eleventh or fifteenth."

"Put in the date you think is correct," Pat said. "Do you know where you were born?"

"Yeah, here in St. Paul."

"Dev, if you could get a birth certificate in the next couple of days, let me know if the date changes."

"Yeah, sure, I'll get on it this afternoon."

"It's not a problem, so don't worry," Pat said to Taylor. "We had a guy in here last month who was a twin, two brothers. Their names were Easton and Weston. One was born at 11:59, and the other was born at 12:03 the following day, four minutes apart."

"Oh, that's just—"

Bang! What sounded like a gunshot, a very close gunshot went off. A voice suddenly shouted, "Everyone on the floor now. Let's go. Come on, move!" A half-second later, a guy in a scary clown mask popped his head around the corner and said, "You three, get out here." He waved a gun at us in case we had any questions.

There was only one other customer in the bank, a blonde woman in blue hospital scrubs. She was lying on the floor by the teller's counter. Another guy in a red wig and a Ronald McDonald mask handed a black cloth shopping bag to Deb the teller and said, "Fill it up and make it quick."

"Oh, no," Taylor said.

"I told you guys to get down on the floor. Do it now," the clown with the scary mask shouted.

We all got down on the floor and placed our hands behind our heads.

Ronald McDonald grabbed an office chair with wheels and rolled it over to the tellers counter. He stepped onto the chair and then up onto the granite counter. He sang a line from a song, "With a little bit, with a little bit, with a little bit of luck, you'll never work," and said, "Now everyone, just stay nice and calm, and this will all be over in—" Bang!

He suddenly jerked, let out a short scream, and fell off the counter onto the floor. The clown in the scary mask frantically looked around and then ran out the front door. Pat was on his feet immediately and picked the pistol up off the floor.

The clown was groaning and rocking back and forth. Taylor hurried over, pulled the Ronald McDonald mask off his face, and said, "Uncle Eli?"

Forty-four

The blonde woman in scrubs turned out to be a surgical nurse and attended to Eli Cummings.

"So let me get this straight, Haskell. You're telling me it was a coincidence that you just happened to be here in the bank when the robbery occurred?" Detective Manning asked again.

"I already told you, Manning. This is my bank. I've had an account here ever since I was in high school. We were opening an account for my friend Taylor, who—"

"Who just happens to be the nephew of the robber wanted in two previous bank robberies."

"Actually, Manning, I believe it's three previous robberies but go ahead. Taylor has been living with me. He was going to open an account and deposit a check. We were in the process of doing that when those two clowns showed up."

"How convenient."

"What's convenient about this? One of them fired his pistol into the ceiling and told us to get on the floor. Then dumb ass Eli Cummings climbs up on the tellers' counter, slips on a half-eaten candy bar, and shoots himself in the foot. The only thing convenient about this is you were able to arrest Cummings, and with any luck, he'll give up the name of his accomplice."

"Oh yeah, the masked man you watched run across the street and disappear."

"Are you suggesting I should have chased him? The guy had a gun for God's sake."

Aaron LaZelle suddenly appeared and asked, "Did you sign your statement, Dev?"

"Yeah, ten minutes ago."

"That'll do it for now. You're free to go. We have any more questions, we'll give you a call."

"You guys finished with Taylor?"

"Yeah, he's back in the cubicle with the bank officer."

"Pat?"

"Yeah. He's a little upset. Not fun, and then on top of that to be related to the robber. Poor kid."

"He's a good guy, Aaron. He didn't have anything to do with those two idiots."

Aaron nodded and said, "Yeah, that's pretty obvious."

I glanced over at Manning and gave him a, *'Told you so,'* look. "We'll head home. Hope you get the second guy," I said and headed back to Pat's cubicle. Taylor was seated at the desk, talking to Pat. He'd obviously been crying.

"How you guys doing?"

"We're okay, just going through some stuff. Right, Taylor?" Pat said.

Taylor nodded but didn't look at me.

"Any chance we can get that check deposited before we head home?" I asked.

"Yeah, just need your signature because Taylor is under eighteen, and then I'll run it through."

I wrote my signature on the application form and handed it to Pat.

"Give me a couple of minutes," Pat said and hurried over to the tellers counter.

"How are you doing, Taylor?"

He looked up at me and said, "I can't believe that was Uncle Eli. He was robbing the bank while I was trying to open a savings account here. They'll probably keep my check and tell me to get lost."

"Nah, they won't do that. How'd you know that was your uncle wearing the Ronald McDonald mask?"

"He'd sing that 'Little bit of luck' line when he scored big on one of his bets, which wasn't too often. It's a song from My Fair Lady. Of course, he ends up not paying attention and shoots himself in the foot."

"The teller I know, Deb, was eating a candy bar and left half of it on the counter. I guess he stepped on it, slipped, and that's when he shot himself in the foot."

"It figures," Taylor said.

Pat stepped back into the cubicle. "Here you go, Taylor. We look forward to working with you in the future," he said and handed Taylor a deposit receipt.

"Debit card, deposit tickets, and account information should arrive within the next five working days."

Taylor nodded and said, "Thank you."

"Thanks Pat. Anything else you need from us?"

"No, that should cover it. Thanks for stopping in, fellas. I promise next time it won't be quite so crazy."

I waved goodbye to Aaron, ignored pain in the butt Manning, and we headed out the door. We climbed into my car and buckled up. I turned the car on, checked in my rearview mirror, and that's when I saw it. A red Chevrolet Chevelle SS with two, six-inch wide white racing stripes on the hood and a 'chrome breather' to use Lyle's term. I adjusted my rearview mirror, read the license plate, and laughed.

"What's so funny?" Taylor wanted to know.

"Look in the rearview mirror and read the license plate on that souped-up red car behind us."

Taylor leaned over and looked in the mirror. "What the hell? Are you kidding me? The guy's license plate says asshole?"

"Yeah, when you see it in a mirror. I'd better tell Aaron about it. This is the car your uncle grabbed from that Lyle jerk."

"That's the guy that got the pan full of hot chili tossed on his face."

"Oh, really. That explains all the blotches and blisters. Big guy with a shaved head?"

"Yeah, Eli hit him on the head with the pan, knocked him out for a minute, and we ran. Of course, my uncle didn't wait for me."

"I better go back inside and tell Aaron. He'll love this story."

We hurried back inside, waited a few minutes until Aaron was done talking to one of the officers. When they finished, he looked at me and said, "I thought you two left."

"We did, but we found the getaway car."

"What?"

"In the parking lot, I'll show you. Taylor, tell him the story."

Taylor told Aaron about Lyle kicking in the door to their unit and Eli throwing the pan of hot chili in his face, hitting him with the pan, and grabbing Lyle's car keys. I told him about my phone conversation with Lyle and his description of the license plate. At this point, we were standing in front of the car looking at the license plate.

Aaron stood there, shaking his head. "Can this get any crazier? The guy slips on a half-eaten candy bar, shoots himself in the foot, and now this is his getaway car. I'm wondering if that means his partner is still on foot?"

"The way things are going, he's probably still wearing his clown mask."

Forty-five

When we finally got home, Taylor hurried upstairs and began to work on the logo for Dennis's pals. I got a call from Barbara and gave
her an update on the day's activities.

"Is Taylor all right?"

"Yeah, he's fine. Right now, he's upstairs working
on a logo for some guys business. I guess the guy is going to stop over tonight and look at whatever he comes
up with."

"My God, Dev, someone attempting to steal an
ATM in the middle of the night. A bank robber shoots
himself in the foot this afternoon. I guess life is never
dull if you're around."

"To be honest, a few dull days would be just fine
with me."

"How's the nose? Are you healing?"

"Yeah, slow but sure. The black and blue isn't quite
as bad as forty-eight hours ago. A few more days and I
should be pretty much back to normal."

"Whatever that is in your world," she said. "Do you
think you'll be able to join us next week in detention?"

"I'm counting on it. The swelling is pretty much gone, and the black and blue is slowly but surely beginning to fade."

"Honest to God, Dev, it all seems so crazy." She more or less finished on that note and hung up.

I heated up some stew and called Taylor downstairs. It was getting close to 8:00, and after twenty minutes, I filled a bowl and brought it up to him. He was at the desk working on the logo for Dennis' friend. There were four different versions sketched out in colored pencil on the desk.

"Hey, Taylor. That guy is going to be here in a few minutes. You better wolf down this stew." I looked at the images he'd sketched out. "This guy's business is called Alley Katz? What is it, some new bar?"

"No, Dev, it's—" Suddenly, someone pounded on the front door. "Oh man, that must be him," Taylor said. He gathered up the sketches and flew out of the room. I was right behind him. There was more heavy pounding on the front door as we rushed down the stairs.

"Tell that guy to take it easy on my front door," I said as Taylor hurried over to the door and opened it. He suddenly flew back and landed on the floor. A second later, Tubby's thug, Lyle, stepped into the entry, followed by two other goons.

"What the hell do you think you're doing? Get your ass—" I was suddenly on the floor next to Taylor.

"Shut up, Haskell. Get them up off the floor," Lyle shouted, and the two goons grabbed hold of our shirts and yanked us up. "Bring them into the back of the house," Lyle said, and they pushed us back toward the kitchen. Morton scurried past and headed upstairs.

Taylor clutched his sketches and hurried ahead of me.

"Lyle," I said. "What the hell are you doing? Are you crazy?"

"Where's my car for starters, and then I want the money you stole from that bank."

"Stole from the bank? What are you talking about?"

"I got it on good authority you two were there while punk ass's uncle robbed the place. I want your half."

"Our half? Are you crazy? We didn't take any money. Eli Cummings shot himself in the foot, and his partner ran—"

"Cut the bullshit, Haskell. They drove my car there and—"

"Yeah, and the police took it down to the impound lot. We don't have it. We don't have any money. And we don't know what in the hell you're talking about."

"So, you're calling me a liar," Lyle shouted and then glanced nervously at the two goons.

"I'm telling you we don't have any money. We don't have your damn car. And we don't—"

Lyle grabbed me by the shirt. Taylor grabbed the boiling stew pot off the stove and poured the contents over Lyle's head. He wound up, slammed the pan into Lyle's forehead, and Lyle dropped to the floor.

"You're going to get your assed kicked, kid," the larger of the goons growled.

"Is there a problem here?" a voice said from behind. The goons turned to face four very large guys with shaved heads and long beards. They wore black leather vests, exposing muscular arms and lots of ink.

"You're Taylor, right? You okay?" one of the guys asked.

Taylor nodded and set the empty pan back on the stove.

Lyle groaned and began to move his head back and forth. The largest of the four in the black leather vests stepped over and bent down next to Lyle. He pulled Lyle's shirt from his belt and used it to wipe some of the stew from his face.

"I recognize you. You're that worthless Lyle bitch. You drive that pain-in-the-ass red car with the racing stripes, don't you?"

Lyle groaned, and his eyes fluttered open.

"That's what we're looking for. We think these two got Lyle's car," one of the goons said and stepped back, putting some distance between him and the leather vests.

"I already told you. The cops took the car. It's down in the impound lot," I said.

The guy in the vest stood and said, "Sounds to me like you got your answer. Might be wise to pick up this piece of shit," he said, placing a large black boot on top of Lyle's righthand. "He could get hurt just lying on the floor," he said as he ground the hand back and forth beneath his boot. Lyle groaned and rolled to his side in an attempt to pull his hand out from beneath the boot. We could actually hear the bones in his hand breaking. The same hand that had been caught in the rat trap in my file drawer the week before.

The two goons stood wide-eyed, not sure what to do.

Eventually, the guy lifted his boot, and Lyle rolled onto his back holding his right wrist and whimpering.

"You best get him out of here and don't plan on coming back, ever. We hear you even drove past this place, we're going to come looking for you. Now get your ass out of here."

The goons quickly picked Lyle up off the floor and headed for the front door. The other three guys in vests followed them out.

"So, you're Taylor. My pals call me Doc," the guy said and held out a hand to Taylor. They shook, and the guy looked over at me. "You must be Hassle," he said and nodded but didn't extend a hand.

"Yeah, very nice to meet you. Good timing. Are you a doctor?" I asked.

He shook his head. "I can't abide violence. Name is short for Doctor Death," he said but didn't go into any detail. I didn't see any point in commenting.

"Really liked the work you did down at Inkredible. Our pal Dennis spoke very highly of you."

"Thanks," Taylor said. "I enjoyed doing the work for him. He was very nice."

"Yeah, and a hell of an artist, which is why we're here," he said as the other three guys strolled back into the kitchen.

"They're gone. Doubt they'll be back," one of them said.

"You got a drawing to show us?" Doctor Death asked.

"Yeah. Actually, I worked on five of them. Feel free to suggest or change anything you don't like. I tried to include everything you told me over the phone," Taylor said. He laid out five different sheets, each with a different drawing. All emblazoned with the name Alley Katz. The designs had a large image of different looking cats some vicious some almost cartoon like.

"Oh, my God. These are fantastic. You digging these?" he said to the three guys standing behind him.

"Each one's better than the next," one of them said.

"Fantastic," another said.

"Would it be all right if I took these and showed them to our members? I could have them back to you in a day or so."

"That would be fine. Take your time," Taylor said.

"I can give you a partial payment now if you'd like."

"No worries. We can settle up once you've made a decision. Just give me a call whenever you're ready."

"Thanks, Taylor. Dennis wasn't kidding. You're great." Doctor Death held out a fist the size of a ten-pound ham, they butted fists, and we all walked toward the front door.

I wasn't sure if we'd see Lyle and his two goons. Fortunately, they were nowhere in sight. "Thanks again, Taylor," Doctor Death called and waved as they headed down the porch steps. He slid the sketches into a saddlebag hanging over the rear wheel on one of the four Harleys parked on the street. They climbed onto the bikes, fired them up, and headed down the street.

"What a day," I said.

"You're telling me. They're going to pay me two hundred bucks for that logo."

"Actually, I was referring to the bank robbery, nutcase Lyle, and now the Alley Katz motorcycle club."

"Yeah, they were nice guys."

"Well, their timing was perfect. I'm going to clean up that stew on the kitchen floor. Good move, by the way."

"Yeah, I didn't like that Lyle guy. As soon as I saw him, I recognized him. He's the guy my uncle threw the chili on and hit over the head with the pan."

"I don't think anyone likes Lyle, Taylor."

When I wasn't sipping a glass of wine, I was mopping up the kitchen floor. Taylor was drowning his troubles in a bottle of root beer and finishing up a grilled cheese sandwich.

"Hey, Dev, sorry I wasted the stew on that loser, Lyle."

"You're not going to hear a complaint from me. That jerk had it coming."

Once I had the kitchen back to normal and Taylor's plate in the dishwasher, we settled in front of the TV and watched a movie on Netflix that I'd seen before. We were both in bed at eleven.

Forty-six

Thankfully, we had a quiet weekend. Annette came over for dinner on Saturday night. She and Taylor talked art for close to four hours, and I pretended to follow the conversation. Taylor worked on his paper all day Sunday.

Monday morning, we were just getting ready to head out to the car when we heard a loud rumble outside. "Now what?" I said and hurried to the front door.

There must have been two dozen guys on Harleys in the process of backing them up against the street curb in front of the house. We opened the door and stepped out onto the front porch. Doctor Death had just climbed off his bike, and he gave a wave. Taylor waved back as the mob followed Doctor Death up the front sidewalk and stopped at the porch.

"You decide which design you want?" Taylor asked.

Doctor Death nodded and said, "Yeah, we chose one, but we'd like to hang on to all five of the samples. Be nice to have 'em framed and hanging in the club-house."

"Sure thing, I'd be honored," Taylor said.

"Well, I got your money right here," Doctor said as he reached into his pocket. He pulled out a roll of twenty dollar bills with a rubber band around them and tossed it up to Taylor. "Little something extra in there. Payment for the other four designs."

"Oh, man thanks. Much appreciated," Taylor said.

"You busy tonight?" Doctor asked.

"You kidding? It's Monday night. I don't have anything going."

"Good, then you'll have time to come over to our clubhouse and be made an honorary member. Long as that's okay with you, Hassle," he said.

"It's up to Taylor. Whatever he decides."

"Oh, that would be so cool. What time do you want me there?"

"Say 8:00, be nice if you dressed in black. A note with the address is in with your payment."

"We'll be there," I said.

They climbed back on their bikes, fired them up, and headed down the street.

"Taylor, I don't know man. You seem to be leading a charmed life. Let's get you to school. I'll pick you up after school, and we can maybe get you a proper shirt for tonight. You can wear your black jeans.

He was all smiles when I dropped him off. I noticed two guys said hi to him as he headed in the door, and a girl waved. Things seemed to be getting better.

I was waiting for Taylor in the school parking lot when the doors opened and kids started walking out. A couple of guys gave a second look at my car, and I wondered if one of them might have been the one who spray painted 'OINK' on the side. Taylor came out the door about five minutes later and headed for the car.

He yelled something to a group. They laughed, and one of them yelled something back. He climbed in, and we headed out of the parking lot.

"How'd the day go?" I asked.

"It was pretty good. A couple guys invited me to sit with them at lunch. It was the first time I didn't have to eat alone."

"That's good. You tell them about tonight?"

"About being made an honorary member of Alley Katz? No. I was afraid they'd think I was lying, so I didn't mention it."

"Probably a good idea. I've got a thought about a shirt. Let me take you to a store. If you don't like what they have we can head out to the mall and grab something."

Fifteen minutes later we pulled in front of a white building with orange trim, the Harley Davidson store.

"We're buying a motorcycle?" Taylor asked.

"No, but they've got all sorts of t-shirts that would be perfect to wear tonight. No pressure."

He seemed to think about that for a nanosecond then grinned and said, "This'll be so cool."

If we looked at one, we must have looked at fifty different t-shirts. At the end of the day, Taylor settled on the second shirt he looked at. A black t-shirt with an orange Harley Davidson logo in the front. Rather than put it in a bag, he wore it out of the store.

We went home, and Taylor took Morton for a walk while I got dinner ready. By the time they were back, I was ready to dish up our meal. Taylor was too excited to eat much, so I finished his portion. We headed over to the Alley Katz clubhouse and arrived maybe five minutes early. The parking lot was full of Harleys and we had to park out on the street.

The clubhouse was a one-story white-stucco structure with a red neon sign on the roof that read ALLEY KATZ CLUBHOUSE. The sign flashed off and on. I found it interesting that there were nice flowers planted along the front of the building.

I held the door for Taylor, and we walked into a sea of black leather. All shapes and sizes, both men and women were jammed into the place. We turned a few heads as we entered.

A guy stepped out of the crowd. I recognized him from the other night at my place. He shook hands with Taylor and gave me a friendly nod. "Follow me. Doctor Death and the crew are in a back room."

We made our way through the crowd. Taylor got a couple of pats on the back from guys and someone pinched my butt. We walked through a door marked 'PRIVATE' and entered a room with Doctor Death and five other guys sitting around a table. Everyone had an open file in front of them, and clearly, a meeting was going on.

Doctor Death looked up as we entered the room and said, "Ahh, Taylor, perfect, right on time." Apparently, that was the sign to close the files in front of them. Everyone stood and came over and introduced themselves. Taylor got a fist bump from everyone, and I got a couple of nods.

"Have them get ready out there," Doctor Death said to one of the guys who immediately headed out to the main room. They chatted some more with Taylor and ignored me. The entire time, the smile never left Taylor's face.

After maybe fifteen minutes, the guy popped his head in the room and gave the thumbs-up. "Okay, looks like they're ready out there. Let's suit up," Doctor Death said. He walked over to a closet, opened the door, and began handing out what looked like judges robes. They slipped them on and lined up at the door. Doctor Death was at the front of the line, and he signaled Taylor to join him. "Hassle, follow us out at a distance. This is gonna be all about Taylor."

I smiled and gave Taylor the thumbs-up.

Doctor Death opened the door, and they stepped into the main room. The lights were off, and everyone held a lit candle. It was quiet as they walked through the crowd toward the front of the room. The guys from the meeting formed a half-circle and had Taylor face them. The crowd inched forward. I stood in the back.

Doctor Death looked around the room and said, "I want to thank you all for being here tonight. We're honored to welcome a talented young man, Taylor Cummings, into our fold. Taylor, you may not know this, but take a look around. You're in a room full of misfits. We're the oddballs. We were the kids no one wanted to be with. The girls no one called for a date. The guys who didn't have friends. We were the kids who sat alone on the bus. We were alone at lunch. We're the kids everyone laughed at and scorned, the Alley Katz. They did that because, in our own way, each and everyone of us had a talent that no one could compete with. You've blessed us with your talent."

"Biggy?" he called, and suddenly the crowd separated, and five guys walked in holding picture frames with Taylor's sketches of the Alley Katz logos. The guy named Biggy looked about a foot shorter than Taylor. Dennis Richardson was carrying one of the frames, and he nodded and winked at Taylor.

"These images will be mounted on the wall here for everyone to see. They'll remind us what we can accomplish if we just put our mind to it. With this, we make you an honorary member. You're welcome here anytime. If you ever have a problem, no matter what, we will be here to help you. It's what we do."

A woman stepped out of the crowd and handed Doctor Death a black leather vest. He grinned and held the vest up, displaying the logo Taylor had designed stitched onto the back. The words Alley Katz across the top. What looked like an orange moon and a black cat peering out.

"This is our first vest with your logo. It's only fitting it should belong to you, Taylor. I might also mention Inkredible is offering the image at a discount." Everyone clapped and cheered as Doctor Death held the vest out for Taylor to slip on. They shook hands and suddenly, the lights came on, and the candles were blown out. Taylor shook hands and butted fists with people for the next ten minutes.

Two guys I recognized approached me, Mike Casey and Buster Brown, both cops. "Hey, Dev, good to see you."

"What are you guys doing here?"

"What are you talking about?" Buster said. "We're members, you idiot."

"But I thought—"

"What? You thought the club was some kind of criminal enterprise? Wrong again."

"What Doctor Death said is correct, a lot of bright folks who didn't fit in as kids. Some of us still don't fit in," Casey said and they both laughed.

"Yeah, but Doctor Death, what does he do?"

"You kidding? He teaches mortuary science. You wouldn't want to cross him, but he's a brain."

We didn't make it home until late. Taylor said he was sore after shaking hands with so many people. He headed up to his room while I got things ready for the morning. I went up to bed maybe a half-hour later. Taylor was sound asleep and still wearing his vest. Morton was sacked out next to him.

Forty-seven

I was up early the next morning. I woke Taylor and Morton at seven and let Morton out while Taylor hit the shower. I made pancakes for breakfast, and Taylor wolfed them down.

While I cleaned up, Taylor went back upstairs. I grabbed my car keys and called upstairs to Taylor. He came downstairs wearing his Alley Katz vest.

"Maybe you shouldn't wear that to school today. You don't want someone stealing it and trying to wreck it."

"I have to wear it, Dev. The Alley Katz are giving me a ride to school."

"The Alley Katz? Hey look, Taylor, last night was great, and they're a nice bunch of folks, but don't you think—" I was cut off by the rumble out in the street.

Taylor glanced out the window and said, "Oh good, they're here. Dev, they came here to give me a ride to school. I want to go with them. I earned this."

There was a knock on the door, and Taylor opened it. Biggy smiled and said, "You all set for your victory ride?"

Behind him stood Buster Brown and Mike Casey, the cops I knew. Buster smiled and said," Doc is over at the school now. He wanted to meet with them just to tell them we'd be giving Taylor a ride to school, so they know what's going on."

I was outnumbered by about twenty to one. "Okay, Taylor. Enjoy your ride. Have a good day at school. Call me if you need a ride home."

"Thanks, Dev," he said, gave me a hug, and headed out the door.

Buster looked at me and said, "Relax Dev. He'll be fine. We've done this before. It's a real win for the kid."

I watched them fire up their bikes. Fortunately, Taylor climbed on behind someone larger than Biggy. I counted twenty-three motorcycles as they drove down the street.

I put Morton in the car, and we headed to the office. Louie wasn't in, so I made a fresh pot of coffee. I had just filled my mug when my phone rang. Barbara Wright.

"Hello Barbara, how are you this morning?"

"I'm fine. More importantly, how are you?"

"Good. Things seemed to have calmed down somewhat."

"How is Taylor?"

"He's doing very well." I went on to tell her about the Alley Katz.

"A motorcycle gang?"

"Not a gang. A club. They've got two cops I know who are members. The head of the club is a doctor who teaches. Very nice people, plus, they really like Taylor's artwork. We all need a win from time to time."

"We certainly do. Are you coming to detention this evening?"

Once again, I'd completely forgotten about it. "Yeah, I was planning on it. It's not canceled, is it?" I asked, crossing my fingers.

"No, it's not canceled, Dev. We would love to see you there."

"I'll be there," I said, and we disconnected.

Louie sent me a text after the noon hour, telling me he was going to be tied up in court for the rest of the day. I was just about to take Morton for our walk when a black SUV pulled up across the street. I watched as Fat Freddy and Tubby Gustafson hurried across the street and into the building. A moment later, the stairs began to creak and groan.

Fat Freddy opened the door and then stepped aside as Tubby waddled in. Freddy pulled out the chair for Tubby, who immediately collapsed in it. Freddy took a seat, and I watched both of them gasping for breath.

Eventually, Tubby said, "Once again, Haskell, you've been keeping something from me."

"No, Mr. Gustafson, I swear, I have not kept anything from you. I—"

"I understand a dear young man is staying with you, and he has just been made a member of the Alley Katz motorcycle club."

I was about to correct Tubby and say honorary member but decided against it.

"These are the sort of things I need to know about, Haskell. Never enough time in the world to be congratulated for our accomplishments. Would the young man happen to be around?" Tubby asked and glanced over at Louie's picnic table.

"No sir. He's at school, as a matter of fact, escorted by about two-dozen Alley Katz bikers. After the incident with Lyle a few days back, they've taken a very protective stance with Taylor. Actually, on both of us," I said, hoping Tubby got the message.

"Well, we just wanted to stop by and give him our congratulations," Tubby said. "Such a promising young man."

"I'll be sure to tell him you were here, sir."

"Yes, and you needn't be concerned about Lyle. He's— well, let's just say he won't be inserting himself again. Frederick," Tubby said. Fat Freddy jumped to his feet and pulled the chair back.

I watched out the window as they waddled across the street. Fat Freddy held the car door open for Tubby. For the first time ever, Fat Freddy didn't look up at me and give me the finger. He simply climbed in behind the wheel, and they drove up the street.

Taylor sent me a text to say he was waiting outside school for a ride whenever I could pick him up. I texted him back, telling him I was on my way. I saw him leaning against the building as I pulled into the parking lot. Morton was in the back seat, pacing back and forth by the time I pulled over. He began licking Taylor as soon as he climbed into the passenger seat.

"Hey, how was the ride over this morning?" I asked.

"Oh, it was a lot of fun. It was really cool when we got here. They lined up along the edge of the parking lot, and everyone was just watching and checking me out as I went into school. I really liked it. The school let me wear the vest all day but said it would probably be a good idea to leave it at home in the future."

"I'm glad everything worked out. Hey, I'm going to serve dinner a little early today. I forgot I have to do detention tonight from six to eight."

"Not a problem. Oh, I got an A on my paper. I wrote about Vincent Van Gogh."

"Way to go. Well done."

We ate an early dinner, and I headed off to detention. Everyone was chatting about the Alley Katz delivering a kid to school that morning. It was a positive-sounding conversation, and I didn't mention anything. Barbara smiled and gave me a wink but never mentioned Taylor to the others. Even Harold Kennedy was mildly pleasant. I had a steady stream of students at my table. All of them eventually asked about the Alley Katz and, in one way or another, hinted that they'd like to get a ride to school. Ramona Williams stopped in and gave me the paper on <u>To Kill A Mockingbird</u>.

When we were finally finished, I chatted for a couple of minutes with the adults. I checked to make sure Barbara had her phone and handed her *'my'* paper on <u>To Kill A Mockingbird</u>.

"Oh, Dev, this is wonderful."

"I loved the book, Barbara," I lied.

"Well, I have to be honest. I really didn't think you'd do it. Thank you. I'll go over it tomorrow."

I begged off meeting at Tiffany's Sports Lounge and headed home.

I called Taylor's name once I stepped into the house, and he answered from upstairs. I climbed the stairs and stepped into the guest room. He was working at the desk, and Morton was stretched out on the bed. There were a number of rough landscape sketches scattered across the desk.

"Oh, working on landscapes now?" I asked and leaned against the doorframe.

Taylor looked up at me and smiled. "Annette called tonight."

"Annette, were you able to score us dinner at her place?"

"That's not why she called," he said, staring at the floor.

"What's up? What's wrong, Taylor?"

"Nothing's wrong. Good news, actually. I ummm, I guess I got that scholarship. I can move in there this coming weekend."

"You did? Oh, that's great, man. Congratulations," I said and then felt the lump in my throat. "I'm really happy, and I'm so proud of you, Taylor. You've overcome a lot to get to this," I said as my eyes began to water. "You gotta do this. It's the ticket to a whole new world, man."

"Yeah, I know. I'm really happy, but I couldn't have done this without you giving me a place to—"

"Taylor, you've always got a place here. That's never going to change. Congratulations! You earned it with that magnificent portrait of me."

"Yeah, I guess. I'll do another one of you now that your nose is more or less back to normal."

We stayed up and chatted until after midnight. Largely Taylor opening up about his life. His parents were killed in a car crash when he was an infant. His uncle Eli gambled, had a history of bad decisions, and, as it turned out, was a mediocre painter. Taylor was the one with the painting gene. I drove him to school for the next few days. I spent the better part of an hour on Friday arranging for his records to be transferred to the Art Academy. We had Annette and Barbara over for dinner on Friday night. I served prime rib with all the trimmings and an apple pie for dessert. When our guests left, I cleaned up the kitchen, and Taylor grabbed a couple of paper grocery bags to pack his clothes.

I went upstairs ten minutes later, pulled my suitcase from the bedroom closet, and took it into the guest room. "Here, Taylor. You're not launching yourself into the world with your clothes packed in grocery bags. Take this suitcase."

"Are you sure, Dev?"

"Very sure. You earned it. You just remember you've been accepted to the Art Academy because of the work you've done and the talent you have."

"Well, and because of Annette and—"

"Hey, Taylor, I'm going to let you in on a little secret. I'll admit Annette was a good contact. But at the end of the day, it isn't someone pulling strings. It's your talent and what you do with it. You did the work. They were impressed enough to want you there and offer a scholarship in the hope you would take them up on their offer. Don't sell yourself short. There's enough people in the world waiting to do that. Your job is to prove them wrong."

We were at the Art Academy at 10:00 Saturday morning. There were maybe a dozen kids in various stages of moving in. Taylor just had the one suitcase to unpack, so it didn't take very long. He had just placed his Alley Katz vest in the closet when the door opened, and a guy stepped into the room.

"You must be Taylor," he said and held out his hand. "I'm David. Looks like we're going to be roomies for a bit. I'm from Chicago. Where are you from?"

"Kind of all over."

"Mmm-mmm, we all really dig your portrait. Great piece." He glanced over at me. "Are you the guy with the black eyes and nose?"

"Yeah, that was me, David. Nice to meet you."

"Hey, I'm meeting some of the gang in the lab building. Why don't you come with me, Taylor? Be a great chance to meet a bunch of us. Everyone will want to ask you about the portrait. We all thought it was really cool."

"I don't know. Dev, did you want to—"

"Go on, Taylor. That sounds a lot better than having to waste your time with a senior citizen like me. David, nice to meet you. Taylor, now don't be a stranger. The door is always open," I said and held out my hand.

He took my hand, wrapped his arms around me, and we hugged for a long moment. "I'll never forget what you've done for me, Dev. Never." We had watery eyes and sniffles as we pulled apart.

"I'll leave you guys to it. Enjoy and stay in touch," I said. I walked out to my car and then sat behind the wheel for five minutes. I had Taylor for a couple of weeks. How the hell did parents do this after raising a kid for seventeen years?

Epilogue

I drove home, took Morton for a walk, and made a sandwich with leftover prime rib for dinner. I watched a movie on Netflix and headed up to bed. Morton wandered into the guest room, looked around for Taylor, and then whined. "Yeah, he's a good guy, Morton. We're both going to miss him."

I glanced at the desk, and there was an envelope with my name on it. I opened the envelope and pulled out a piece of paper folded in half. On one side was a lovely sketch of flowers, roses and daisies, and on the inside was a simple note.

Thank you, Dev.

I hope I'll be able to help someone like you've helped me.

Taylor

I continued attending the detention meetings and had a steady stream of students. Barbara handed back the paper Ramona Williams wrote for me. She gave me an 'F' with an exclamation point. It was written in red marker and circled.

"An 'F'? Why? I spent a lot of time on this."

She shook her head and said, "Oh please, some things never change. You copied it word for word from the Cliff Notes, Dev." She gave an audible exhale and said, "We've got a lot of work to do."

Annette called me about a week and a half later, and I invited her over for dinner. We were having a dessert wine in the den, talking about Taylor.

"Have you heard from him?" she asked.

"Oh yeah, a couple of phone calls. He sent me a text yesterday. He's getting on, very busy, and more importantly, he has friends. Maybe the school is a version of the Alley Katz."

"I'm not following."

"You know, the kids at the Academy are all talented. Maybe not everyone, but certainly a number of them were probably social outcasts in schools. Now they're in a school where that's a common bond. Just like his roommate, David. He gave Taylor more social interaction in ten minutes than he would have gotten in a month in high school."

"And his artwork. Think what he'll be able to create."

"Yeah, truly talented. He sketched roses and daises on a card he left for me."

"Mmm-mmm, speaking of which, did I tell you I had some work done on one of his sketches?"

"Work done? No, you didn't."

"Let me show you," she said, stood, and unzipped her skirt. She let it fall to the floor and then turned around. There, across the lower portion of her back were the two blue hummingbirds facing one another that she had designed. Below them was a chain of roses and daisies, just like the one he'd sketched on my card, only running all the way across her lower back.

"What do you think?" she said.

"What's not to like Annette? They're gorgeous."

"I think they'd look even better up in your bedroom…"

The End

Hope you enjoyed the read. Thanks for taking the time to read **Alley Katz**. If you enjoyed the read and leave a review I'm indie published so your review really helps.

Thank you, much appreciated…

Don't miss the sample of **The Big Gamble,** the next book in the Dev Haskell series, on the following page.

Sneak Peek

The Big Gamble

Second Edition

MIKE FARICY

Alley Katz ◆ 333

Prologue–June 2018

The minister forced a smile and said, "Ladies and gentlemen, I would like to present, for the first time, Mr. and Mrs. Colton Ferral." There was a pause before a few hands slowly applauded. "You may kiss the bride."

Colton wrapped his arms around Maddie in a bear hug, plastered his mouth over her lips, and bent her backward. He held that position for an uncomfortably long time. There were a couple of gasps. Maddie finally beat her bouquet against his shoulder three or four times before he uprighted her. He ran the back of his hand over his mouth and grinned.

The minister leaned forward, said something to the couple, and they left the altar. As they headed out of the church, Colton gave the thumbs-up with both hands. Maddie had a look on her face suggesting, *'Someone do something, please.'*

I was seated in the back, watching more than a few heads shaking as the couple made their way down the aisle. The minister fled into a side room, and the congregation began to follow the wedding couple out of the sanctuary. Maddie's eyes flared for a half-second as she spotted me. Her new husband sneered, pulled her arm, and they disappeared out the door.

Her parents looked heartbroken. Both her sisters appeared to be in shock. Since I was seated in the back, I was one of the last people to exit.

Her parents were accepting congratulations, or maybe it was condolences, in the vestibule. Apparently, the groom's mother had already left. I waited as the line slowly moved forward. Finally, facing her folks, I said, "Hi, Mr. and Mrs. McGuire. I'm Dev Haskell. Congratulations on the wedding. Colton's a lucky guy. Maddie's a wonderful woman."

"Haskell? You went to high school with Madeline. I thought you were in the army?" her mother said.

"I was, but now I'm back in town."

Her father shook his head and said, "This guy makes even you look good."

"Terrence, now stop. That's enough. Nice to see you again. Thank you for coming, Mr. Hassle," her mother said and turned to the elderly couple behind me. I saw no point in correcting her on my name.

I'd been surprised to receive the wedding invitation, debated about attending, and in the end, skipped the reception and headed down to a new bar I recently discovered.

This year
One

It was cold outside. Morton and I hurried into The Spot. The temperature had dropped to around ten, and we were only halfway through the eight inches of snow forecast. I closed the door behind us and stomped my feet, knocking off the snow. Morton spotted my office mate, Louie Laufen, sitting on his usual stool at the end of the bar.

Louie gave Morton a nod and proceeded to open a bag of pork rinds. Morton took off, damn near pulling my arm out of the socket as he made his way toward Louie. His tail bounced off every other person standing at the bar.

"Well, Morton, thank you for helping Dev find his way across the street. How are you? Did you miss me over the last fifteen minutes?" Louie said, leaned over, and served up a handful of pork rinds. Morton had licked his hand clean in a second or two and was searching the floor for any errant crumbs.

"Usual, Dev?" Mike, the bartender, asked.

"Yeah, a Summit, and you better give Louie a refill, so I don't have to listen to him bitching."

"Still snowing outside?" Louie asked.

"Afraid so. Not looking forward to shoveling this stuff tomorrow morning. How'd your case go this afternoon?"

"About what I expected. License revoked, and my client will be spending weekends locked up. It was his second DUI, and they don't look kindly on that."

"Wasn't he going to agree to treatment?"

"Correct, he was. It seems he had a last-minute change of heart, even after I warned him. I get paid whether or not he follows my advice, but apparently, he knows the system better than I do. What were you working on?"

"Just verifying information on job applications for my insurance client. You know, where people worked and how long. I'm checking on arrest records, DUIs, the usual bit. It's boring work, but who cares? I wish I had a few thousand additional applications to verify."

"Things still slow?" Louie asked, just as Mike delivered the drinks.

I pulled out the last two bills in my wallet, a ten and a one, and gave them to Mike. "Keep the change, Mike."

"Gee, thanks," he said and gave me a look.

"You know, you and Morton are rattling around in that big old house. You ever think of doing an Airbnb or something?"

"Airbnb? No thanks. I don't want to be cooking meals for folks. Having to listen to someone complain that the sheets aren't starched, or the towels aren't soft."

"You might want to check it out, Dev. I don't think it's like that. From what I read, the vast majority of guests are pretty nice and not demanding. You could set out some fruit and cold cereal for breakfast, and that's all they expect. They aren't looking for some fancy. over the top place. That's why they aren't booking into a hotel. You could pick up maybe seventy-five bucks a day for pretty much doing nothing except changing sheets."

"You don't have to cook them dinner?"

"No, not at all, and with a restaurant right across the street and a half-dozen other places within walking distance, you'd be the perfect location. Think about it, historic neighborhood, close to downtown, fifteen minutes from the airport. You'd be a natural."

"Hmm-mmm, I might have to give it some thought."

Louie bought a round, gave Morton the rest of the pork rinds, and we were home an hour later. It was still snowing, and I was glad there wasn't much traffic. I grabbed some leftover pizza from the fridge, settled in front of the TV, and opened my mail. There were four envelopes. One was a schedule for the next six months of recycling pick up. The other three were bills, one of which I'd apparently missed last month. Now I had two monthly payments plus a past due charge. I could make the payment, but I'd be running on financial fumes for the next week or two.

Louie's Airbnb suggestion started bouncing around in my thick skull. After thirty minutes of failing to focus on the movie I'd chosen, I wandered upstairs and looked at my spare room. The double bed featured a pile of summer clothes I'd tossed there two months ago—same thing with the sandals and tennis shoes scattered on the floor. The chest of drawers was filled with clothes I hadn't worn in over three years. The top drawer held, among other things, four framed photos of women who had dumped me over the years.

The closet was no different. I couldn't even remember where or when I got the tux. There were four out-of-date sport coats and a half-dozen ties I figured were mine, although it had been so long since I'd worn them, I couldn't be sure. Two of the ties played a Christmas carol when squeezed. There was a small pile of lingerie on the closet shelf, all different sizes.

I began carrying everything downstairs and piling it by the front door. I'd donate it all to a facility tomorrow. I went online to the Airbnb site and registered.

The following morning, I was up early and ran the snowblower on the driveway and sidewalks. I loaded up the car with old clothes, left Morton in the kitchen. We'd gotten almost nine inches of snow overnight, and there was a snow emergency in effect. One of the benefits of living on a busy street is we're one of the first streets plowed.

I backed out of the garage, down the driveway, and headed to the donation site. All the clothes were clearly going to waste, collecting dust in my spare room. Hopefully, someone would get some value from them. I drove back home, grabbed Morton, and we headed down to the office.

Louie was at his picnic table desk tapping keys on his computer. "Sleeping in late?" he asked without looking up.

"Actually, no. Hard as it may be to believe, I took your advice from last night."

"You're running an ad on the Hot Hookups dating site?"

"No, I'm going to do Airbnb. I just took all the clothes out of my spare room and donated them this morning. There's a double bed in the room. I'll pick up a couple sets of sheets and some new pillows. I probably should get some bath towels too, come to think of it. Anyway, I'll be up and running in no time. Thanks for the idea."

"You're really going to do this?"

"Yeah, I checked it out online. Based on what I have to offer, you know, one room, I'm limited on what I can charge. But, with some coffee, fruit, and cereal in the morning, it's not like I'll have to be cooking breakfast, lunch, and dinner. This is going to be good. Thanks again for the tip."

"My pleasure. I didn't really think you'd want to do it. Good for you, Dev. It may be just the thing to get a somewhat even cash flow going in your life."

"We'll see. I'm looking forward to it. I've got a couple of things to line up, starting with I have to get a key for the lock to the room. The lock in the door is original, so it's a hundred and forty years old, but I got a pal in the lock biz. In fact, I should give him a call, now."

"Good luck."

I ended up leaving a message for Reggie, my locksmith pal. I fooled around in the office, made a couple of phone calls, and took Morton on a short walk. Reggie called me back just before 4:00.

"Yeah, Dev, returning your call. You locked out of the house again?"

"Surprisingly, no." I went on to explain what I needed.

"Shouldn't be a problem. This is the original door hardware, right?"

"Yeah, as far as I know. I'm thinking one of those skeleton keys."

"Yeah, probably. You home now?"

"No, but I can be there in about ten minutes."

"Take your time. I'll be there in a half-hour."

"Just pull into the driveway. I'll park in the garage," I said, and we disconnected.

TWO

True to his word, Reggie pulled into the driveway a half-hour later. He opened the rear of his white paneled van, grabbed two small boxes and a tool belt, and headed to the front porch. I was watching him and opened the door as he climbed up the steps.

"This snow could leave anytime, and it would be okay with me," Reggie said and stomped his feet on the porch before he stepped inside.

"With any luck, four more months, and most of it should be gone."

"Yeah, right," he laughed. "Want me to take my shoes off?"

"No, don't worry about it. Come on upstairs," I said, and we headed up to my spare room.

"So, you're going to be renting this out?"

"I'm gonna try Airbnb. Maybe have someone in here for one or two nights. Renting the room to someone for an extended period would be more of a pain for me."

"Well, you got a nice place, in a nice part of town, so you should do all right." He was down on his knees, shining a flashlight into the keyhole. He nodded as he examined the exposed lock mechanism. "Yeah, pretty standard cast iron horizontal rim lock. With any luck, I got just what you need," he said and opened one of the small boxes. It was full of brass skeleton keys. He inserted a key in the lock and turned it. A brass deadbolt suddenly appeared on the side of the door.

"Oh, man. That's great," I said.

"Yeah, chances are this hasn't been operated since the first world war. Let me just squirt some graphite in there to make sure it remains operational," he said, then produced a small tube and squirted some black powder into the lock.

"I'll leave this graphite with you. The key is fifteen bucks. I'd recommend you get three or four of them. They have a habit of disappearing."

"Better give me four," I said.

He smiled at that, pulled out three more keys from the box, and handed them to me. "Cash, check, or credit card, whatever is easiest for you."

"Credit card would probably be the best," I said, remembering my bank balance. "Can I talk you into a beer?"

He checked his watch, nodded, and said, "Yeah, I can do that."

We headed down to the kitchen. I handed him my credit card and grabbed two beers out of the refrigerator. He pushed some buttons on a white credit card machine not much bigger than my cellphone, and I inserted my card. A moment later, my paper receipt rolled out, sixty bucks for the keys and another sixty for the house call. A hundred and twenty bucks total. I couldn't rent the room without a key, so I chalked it up to the cost of doing business.

We stood in the kitchen sipping beers. Reggie told me he was making an Airbnb call at least once a week. Folks like myself just getting started or homes needing more keys or, in some cases, new locks.

He left after one beer. I put three keys in a kitchen cabinet and placed the fourth one in the lock on the spare room door. I climbed in my car and drove to a discount store where I picked up two pillows, two sets of sheets, and two prints on canvas, a sky with clouds and a stream in a forest. I was tempted to get the naked blonde woman sitting in a giant martini glass but, after some internal debate, decided that may not be the best idea.

Three

I was on my computer the next morning when the phone rang. The number came up as 'unknown.' "Dev Haskell," was how I answered, thinking if I said Haskell Investigations, it might scare a potential Airbnb customer away.

"Hey, Dev, it's Wink," the voice on the other end said.

Wink. Luther Winkler, an old high school pal. I'd been involved in his attempt to impersonate Bono a couple of years back. Pretty much a disastrous experience, but I still considered him a long-term pal. I hadn't talked to him in over a year.

"Hey Wink, how's it going? Before you answer, if this has anything to do with another Bono gig, count me out."

"Oh, man. Don't even bring it up. No, I just came across some bad news in the paper and wondered if you'd seen it."

"Bad News? What, is the IRS going to be investigating my taxes?"

"Stop it, something else I don't want to hear about. No, I was reading an article about a woman who was skating down on the river. She ended up falling through the ice."

"Eeew, she okay?"

"There's no sign of her. They figure the current probably moved her downstream somewhere. They're thinking it might not be until spring before they find the body."

"Oh, gee, that's too bad. What was she thinking? You know, even as kids, we knew it wasn't safe to skate on the river."

"Yeah, but that's not why I'm calling you."

"I'll check out the article and—"

"Dev, the woman who fell through the ice. It was your high school sweetheart, Madeline."

"You mean Maddie McGuire? The girl in our high school class. She married some thug with the last name of Ferral."

"Yeah, the girl that dumped you. She invited you to her wedding, didn't she?"

"Ahh, yeah, yeah, she did," I said, and suddenly, the image of her being dragged down the aisle and out of the church with a shocked look on her face flashed into my mind. "Tell me again. She was skating on the river?"

"Yeah, and apparently, she fell through the ice and got carried away. Probably couldn't get out from beneath the ice. I don't know how long she could stay there before she drowned."

"Not very long. What the hell was she thinking? She was a really good skater. I think she got a scholarship to the University of Wisconsin or somewhere for synchronized skating. I can't believe— You sure it was her, Wink?"

"That's what the article said. They referred to her as Madeline Ferral."

"Yeah, that was her husband's name."

"And that's the name of the woman in the article."

"Wink, thanks for the call. Let me check out that article, and I'll get back to you."

"Yeah, okay. Let me—"

I hung up on him and Googled Madeline Ferral. Halfway down the page, I found the link to the article and clicked on it. It was actually in yesterday's paper and wasn't much of an article, about a half-dozen sentences that basically told me what Wink had said. Her car had been spotted. There was a hole in the ice, and her purse and shoes were found on the shore. Based on the rough description, I had a general idea of where this happened.

I turned off my computer and kicked myself for not contacting Maddie over the last few years. How hard would it have been to see how she was doing and to wish her well? I called Wink back. We chatted for maybe ten minutes, exchanging a couple of stories, and then Wink had to ring off. I put Morton in the car, and we headed down to the office.

Louie wasn't in, but the coffee pot was on, and there was about a half-cup of coffee in the pot. I turned it off, dumped the coffee in the sink, and let the pot cool down before I refilled it.

I went online to check my Airbnb ad, but after twenty minutes of never finding it, I gave up.

I placed a call to my pal Aaron LaZelle. He headed up the homicide division in the St. Paul Police Department. I was ready to leave a message when he answered. "LaZelle."

"Hi Aaron, it's Dev."

"Hi Dev, I was going to give you a call. Did you read about Maddie McGuire?"

"Yeah, Wink called me, and I read the little article a couple of minutes ago. Are you guys investigating it?"

"There's nothing to investigate. She wasn't robbed. Her purse with her billfold and car keys and her car were still there. It looks like an unfortunate situation, but there's no indication of anything criminal."

"But even as kids, we knew not to skate on the river, and she was quite the skater. She got a college scholarship for skating."

"When was the last time you saw her?" Aaron asked, ignoring my last statement.

"I went to her wedding a few years ago. Never did talk to her. Maybe caught her eye on her way out of the church. The guy she married seemed like a jerk."

"Colton Ferral. He's been a person of interest in a few matters. As far as I know, that's it. I don't believe he's been charged in the past few years."

"What was he suspected of doing?"

"The usual, stolen good and drugs, he graduated up to more financial scams. His name came up a couple of times in the murder of some undesirables, but nothing ever stuck. And, I would have to add, he wasn't the sole suspect."

"He sounds like an up-and-coming Tubby Gustafson. Was Maddie still married to him?"

"I'm presuming they were still married, but I don't know that. Your assessment sounds correct. I'm sure Gustafson views him as potential competition."

"You think someone might have murdered her to send a message to her husband?"

"No, Dev. Absolutely not. There's nothing in any way, shape, or form to suggest anything other than a most unfortunate accident occurred."

"Did anyone on your team investigate the scene? It would seem to me—"

"Hello, is anyone listening? Let me state it again. Nothing indicated anything but an unfortunate accident. She was skating on the river, Dev. We've known since we were kids that it's not safe to do that. Unfortunately, Madeline seemed to forget that."

"Yeah, I guess you're right. Well, thanks for taking my call."

"I wish I had better news for you, Dev. Maybe look at it this way. If she had to die, isn't it better it was an unfortunate accident that happened while she was doing something she loved doing? As dark as it is, that seems a lot better option than having her throat slit or being shot or raped."

"Yeah, I guess you're right. I'm just kicking myself for never getting in touch with her after her wedding. Still have a soft spot for her in my heart, I guess."

"Probably a good idea you didn't get in touch. You know, the old boyfriend thing. No offense, but it works both ways. If she was interested, she could have gotten in touch with you."

"Yeah, you're right. Hey, Aaron, we need to get together for dinner sometime. If memory serves, it's your turn to buy, so I'm thinking of some really expensive place."

"Yeah, or we could just meet at McDonalds, since it's really your turn."

"That works, too."

"I'll give you a call when things loosen up. Thanks for calling, Dev," Aaron said and disconnected.

I thought about what he said. He was more or less right, except for one thing. Maddie had contacted me. She sent me a wedding invitation. But, other than watching her being dragged down the aisle on the way out the door, I never did anything.

Four

I slept off and on that night and was up just after 5:00 the following morning. I didn't learn anything new scanning the internet for two and a half hours. Morton eventually wandered into the kitchen. I gave him his morning head scratch and then let him out the backdoor. He stood on the back porch looking at all the snow then slowly made his way down the steps and maybe three feet into the yard where he did his business. I couldn't really blame him. Three minutes later, he was scratching at the backdoor.

I let him inside, and he promptly shook off all the snow onto the kitchen floor. When he was finished with his breakfast, we climbed in the car and took a roundabout way to the office.

I drove through downtown and across the Mississippi on the Wabasha bridge. I took a right at the second stoplight and followed the road upriver. In a couple of short blocks, I was past the St. Paul Yacht Club and in Cherokee Regional Park. The only tracks in the snow were from deer, fox, and the occasional coyote. After maybe a mile, I passed an area with tire tracks. The tracks led to the river no more than twenty yards from the road. I pulled over, climbed out, and walked toward the river.

The tracks were in the snow we'd gotten three nights ago. From what I could determine, maybe a half-dozen vehicles had been here. It was clear by the tracks that four different cars pulled off and stopped close to the river's edge. I took them for probably police cars. The heavier set of tracks, with duel rear wheels, had clearly backed into the area.

The tracks stopped at a point, and there was snow piled behind the end of the dual rear wheels. It was probably a tow truck that had loaded a vehicle, most likely Maddie's car, and hauled it out of the area. I made a mental note to check the impound lot.

I walked to the river's edge. The river was frozen, but the wind had blown most of the snow off the ice. I could see the area with thin ice where Maddie had fallen through. If she'd gone all the way under, the river current could have swept her downstream. Even if she'd only drifted a few feet, given the shock from the cold, the weight of soaked winter clothing, and the river current, it would be damn near impossible to find your way back to the hole in the ice. She could have hit her head on the edge of the ice and been unconscious. She certainly would have been in severe shock from the cold. It was a hell of a way to go, damn it.

There was nothing else to see. All the footprints pretty much trampled the snow. I couldn't see anything that looked like it might have come from a woman's dainty foot. I don't know what I had expected to find. A note in a bottle? A heart drawn in the snow with my name in the middle? To be honest, I hadn't thought about Maddie since her wedding, and I was pretty sure, other than inviting me to watch her get married, she'd never thought of me.

Life works in strange ways.

I walked back to my car, followed the park road through the park heading upriver and past the Pool and Yacht Club. I took the 35E bridge across the Mississippi and turned on the Randolph Street exit down to the office. Louie wasn't in, and amazingly, the empty coffee pot had been turned off. I made a fresh pot, worked at not thinking about Maddie McGuire, and got back to vetting employee applications for my insurance client.

Louie wandered in that afternoon. He gave me his usual wave as he set his briefcase on the picnic table then removed his coat. As he sat down, I got up, poured him a coffee, and set it in front of him. After a couple of sips, he'd recovered from the stair climb up to the office and said, "How's your day going?"

"Okay, I guess. Not much shaking. Just working these job applications."

He nodded, took a few more sips, and said, "You okay? You're sounding a little down."

"It's nothing," I said and went on to tell him about Maddie.

"Oh, she sounds like she was pretty nice."

"She was. Too bad I never really picked up on it. At least she had the good sense to ditch me."

"But she sent you an invitation to her wedding, and you went?"

"Yeah. Not sure why I went. Maybe just to see who was lucky enough to marry her. Turns out the guy's a real jerk. Aaron LaZelle described him as a competitor of Tubby Gustafson's. I guess I'll always wonder if maybe she didn't want my help to get out of that predicament, you know, marrying Colton Ferral, and I completely missed it."

"Dev, you didn't even have your P.I. license then, did you? Quit beating yourself up. You ever think maybe she just wanted you to know that she was marrying someone. The guy may be an awful person, but at the end of the day, she made the decision of her own free will."

"Yeah, I know. It just seems like such a waste of a really classy person. God, she didn't deserve the way she died, and she sure as hell didn't deserve to be married to that prick Colton Ferral."

"Yeah, okay. But she made the choice to marry the guy. She could have said no. And as far as not deserving to die that way, yeah, you're right. I don't want to push this, but did you ever think maybe she knew what she was doing?"

"What do you mean?"

"She's a big skater, right. But you said it yourself a few minutes ago. Growing up, we all knew you don't skate on the river. It was beaten into us. You don't walk on river ice. Yet, there she is, an adult. A smart, educated individual, and she's skating all by herself on the river. I mean this nicely, and I'm not condemning her. But do you think that maybe she was hoping that's what would happen? Maybe she was in a dark place, and that seemed to be the logical way out."

"You mean she committed suicide?"

Louie nodded and said, "Yeah, maybe. Every park in town has an ice rink or two. Yet she goes down on the river?"

I gave a long exhale and thought about that.

Louie waited a minute or two, then turned on his computer and started tapping keys.

Eventually, I said, "You know, I never thought about it that way, but maybe you're right. Maybe, for whatever reason, she found herself in a dark place, and, unfortunately, that seemed like the logical way out."

"We'll never know for sure. Maybe she left a note somewhere. Who knows? It's just another yank of the chain for every one of us to realize that we don't have anything to bitch about. No matter how bad we think things are, there's always someone who has it worse. All we have to do is look out the window, and we'll see them," Louie said.

I nodded and said, "Yeah, you're right. We both know good folks who are no longer with us. It's just that I keep thinking if only I'd checked in with her. Asked how she was doing, you know?"

"Yeah, and I'd say that's pretty normal. But the second half of that is if only she'd touched base with you. You would have offered support, comfort, whatever she needed. You would have, Dev. It's the type of person you are. But she didn't get in touch, and there's only so much you can do. Beating yourself up, now, when something happened through no fault of your own, doesn't help. Maybe look at all the clothes you donated the other day and know that there are folks out there who will consider themselves very lucky to have gotten them. You'll never know who they are. They'll never be able to thank you in person. But by donating, you helped them out in a big way. You did more for them than most people on any given day, and you're a good guy for doing it. Focus on that, rather than this unfortunate situation."

"Yeah, thanks, Louie. You're right, as always," I said and went back to going through the job applications.

To be continued . . .

Thanks for checking out the sample of **The Big Gamble**. Things are about to go crazy, Dev Haskell style. Better grab your copy and check it out!

Books by Mike Faricy
Crime Fiction Firsts

A boxset of the first four books in four crime fiction series:

Russian Roulette; Dev Haskell series
Welcome; Jack Dillon Dublin Tales series
Corridor Man; Corridor Man series
Reduced Ransom! Hot Shot series

The following titles comprise the Dev Haskell series:

Russian Roulette: Case 1
Mr. Swirlee: Case 2
Bite Me: Case 3
Bombshell: Case 4
Tutti Frutti: Case 5
Last Shot: Case 6
Ting-A-Ling: Case 7
Crickett: Case 8
Bulldog: Case 9
Double Trouble: Case 10
Yellow Ribbon: Case 11
Dog Gone: Case 12
Scam Man: Case 13
Foiled: Case 14
What Happens in Vegas… Case 15
Art Hound: Case 16
The Office: Case 17

Star Struck: Case 18
International Incident: Case 19
Guest From Hell: Case 20
Art Attack: Case 21
Mystery Man: Case 22
Bow-Wow Rescue: Case 23
Cold Case: Case 24
Cash Up Front: Case 25
Dream House: Case 26
Alley Katz: Case 27
The Big Gamble: Case 28
Bad to the Bone: Case 29
Silencio!: Case 30
Surprise, Surprise: Case 31
Hit & Run: Case 32
Suspect Santa: Case 33
P.I. Apprentice: Case 34
Rebel Without a Clue: Case 35
Puppy Love: Case 36

The following titles are Dev Haskell novellas:
Dollhouse
The Dance
Pixie
Fore!
Twinkle Toes
(*a Dev Haskell short story*)

The following are Dev Haskell Boxsets:
Dev Haskell Boxset 1-3
Dev Haskell Boxset 4-6
Dev Haskell Boxset 7-9
Dev Haskell Boxset 10-12
Dev Haskell Boxset 13-15
Dev Haskell Boxset 16-18
Dev Haskell Boxset 19-21
Dev Haskell Boxset 22-24
Dev Haskell Boxset 25-27
Dev Haskell Boxset 28-30
Dev Haskell Boxset 1-7
Dev Haskell Boxset 8-14
Dev Haskell Boxset 15-19
Dev Haskell Boxset 20-24
Dev Haskell Boxset 25-29

The following titles comprise the Jack Dillon Dublin Tales series:
Welcome
Jack Dillon Dublin Tale 1
Sweet Dreams
Jack Dillon Dublin Tale 2
Mirror Mirror
Jack Dillon Dublin Tale 3
Silver Bullet
Jack Dillon Dublin Tale 4
Fair City Blues

Jack Dillon Dublin Tale 5
Spade Work
Jack Dillon Dublin Tale 6
Madeline Missing
Jack Dillon Dublin Tale 7
Mistaken Identity
Jack Dillon Dublin Tale 8
Picture Perfect
Jack Dillon Dublin Tale 9
Dublin Moon
Jack Dillon Dublin Tale 10
Mystery Woman
Jack Dillon Dublin Tale 11
Second Chance
Jack Dillon Dublin Tale 12
Payback Brother
Jack Dillon Dublin Tale 13
The Heist
Jack Dillon Dublin Tale 14
Jewels To Kill For
Jack Dillon Dublin Tale 15
Retirement Scheme
Jack Dillon Dublin Tale 16
The Collector
Jack Dillon Dublin Tale 17

Jack Dillon Dublin Tales Boxsets:
Jack Dillon Dublin Tales 1-3
Jack Dillon Dublin Tales 4-6

Jack Dillon Dublin Tales 1-5
Jack Dillon Dublin Tales 1-7
Jack Dillon Dublin Tales 6-10

The following titles comprise the Hotshot series;
Reduced Ransom! Second Edition
Finders Keepers! Second Edition
Bankers Hours Second Edition
Chow Down Second Edition
Moonlight Dance Academy Second Edition
Irish Dukes (Fight Card Series)
written under the pseudonym Jack Tunney

The following titles comprise the Corridor Man series:
Corridor Man
Corridor Man 2: Opportunity knocks
Corridor Man 3: The Dungeon
Corridor Man 4: Dead End
Corridor Man 5: Finger
Corridor Man 6: Exit Strategy
Corridor Man 7: Trunk Music
Corridor Man 8: Birthday Boy
Corridor Man 9: Boss Man
Corridor Man 10: Bye Bye Bobby

Corridor Man novellas:
Corridor Man: Valentine
Corridor Man: Auditor

Corridor Man: Howling

Corridor Man: Spa Day

The following are Corridor Man Boxsets:
Corridor Man Boxset 1-3
Corridor Man Boxset 1-5
Corridor Man Boxset 6-9

All books are available on Amazon.com
Thank you!

Contact the author:
- Email: mikefaricyauthor@gmail.com
- Twitter: @Mikefaricybooks
- Facebook: Mike Faricy Author
- Website: http://www.mikefaricybooks.com

Published by

MJF Publishing

www.ingramcontent.com/pod-product-compliance
Lightning Source LLC
Chambersburg PA
CBHW070339010826
48976CB00017B/294